Twice as Fatal

A Jarvis Mann Detective Novel

By
R Weir

All thebrzt

RWu

Copyediting by Gabriella West at EditforIndies.com

Cover Design by:
Victoria Robinson
Cover Smartz
http://www.coversmartz.com
info@coversmartz.com

To Kim and Dakota
Third times a charm

Chapter 1

Contemplating the hole in my bank account created by new brakes and tires for my Mustang, I drove to my home office where I saw her at the top of the stairs. Kate, the owner of the beauty salon that occupied the upper space of the building, was my landlord. She stood with her arms crossed soaking in the Saturday afternoon sun, which remained unseasonably warm for this time of year. She might have been there for some pass-the-time chit-chat, though our relationship hadn't been overly social over the years. A serious expression meant she was all business.

"Hi, Kate," I said with a smile. "Are you hanging out enjoying the nice weather and working on your tan?"

She smiled back weakly.

"Not today," she replied. "I came to talk to you. I need your professional help with something."

I walked around to the passenger side and grabbed the groceries I'd picked up at the store. I headed down the steps, opened the front door and allowed her to walk in first. Placing the reusable bags on the kitchen counter, I organized the food into the refrigerator. I motioned for her to take a seat at my small two-seater kitchen table.

"Would you like a beer?" I asked.

Beer was the one item always on hand and cold.

"Sure," she answered, looking the place over. "I don't think I've been down here since you rented it. Going on what, six years now? You keep it attractive and clean for a bachelor."

"Thanks. I do what I can."

She smiled lightly and sat down, taking a long drink from the bottle. She was a pretty woman, probably in her middle-to-late forties, nice figure in her five-foot-seven frame. Her deep black hair was long and braided into a single ponytail, draped over her right shoulder. Today she wore a shirt with sleeves and crossed her faded jean-covered legs while sitting, the black-heeled boots nearly reaching her knee caps. I'd seen her in tank tops and shorts many times over the years, and she featured numerous tattoos on various parts of her body, many custom designed. On some women the skin paintings didn't look good, but for her it was just right and added a little zing to her appearance. She had several piercings along each ear lobe filled with shiny gold, silver and diamond rings, and a small diamond stud in her nose sparkled in the light. I knew in the summer months she rode a Harley Davidson, the full-throated, piston-thumping roar announcing arrivals and departures. Today I saw her Toyota RAV parked outside, the motorcycle shut down for the inevitable winter on the horizon.

"What can I help you with?" I asked while parking it in the other kitchen chair after a long pull on my own beer.

"I need you to check into something personal," she said. "I want assurances you will keep this in confidence. I don't want any of the ladies at work knowing about this until I'm ready to tell them."

She was aware I often talked and flirted with some of her employees when the mood struck me. I'd even dated a couple of them, though they had long since moved on.

"My lips are sealed. In this business, confidentiality is vital. I wouldn't have clients long if I blabbed. I'm assuming you are in need of my detective services?"

She stopped and drank another third of the bottle. "Yes. I need to learn what my husband is up to. He is either cheating on me, drinking heavily or gambling. I'm not sure which, but he was raiding my business account for money and I need to know the reasons for his behavior."

"How have you drawn this conclusion?"

"Because of past problems in all those areas. His current behavior is a dead-giveaway they are back."

"You want to hire me?"

"Yes. You are the only detective I know, and I figure I can trust you, since I'm your landlord."

"Even if you weren't, you could."

I got the hard part out of the way by stating my rates to her, which she found agreeable. It wouldn't take more than a day or two to find out what he was up to. Anyone with either of those problems isn't difficult to track down and retrieve evidence against. Those addictions were hard to conceal.

"I'll need as much information as possible on him, and anything else you believe will help me gather what is necessary. Is it OK if I take notes?"

She nodded so I snagged my little notebook and pen. Her beer was finished and I offered her another, but she declined. I polished

2

off mine, grabbed both bottles and placed them in my recycling container after rinsing them out. I am the environmentally friendly detective. *A new tagline for my business card.* On recycled card stock, of course.

"So what behavior are you seeing?" I asked.

"Well, taking money from my business account is the biggest one," she stated bluntly. "Several thousand dollars over the last few weeks. Also, he is rarely ever home these days, staying out until all hours."

"Have you confronted him about this?"

"Yes, and all he does is brush me off and walk away. I grabbed him the other day and said to either 'fess up or I was leaving him. He called me a 'bitch' and left. I've hardly seen him since. When he comes home late at night, he sleeps in the guest bedroom in the basement."

"He has access to your business finances?"

"He did, but he doesn't anymore. He was a secondary on the account and I had him removed. His bank card was also cancelled. He is cut off. There are limits to my financial fortune."

"What about personal finances, credit cards and such?"

"He still has those, some of which are in his name only. I'm trying to get untangled from him, but this takes time and money."

"Have you enlisted a lawyer?"

"Yes. He is doing what he can, but I can't pay too much, so he is probably not the best I could get."

"Will you be able to afford me? I hate to ask, but I've experienced issues with getting paid by some clients in the past. I trust you, but one can't pay what one doesn't have, no matter how honest they are."

"If I can't, we can work out the difference in your rent. I don't foresee this being a problem now that his access to my business account is terminated."

"No hope for reconciliation?" I asked. "You mentioned you went through this before and were able to reconcile. Is this the last straw?"

She stopped and thought for a couple of seconds. "No. I'm finished with him. I stayed with him the last time because he said he'd change, and for the kids. They are grown up now, one in college the other a senior in high school. They understand clearer what he is like; no more of that idealized bullshit younger kids can

3

have about their parents. They know he is a dick and they want me to be happy. I make a good living with my salon, but he will ruin me financially if I don't get him out of my home and hair. Time to start my life over. A new beginning to challenge myself with."

I'd dealt with this type of client regularly. Cheating or addicted spouses ruining the other's life, along with their children's, and running around foolishly. Cases like this one were challenging, though, with many pitfalls. I knew Kate well enough to be happy to help her and trusted her enough to think I wouldn't be in the same mess as I was in my last domestic case. Her starting over was easier said than done.

"I'll take the case and gather evidence you can use against him. It may require me to dig into your life and background, if necessary. Generally, it's clear-cut but I want to make you aware of the possibility, depending on what facts I find. Are you OK with this?"

"I have nothing to hide. I smoked pot occasionally when I was in high school and college, and enjoyed an active sex life before meeting Jack. Nothing too shocking for a teenager and young adult, especially by today's standards. Married and family life have been pretty boring other than my jerk of a husband."

"Fair enough," I answered. "Tell me all you can about Jack. His comings and goings, places he frequents, what he drives and anything else to help me. I'm working a minor case for someone else in my spare time, but I can work this in and start on Monday. Tomorrow I'm entertaining a friend."

She happily gave me all the details, which I stored to memory and to paper. It was often therapeutic for clients to bare their souls when starting a case, a relief to unburden themselves. *Another new tagline: "The Psychologist Detective. Unburden Yourself and Case Solved for One Low Fee!"* I'd get facts from some clients that would make a lesser detective blush. Kate's were straightforward and generic, yet detailed enough to get started. I was happy to help her out and even happier to be staying busy with a paying client. Once she'd finished, she wrote me a check as a retainer and walked back upstairs to the salon. It wasn't enough to replenish what I'd spent on my new brakes and tires, but it was a start.

4

Chapter 2

After numerous conversations, a couple deliveries of flowers, and various apologies for believing the lies spewed by a woman on my last case with an ax to grind, Melissa had agreed to start seeing me again. We kept our dates together simple. No hot, passionate nights: only the two of us going to dinner and a movie; a day of shopping; and some quality time spent together. Afterwards, a simple kiss and hug goodbye, agreeing to take the relationship slow. Today she was coming over to relax, converse about whatever we cared to talk about, and savor some beer and pizza for lunch. A quiet and uncomplicated day together.

Having slept well the night before, I was freshly showered, shaved and anxious for a relaxing Sunday. I had on broken-in jeans, a long-sleeved beige sweater and white Avia running shoes, in which I was pacing the floor. She was set to arrive at any time and I had to admit, I was still nervous at the thought of seeing her. Screwing up big-time with her previously meant no more major mistakes. I wanted to make it work.

Her car pulled up and I viewed her coming down the stairs. She was beautiful as always, wearing blue jeans, a pink blouse unbuttoned enough to show a hint of cleavage, and black boots, all covered under her warm, lengthy black coat. She wore no makeup from what I could tell, but if she did, it was applied so as not to notice. Her straight brown hair draped over her shoulders, a colorful butterfly barrette on one side. Her bright green eyes full of life and happiness glistened in the sunlight. She walked in gracefully and brushed past me smiling, a six pack of bottled beer in her hand. She placed the carton in the fridge, came up and kissed me softly, our arms wrapping around each other in a simple embrace. Her body was warm to the touch, the hint of perfume lingering in my nose. I smiled back at her, trying not to show nervousness. I was lucky to be given a second chance, which was a rarity in my love life.

She had been to my place a couple of times before and she looked around. She stopped to stare at the bubble gum card placed in front of the fall mountain leaves photo gracing one of the walls. The souvenir was one of my prized possessions, earned on one of my memorable cases lasting only one afternoon.

"Willie Mays," she said out loud. "I've noticed the picture and card before but never asked what it was for?"

"Payment from a past case," I answered. "I helped a young man, Dennis Gash, find an Ernie Banks rookie card which was stolen, we discovered, by a friend…" I went on and told her the story.

"Wow, what a special memory. Do you ever see him?"

"I actually watched him play football a couple of times this year at All City Stadium. He is a pretty decent running back, though they lost both games. Probably not pro material, but could compete at a small college and parlay a scholarship."

Two beers in hand, I joined her in the living room. Sitting down on the sofa, I placed both bottles on coasters on the coffee table. I motioned for her to join me and she sat down, but for now kept some space between us. It was possible she was nervous too.

"How was your week?" I asked.

"No major cases or trips to court this week," she stated after taking a short sip from her bottle. "Mostly research. What about you?"

"I was hired for a new case. Kate upstairs wants me to gather evidence against her husband. Apparently, he is up to something and I need to determine what it is."

"Domestic cases have to be difficult."

"Yes, they can be. I've had some go sideways on me before, and you feel like a peeping Tom prying into their lives. But those are the cases which put bread on the table."

"We deal with them all the time at Bristol & Bristol. It's hard to believe two people once so full of love for each other becoming so bitter. What does Kate think he's doing?"

"One of several things…" I recited a few basic details Kate had given me.

"A shame it's come to this. It is difficult to trust a man with a history of promiscuity and other unpleasant habits."

I ignored the comment, for I'd had a history of my own. Mending one's ways wasn't easy.

"Are you getting hungry?" I asked.

"Yes, I am," she answered.

"Where shall I order from?"

"How about Domino's?"

"Surprising. I would have not guessed."

6

"What can I say, I like their pizza. Need to get extra cheese, for they are skimpy on the mozzarella but quick to deliver."

"Probably from a deep-seated fantasy about the hunky deliveryman delivering more than pizza."

She smiled. "Possibly, but I've found the deliveryman never lives up to the fantasy and often disappoints."

"Domino's it is."

We agreed on ingredients and a side, so I went online and ordered.

"I'm chilly," Melissa stated.

I got off the sofa. "I'll turn up the heat and grab a blanket. They are predicting a nippy night with some snow."

She gave me a disappointing glare.

"You realize I wanted to snuggle with you?" she said flatly. "It's one of those signals we girls use to let the guy know what we want. Or was this overly coy on my part?"

"I'm being cautious," I answered while sitting back down. "I'm trying to take it slow per your request."

"I'd like to think you can put your arm around me without thinking about sex. Or can you?"

Shrugging a "maybe" with my hands, I draped an arm around her and she rested her head on my shoulder, a blue blanket covering her lap and mine. Some soft music was playing in the background from a local radio station, filling a silent void in the room. A connection was building between us again. I did my best to temper my urges, which was challenging.

Passing the time, we talked some more about her work and mine before the food arrived. The deliveryman was exactly like Melissa said—not fantasy material, but the pizza was hot which was most important. I paid him and brought the large pizza into the living room with two more beers. I cherished the view of her while I ate two pieces in the time it took her to eat one, her bites smaller and more deliberate, careful not to overeat. She wasn't a skinny minnie and had some meat on her, though firm from a solid exercise routine. Memories of her undressed flooded my mind. *Damn, I need to dispel those naked thoughts!*

In time we had sufficiently filled ourselves with enough food and beer, and the leftovers were stored away in the fridge. I returned to the sofa and snuggled up against her. She smelled wonderful: soft hair, pretty face and the curve of her marvelously enticing body. I ached to kiss her, but resisted. She needed to make the first move.

"What would you like to do?" I asked.

"I get to decide?" she said.

"Yes, you are in charge. Name it and I will be right beside you."

"Well…"

She turned into me, took my face in her hands and kissed me passionately for about a minute. My heart raced as her soft lips met mine.

"Any more questions?" she stated with a seductive voice. "Another one of our signals. Do I need to translate what it meant?"

We locked lips again for several minutes, making out like teenagers on the sofa.

"No. Signal received loud and clear," I replied, catching my breath. "Are you sure you're ready? You wanted to take it slow and I'm OK with that. I want you to be certain this time after what happened before."

"Yes," she said while pushing me back and lying on top, kissing me with the hunger of a desire-laden woman. "I can feel how ready you are. We better get those jeans off you or you'll likely burst your denim!"

She got up from the sofa, grabbed me by the hand, and walked me to the bedroom. We undressed one another, starting slowly, touching with fingers and mouths all over in various positions, creating an extreme state of arousal for us both before she climbed on top, our bodies in a continuing motion until each of us cried out in satisfaction. We labored to fill our lungs with oxygen, the deep-breathing sounds lifting to the ceiling. Lying there next to me, she fell into a blissful sleep. It was a wonderful moment and I enjoyed gazing at her naked body, thinking this was perfect and how lucky I was to have her here with me again.

A while later she woke up and went to the bathroom, then returned with an inquisitive glance on her face.

"Can you do me a favor?" she asked, standing naked before me.

"I think I already did," I responded. "But I'm happy and ready to help again."

"Put on some pants, go to my car, and grab the overnight bag from the front seat and bring it in."

"Overnight bag," I said, surprised. "Anticipating spending the night, were we?"

"A girl always needs to be prepared," she answered with her now-familiar sheepish look. "You never know when a hunky guy will come along and present a hot woman with something she desires. If the pizza deliveryman had been better looking, it might have been him!"

"Why, you!" I stood up and grabbed her as we both fell onto the bed. I started kissing her again, starting at the lips and working my way down.

Another passion-filled hour passed before I went to get her bag.

Chapter 3

Monday was the first day on the case for Kate. Her text said he had stayed the night in the basement bedroom, coming home close to midnight, which had been his pattern. He normally left between 9 and 10 a.m., off doing whatever it was he did. A straight follow-and-surveil case to gather evidence.

I had her home address, and I was off after clearing the two inches of snow from the Mustang that fell overnight. I packed a digital SLR with a telephoto lens and spare battery, fully charged for capturing evidence. In a small soft cooler, I placed some water, a can of soda, and leftover pizza to snack on, knowing a long day was ahead. I dressed in a heavy winter coat over jeans and sweatshirt, with a plain black Colorado Rockies hat, warm gloves and boots for stepping through the snow. Heading west on Evans, past Federal, I found her residence about a mile or so west of where I lived, claiming a good parking spot from which to observe. The pickup he drove was parked out on the street. It was around 9 a.m., the Mustang sitting silently with a full tank of gas. I was a patient man who would wait whatever amount of time needed to complete the job. The nothingness of surveillance was a key skill-set for a detective. I excelled at doing nothing.

I went over my notes from the information Kate gave me about her husband, Jack, whom she had less than fondly called Jack-Ass. He was around 5'10" and 200 or so pounds, with thinning, short red hair and graying temples. He was fifty-one, though he would never admit it, and had gone through a serious midlife crisis shortly after passing forty, wanting to try to recapture his youth in any way possible. This led to drinking, gambling and womanizing issues with ladies in their twenties. The gambling and drinking put them in debt, as he had been jobless for some time. It nearly tore them apart then, but they worked through their troubles. With counseling, he'd straightened himself out, finding steady work. He was a good husband and father again, their debt issues resolved. His personal issues returned when he passed fifty and this time, she wasn't giving him another chance and wanted him gone. Nothing was going to save this marriage anymore. She needed the evidence to run him out of her life for good and start anew.

Nearing ten, I saw him exit the side door. He was wearing a black leather jacket, matching jeans and boots, with a skull cap covering his balding head. He appeared heavier than Kate had mentioned and squeezed into the older blue Ford Ranger pickup truck he was driving, throwing a black duffle bag on the seat. He sat for several minutes, waiting for the snow to melt enough for the wipers to clear the windshield. He didn't get out to remove any powder from the windows and rolled each down and back up again in an attempt to clean them. He pulled out, driving north and I was off behind him, doing my best not to be noticed.

His truck would not be too hard to follow, emitting a fair amount of smoke from its tail pipe, leaving a nice trail. You could see and smell the rich and gassy fumes flowing out the back and into the air unburned. He certainly wouldn't be outrunning me in a chase.

Traffic was heavy, and many people were driving slowly, as the streets hadn't been cleared of the overnight precipitation. Apparently, State road crews had been surprised by the snow and hadn't gotten their CDOT equipment out until late in the morning. This created a messy rush hour drive from what I was hearing on news radio, though they tended to make every little thing sound like a major ordeal. Following him was easier, thanks to the conditions.

We traveled for about twenty minutes before we came to our first stop. Jack had pulled off onto Federal Boulevard where three men were standing. He got out of his truck and approached them. I found a spot about a half-block back and parked, giving myself a decent angle to view them. With my camera and the telephoto lens, I zoomed in to see all of them, a clicking sound telling me the pictures were being captured. He talked with them for several minutes, cash being passed to Jack, while he handed them back something, though I couldn't tell what. All was cordial and he headed to his truck and pulled out.

This happened at two other locations, an exchange of money and some product was made. I took the best shots possible, once seeing a rolled-up plastic bag he was giving them. Each time the men were maybe in their thirties to forties, dressed poorly and certainly not affluent in any way, and of varying races: Caucasian, Black, Asian and Hispanic. At the last stop Jack got into an argument with one of the men. He shoved him around some, and the other man pushed back. He opened his coat, flashing a gun. I read his lips: "Pay up or else!" Reluctantly, the man turned over the money, but this time Jack didn't give him anything in return. A debt was being paid in this case, and he was warning him of the consequences of non-payment next time. The man was shaky, as if in need of a fix he wasn't going to get. He stomped his feet, cursing profusely behind Jack's back.

From there we headed south and then east before connecting to Broadway Avenue. Thanks to all the streetlights I was able to stay behind him and not be seen. Riding in a yellow and black Mustang made surveillance tougher, as it stands out from the other four-wheel-drive SUVs and sedan cookie-cutter cars on the road. Today the harsh weather was helping me; the dirt and snow from the streets were dirtying up my car, making it less recognizable. We had driven a while and soon he parked along one of the older sections of Broadway. I had to pull past him and swing around and park on the other side. In the mirror I saw him get out and stroll into a bar called Eddie's.

While sitting there, I decided it was lunchtime. Cold pizza and soda filled my stomach while I was hanging out watching the front door. Several people went in and out, but what got my attention was a brand-new BMW parking behind Jack's pickup. Out walked two men, both large in size, football-big and looking mean, as you'd expect enforcers to appear. The one on the driver's side flashed a large gun in a shoulder holster under his coat. I jotted down the license plate number, guessing these were bad men. I wanted to get a closer look and the only way was to walk into the bar. It wasn't something I would enjoy, but must be done. I needed to change my getup a little bit, so I got out and removed my jacket and sweatshirt, tossing them on the passenger seat. From my trunk I grabbed a full-length one-piece insulated coverall I wore when doing maintenance on the Mustang in the wintertime. I added a gray hat adorned with a bald-eagle head over an American Flag design. Both were dirty, making me look like an ordinary working stiff. Since no one knew me I would be another patron staggering in asking for a beer on a lunch break.

The snow was turning to slush, the temperatures were rising and so I crossed in between the traffic, entering through the front door. The outside was old and dingy, the building probably built in the forties, but the inside wasn't a total dive. Laid out like you'd expect: the bar with stools taking up the left side with tables and booths covering the right. Being in Denver, of course the walls were covered with Bronco's memorabilia highlighting their best players throughout the years. It was dark inside, but bright enough to see Jack in the back booth with the two big men, talking. They stared at me and I took a seat at the bar. The place was mostly empty, with two people sitting on stools and a couple in a booth on the other side, ignoring each other. The bartender came over, seeming to size me up. I gave him a happy smile and ordered a draft, putting a five-dollar bill on the counter. He rang up the order and left a whole fifty cents in change. I saluted him with the mug and drank down half. It tasted watered-down, a lighter-than-lite beer.

"Wow, $4.50 for a beer?" I stated to the bartender.

"Ambiance," was all he said.

Looking around, I didn't see a lot of ambiance. There were only three televisions in the place, an old tube TV behind the bar and a couple of newer large flat screen LCDs behind me, a small number for a sports establishment of this size, and of inferior quality judging by the lousy picture. One was at the end where Jack was sitting, so I turned to watch. They had on ESPN Classic, which showed older sports events considered classics by the program manager. This one happened to be the Broncos against Cleveland in the AFC Championship back in the eighties, a game simply known as "The Drive."

"Go Broncos!" I said out loud so those around heard me. "Man. Elway was something, wasn't he?"

Getting up, I moved down the bar, finding a seat next to one of the other patrons to get a better view of the TV and of Jack in the booth. The man turned around and eyed me, then checked out the screen. He showed a half grin, the potent aroma of beer on his breath. He was certainly swimming in the booze and had probably been drinking since the place opened. I wondered how many $4.50 beers he'd had. Might have received a volume discount.

"Hell of a game," he said with a slight slur. "I poked the old lady good that night I was so pumped we'd won."

"Easy to get it hard after an impressive performance," I answered, though the sight of him and his wife wouldn't do much for my virility.

"Don't think I've seen you in here before," he asked.

"First time. I was on my lunch break and decided I required a cold one before returning to the grind."

"You work on cars?" he stated.

"Yep, I'm into the grease and grime," I answered. "I love getting the motor purring like my lady. Stroke them both right and they howl."

He laughed out loud like I was speaking his language. I watched the game but was keeping an eye on Jack and his two friends. Their conversation appeared civil and businesslike. I saw the exchange of a couple of folders, and the two men got up from the table. They walked by, looking my way, and I sensed the man next to me turn away, not wanting to look at them, genuine fear on his face. I showed them my happy smile, holding my mug in salute, and they were out the door soon, driving past the glass doorway.

"Wow, those guys were huge," I said softly. "Might have played for the Broncos?"

"Best not to talk about them. Only leads to trouble," was all he said, turning on his seat and remaining silent.

Jack peered into the envelope and seemed satisfied by the contents. He pulled out his cell phone and appeared to be typing out a text message. I needed to run to the restroom and found the sign down from me. I strolled by, probing eyes upon me. After I returned, I took my seat again and ordered another draft. Good thing I was working a case, as their alcohol prices would break the bank.

I downed the beer quickly this time and decided I should head on out. Before I got up, Jack stood and left for the door. On my way out, I slapped the back of the man at the bar as if we were best friends and strolled out slowly. Exiting, I saw Jack climb into a new Mercedes, a female behind the wheel. They were kissing before the car was put in gear, the tires spinning loudly, leaving a tread trail down the road and nearly causing a two-vehicle accident in their wake. The plate was covered with snow and ice, so I couldn't register any letters or numbers. I stood cursing myself for letting them get away. The do-nothing detective had done something, and it cost me. *One beer too many.*

Chapter 4

With nothing else to do but stand there with a stupid expression on my face I headed back to my part of town. Bill Malone and I were supposed to meet at Boone's to talk over my other case. This one I was doing as favor to him as payback for the information he'd always provided me in the past. He was covering expenses and offered to buy me dinner tonight to discuss the latest.

On the drive I called Melissa to see how her day was. She answered on the second ring, her voice sounding happy to hear mine.

"I was wondering when you were going to call," she said.

"Don't tell me things are so slow you were waiting by the phone," I stated.

"No, there is plenty to do. It's always good to hear your voice."

I had stopped calling her once previously after a client bad-mouthed her, and it would take a while to get over the possibility of it happening again.

"What did your day consist of?"

"Research, research and more research; the Bristol Brothers are burying me in work."

It sounded boring to me, but I know she lived for it, even when buried in it.

"What was the detective up to today?" she asked.

"This detective started his surveillance on Kate's husband." I gave her details, even the part about being left at the curb with a stupid look on my face. "Please don't mention this to Kate. It might ruin her stellar image of me."

"My lips are sealed," she replied. "So, you were acting the part of a greasy mechanic. You know, I've always had this fantasy about the hunky car tech doing bodywork on me!"

"Wow. Pizza delivery guys and now the greasy mechanic; what a healthy imagination! It appears I need to expand my wardrobe for role-playing."

"It's all those years of sexual frustration coming to bear."

"When will I see you again?"

"It will be a busy week. Maybe Friday we can meet up for dinner."

"Yep, I will mark it on my calendar in digital ink."

We said our goodbyes and the call ended.

Boone's was my kind of place, a neighborhood bar with tasty food and friendly people. Unlike Eddie's, a beer wasn't five dollars, though some of the local brews they carried were close. I parked out back and walked around Evans, entering through the front door. Nick the bartender nodded at me and pointed to the right. Over in the booth was Bill, nursing a brew. I sat down across from him and he glanced up without a smile, which was common for him. It was always hard to tell if he was in a good mood or a bad one. His attitude was always even-keeled whether his day went well or went south. Our relationship was always professional in nature, with simple social interaction, and if he was angry I could never tell. Julie the waitress was quick to arrive, so I decided on Sprite since I'd already had two beers and I rarely drank more than that in a day. I pulled out a piece of paper with the license plate number of the BMW and slid it over to him. He picked it up and placed it in his pocket without comment, knowing what I was asking. He was still in his police uniform but was off duty.

"Tough day at the office?" I asked.

"Aren't they all!" he groaned. "I got a call today from the University of Northern Colorado Dean of Students. He says Ray dropped out and left, as far as they can tell. No one knows where he went."

Ray was Bill's son, who had gone missing twice in the last month.

"No answer on his cell?"

"Straight to voicemail. Rachael is worried sick. She can't seem to sleep. He is her baby."

"And you?"

He glared at me hard to provide a wordless response. It was about as emotional as I'd ever seen him. Anyone else looking wouldn't see it, but there was worry deep in his eyes when you looked closely enough.

"Did you talk with his roommate in school?"

"Says it appears he packed a duffle bag with some clothes and left. No word; there one day and gone when he got back from classes."

"What about his coach?"

16

"After his latest injury he wasn't the same. Seemed lost and they were trying to get him some help. He was being stubborn."

"Takes after his dad," I stated.

It wasn't meant to be a put-down.

"Yeah, hard-headed like me."

The waitress returned with my drink, and we both decided on dinner. I picked the ribs with a side of fries, no salt. I enjoyed the taste of the potato and not the salt. Bill ordered the works on a burger with fries. I'd seen him put one away in four or five bites in the past. I wondered if tonight would be different.

"What should we do?" he asked.

"I will drive up there tomorrow and nose around. I tracked him down last month, so I can probably find him again. He's got to end up somewhere."

"I can take some time and help, use some sick days."

"Use them to comfort Rachael. I can handle this. Anything comes up, I'll call you." I was making excuses, as I was worried how he might act. Besides, I worked better alone.

"It's rough with kids. Even after they are grown you fear for them, worry what could happen. He's had it tough the last couple of years. When he can't play football, it kills him. He can't seem to see there is more to life than the game. I try to help him…"

"How's your daughter taking it?"

"It's hard for Monika, too. They were always close, even though they are several years apart in age. Her 'big bro,' as she calls him, was there for her whenever she needed him. I know she wants to be there for him too. Like us, she isn't sure what to do because we can't understand all he is going through."

As usual, the food was promptly served. I did my best not to get sauce on my face but failed when digging into the tender ribs. *Isn't that what napkins are for?* Bill didn't wolf down his burger like normal. He had a couple of bites and left the rest, nearly half, sitting there. They brought him another beer and even it sat unwanted after three short sips. It was clearly hard to eat when your child was missing, even when they are twenty years old.

"Bill, I'm good at what I do. I can track him down. You go home and take care of the family. I'll call you tomorrow if I come up with anything."

He stood up and tossed down three twenties to cover the meal. As

17

he walked by, he stopped, put his hand on my shoulder for a minute without looking at me and left. This might have topped the earlier glare on the emotion meter.

Chapter 5

The next day required a trip up to Greeley to visit the University of Northern Colorado campus. Surveillance on Jack would wait for another time. Calling Kate, I explained what I needed to do today. One or two more days and I'd have her evidence, which she was fine with. He wasn't likely to clean up his act overnight.

Greeley was north and east of Denver, about sixty or so miles away. I got an early start to try and beat rush hour and failed, since there is traffic twenty-four hours a day now, and proceeded on I-25, then took I-76 to State Highway 85, which passed through Brighton, Fort Lupton, La Salle and Evans before entering Greeley. It was roughly an hour before I hit the town I knew fairly well since I'd been there a month earlier looking for Bill's son.

Ray Malone was a young man who had lived a rough life the last couple of years. He had been a promising tight end at Abraham Lincoln High School, sought after by many Division 1A schools, including CU, until in his senior year when he tore his ACL midway through the season. After nearly a year-long rehab, he received an offer to play for the UNC Bears in Greeley. They were a solid football institution with a rich history of developing excellent student athletes, a few of which had made it to the professional ranks, long a goal of Ray's. After redshirting his freshman year to allow him to achieve full strength in his knee, acclimate himself to the college life, and get his school grades in line with an academic school's expectations, he suffered a concussion in his second game in a head-to-head collision. After going through a series of tests, he was cleared to play after an off-week but two more games later another concussion put him out for the remainder of the season. This completely changed his whole demeanor and state of mind. He stopped going to classes, started getting into scuffles with other students, campus security and local police. Bill had driven up on two occasions to bail his son out. A flash of his badge and Ray's status as an athlete had been enough to get him released and back to school. But this didn't last long.

A week had passed and Ray's roommate contacted Bill to tell him he'd not been to his room for a day or so. Calls went unanswered and Bill, unable to get away from work, called me in to see if I could find him. I spent two days in Greeley going from place to place, showing his picture around before tracking him down. He had been staying with a young woman living off campus who appeared to be his girlfriend or someone he hooked up with. Once I found him, Bill came up and, after much conversation, we persuaded him to go back to school and to see the sports athletic trainers. He wouldn't or couldn't admit to us he was having judgment issues, possibly related to the concussions. A month passed and all seemed OK until this latest news of him missing. I would retrace my steps from before, with the first stop being at the home of the girl he'd been shacking up with.

She lived two miles east of the campus in a simple brick two-story apartment complex. I had learned very little about her other than her name, Ariela Martinez. She worked at a local bar and dance club, which is where they met. It didn't appear as if they were a couple per se, just two people looking for an enjoyable time. She was a few years older than Ray and acted as if she was a little fearful of him when I arrived at her place, cowering and cringing when he got upset. Of course, I was a little fearful of him myself, as he wasn't happy I'd come to bother him or call to tell his dad I had found him. He threatened to kick my ass if I didn't leave him alone. At 6'4" and 250 pounds, he was an imposing figure to reckon with.

I approached the house, searching to see if I could find Ray's car. He drove a 2003 black Chevy pickup, but it was nowhere to be seen. Knowing Ariela worked nights, I expected her to be home. I rang the doorbell vigorously; it took a few minutes for her to answer. I had awakened her, as she answered in her underwear, but topless, a thin brown blanket wrapped around her to cover her up. The door opened on a security chain and she peered through it. Once her eyes adjusted she remembered me and swung it wide open, my engaging smile like a key in the lock.

"Sorry to wake you," I stated, closing the door behind me trying to block the chill of November in the air today.

"Searching for Ray again?" she said while sitting on an old, dirty brown sofa.

When she sat down the blanket came off and she flashed lots of brown skin. She had nice firm legs, average-sized breasts, and I could see a butterfly tattoo on her right thigh. It didn't seem to bother her to reveal herself for she didn't cover herself back up. It didn't bother me either as I took in the view.

"Yes. He is missing again."

"I haven't seen him for several days."

"Has he been in the club lately?"

"Last saw him on Wednesday. He wanted to hook up, but I told him to beat it."

"Why?"

"Because he only cares about one thing. Which was fine at first, but a girl needs more after a while."

"You broke up?"

"If you want to call it that. All it had to do with was sex and him trying to impress his friends. Someone he was banging to show off at the club."

"Sorry to hear it didn't work out."

"It was enjoyable at first, an attractive guy spending money on you, good in the sack. But he had his scary moments, too. Waking up in a cold sweat, as if demons possessed him. It would go away and he'd be OK for a while and then return with a vengeance."

"When was he last here?"

"The weekend before I told him to buzz off. He had a major meltdown on Sunday morning. I had to call the cops. By the time they arrived he had already gone. He smashed up some of my stuff and pushed me around. I knew I couldn't be with him anymore."

"You last saw him at the club on Wednesday. What about his friends? Do they still come into the club?"

"Yeah, most nights."

"If I stop in tonight can you direct me to them?"

She stopped for a second, a look of concern on her face.

"I promise they won't know. Discreetly point them out."

"I make my living there as a dancer. Come over by the stage where I can see you and I'll put on a show for you while pointing them out without them knowing. I expect a decent tip."

"This can be arranged. What time do you work?"

"Five to closing. I'm on the stage at the top of every other hour for about twenty minutes."

"What are you doing after?"

She smiled lightly. "Whatever someone is willing to pay me well enough to do."

It didn't take much to understand what this meant.

21

"What's the name of the club?"

"The Hustle. It's a gentleman's establishment."

"And they pay a membership to act like a gentleman?"

"If they come across with the right amount of cash, they can act however they damn well please!"

"OK, I'll be there tonight. Thanks for the info. If you hear from Ray, give me a call." I handed her my business card.

As I started to leave, a large Hispanic man walked into the room wearing only his blue-striped boxers. Not a single button was in use, his junk hanging out of the opening. He saw me and seemed to be mad I was there.

"Who the hell are you?" he demanded loudly.

"Pest Control. A snake is loose and I think I just found it."

Chuckling to myself, I slammed the door behind me.

Chapter 6

My next stop was to speak with one of the coaches. I headed towards the campus and Butler Hancock Hall, where all the intercollegiate offices are located. I had a map of the facility and made my way around with ease over the large area it covered. There are over 12,000 students at UNC, and I tried to blend in the best I could. With jeans, boots and leather jacket I probably fit in well with everyone else, other than age; though I wasn't the only mid-thirties-aged person traversing the grounds. Maybe I'd pass as a teacher: *Professor Jarvis Mann at your service.*

When I arrived at the offices I flashed my ID to talk with the head coach. Of course, he was too busy, but they said one of the assistant offensive coaches and possibly the trainer could squeeze me in. I found a chair and a copy of the campus periodical, *UNC Mirror*. After an hour of reading the newspaper cover to cover, along with a couple of several month-old *Sports Illustrated* magazines, I was led to the office of the coach.

Entering the room, he stepped around his desk and shook my hand, introducing himself. He was tall and athletic, dressed in Dockers and a team polo. I showed him the ID, but he waved me off as if to say not to bother. I took a seat.

"You're looking for Ray," he stated. "Damn shame what happened. He has a lot of talent."

"How well did you know him? Can you point me to somewhere he might have gone, any friends of his?"

"As coaches we are tight with our players on the athletic field, but personally we keep our distance. Not enough time to be social. Generally, these kids are here and gone before we know it. We want to make sure they are solid student athletes, which is most important."

"How about his latest injuries? What information can you give me?"

"Well, I'm no doctor, but he suffered two concussions over a three-week period. In the old days we'd have put him back on the field. Now with all the evidence of problems they have afterwards, we have strict protocol on how to handle it and the doctors make the final call. After the second one he wasn't cleared to play again this year, as he failed many of the tests. He didn't accept the news very well. Said everything was fine but they wouldn't clear him. The brain requires time to heal. No amount of pain medication, braces, whirlpool treatment or physical therapy can get you playing again."

"Is he allowed to practice?"

"No, can't take the risk."

"That means he is basically cut off from the other players."

"Not completely. He needs to do rehab work, which would involve teammates who have been injured. Light workouts in the weight room and running on a treadmill. Of course, it isn't the same as competing on the football field. Like most athletes, he was extremely competitive and lived for the confrontation with the other teams and players."

"Can I talk with the doctor or doctors who diagnosed him?"

"Due to the strict HIPAA laws these days they can't disclose anything to anyone other than Ray and those he has given permission to share medical info with. All they can tell you is what is in the standard press release on injuries the NCAA requires us to post."

"Even his own family?"

"Since he is of legal age, no."

"How about his roommate? I'd like to speak with him, if possible."

"Sure. Let me call and find out what class he is in. You may be able to get him between periods or at lunch."

The coach tracked down the roommate's schedule and provided a picture of him and a list of the various buildings he'd be in. I thanked him and headed out. With the map I got my bearings and walked towards Candelaria Hall, where his next round of classes would be. He had an Economics class coming up in the next hour, so I hoped to catch him going in if I could spot him among the masses. I found the room and leaned outside one of the entrances and waited. Once released, students were everywhere. I was good at spotting people in a crowd and within a couple of minutes I noticed him. It wasn't real hard because of his tight end stature: an African American standing 6' 3" and 230 pounds.

"Casey," I called out to get his attention.

"Yes," he answered with a deep baritone voice.

"I'm looking for Ray. His father sent me. Do you have some time

24

to talk?"

"I'm heading to class. I have open period next, so we could meet in the Holmes Dining Hall if you want. Are you familiar with the campus?"

"I should be able to find it on my trusty map."

He excused himself politely and moved on. With not much else to do for an hour I made two phone calls. The first was to Bill to let him know what I had, or more likely hadn't, discovered.

"Any luck?" he asked when answering.

"He isn't at the dancer's anymore. She said they are no longer seeing each other."

"And you believe her?"

"She didn't appear to be lying."

Since I had been staring at her naked chest most of the time, I could have been wrong.

"Anything else?"

"I talked with one of the offensive coaches, and he didn't have much to say. Knew he was gone and struggling with his latest injury. I'm going to be eating lunch with Ray's roommate here in a while. Hopefully he can fill in some blanks."

"Well, we haven't heard from him either. We've contacted everyone we know who might have seen him, and nothing."

"We'll find him," was all I could add for now.

After hanging up I called Melissa to see what she was up to. I got her on the move and couldn't talk much.

"I'm heading to court and running late. Are you staying busy?"

"In Greeley trying to find Bill's son; he's gone missing again. I'm roaming the campus talking to people he knows."

"Well, you stay away from those college co-eds," she stated with a laugh.

"I doubt any of them would be interested. Keeping up with them would be challenging."

"Save your strength for Friday. I've got to go. Maybe we can talk again tonight. Be safe."

After hanging up I needed to kill time, so I traversed the campus looking at the buildings. Some were recently built while others had been there for many years. Housing and classrooms comprised most of the structures. Ray lived in one of the newer facilities, Turner Hall, which stood thirteen stories high with modern rooms and excellent amenities. Walking past it on the way to the Holmes Dining Hall, I'd wondered if college life had changed much through the years. Once I arrived I found a bench outside and waited. Using the Windows Smartphone, I searched for the address of the gentleman's club and stored it in my maps' location. It got several four-star reviews, but the people who wrote them sounded sleazy with their graphic descriptions. The phrase "Gentleman's Club" was obviously a marketing expression some genius came up with long ago, with the term "strip club" no longer being politically correct but a more accurate description.

After a fair amount of time I saw Casey walking with some of his friends. Each appeared to be football players: by their size, likely lineman on either side of the ball. He spotted and waved me over, and we walked in. Being hungry I nabbed a tray and found something edible to eat. I offered to pay for their meals, but for students it was all part of the tuition. We grabbed a table and he introduced his buddies.

"This is Brad, Parker and Stoney. They play football for the Bears. You can probably tell they are offensive lineman. This gentleman is looking for Ray. I'm sorry I didn't get your name before."

"Jarvis Mann," I stated. "I'm working for Ray's parents trying to locate him. Anyone have any thoughts on where he might be?"

"Are you a cop?" asked Brad, a large white man with farmer hands, big and calloused.

"Private detective," I replied.

"Cool," said Stoney, who was African American and slightly smaller than Brad.

"Bet you get all the chicks!" said Parker, the largest of them all, who appeared to be Hawaiian or Samoan.

"I think jocks get all the chicks," I answered. "What about Ray?"

"He was a stud and always got tail!" Parker joked, while high-fiving his friends.

I gritted my teeth, smiled and counted to ten. *Patience, Jarvis…*

"Any thoughts on where Ray might be?" I repeated.

The laughter subsided.

"I know he was hurting," said Casey. "He was having a tough time sleeping after the last blow to his head. It bummed him out not being able to play again."

26

"How did he feel about you replacing him?" I asked.

"He understood," replied Casey. "It's part of the game. I would have preferred winning the job on the field, but one always has to be ready to take over—next man up, as they say."

"Ray was damn good," said Stoney. "Might be good enough to make pro with the right breaks. We all understand the risks, but we also think it won't happen to us. I tweaked a knee earlier in the season and wondered if my year was over. Luckily, I only missed a couple of weeks. Taped it up, wore a brace and I was back on the field. It sucks what happened to Ray. Only so much you can do when it's your brain."

"Anyone know where he might have gone? Any other male or female friends he might be with?"

"He does have a girlfriend," said Parker. "A hot one, too."

"I've already talked with Ariela and she says they are no longer involved."

"Ariela wasn't his girlfriend," replied Casey. "Just some fun on the side he screwed. His real girl is Shawna. She is one of the school cheerleaders. I would say talk with her."

This was news to me, as I'd not learned this from my last trip up.

"How long have they been together?" I asked.

All three looked at each other, trying to come up with the proper answer. "Less than a year, I'd say," said Brad. "Ray was a hound with the ladies. He could get anyone he wanted. He was like a rock star when he came here. Nailed a few others before he settled down with Shawna. Well, maybe *settled down* is too strong a word. She was his most consistent relationship."

"Where can I find her?"

"They practice at Butler Hancock in the afternoon about the same time we do, which is 3 p.m. If the weather is good, they train on the field with us at Nottingham."

"Probably too chilly for them today," stated Parker. "Their tits would be extra hard in the freezing air and stick through their outfits, distracting us players. And the coaches don't like us distracted."

The three of them laughed out loud with more high-fives exchanged. *Oh, the sweet bird of youth!*

I finished up the sandwich, which wasn't bad for school food. I reached into my wallet passing out business cards.

"Thanks for the info, gentlemen. If you think or hear anything about Ray, give me a call. His parents are worried and want to make sure he is safe."

"All kidding aside," said Casey. "We do like the dude and hope he is OK."

"Yeah, he is one of our teammates, so we do care about him," added Parker.

I shook each of their hands and walked out of the dining hall. I had a couple hours until practice, so I wasn't sure what to do next. While walking I sensed someone following me. I took my time and rounded a corner near the side of the building ducking down behind a trash can. Shortly, along came a young lady dressed in black with black and red hair. She passed by and stopped, trying to figure out where I went. I stood up behind her, startling her. She wasn't sure what to do but in her defense, she didn't run. She had a long strand of hair covering the entire right side of her face, but I could see she had a nose and lip ring. She glared at me, straight in the eye, and gave me a big frown.

"Looking for me?" I asked.

"I wasn't trying to stalk you or anything," she answered. "I wanted to speak with you some place others couldn't listen in."

"Where would you like to go?"

"Can we walk and talk?"

"Sure. What do you want to discuss?"

"Ray. He is my best friend and I'm worried."

Chapter 7

I followed along beside her walking the grounds. She was mysterious looking and I certainly would have never guessed she had been Ray's best friend. Her long black coat nearly dragged on the ground; black stretch pants covered her slender legs, with a meshing over top. She had various symbols on a cut-short black shirt leaving her navel exposed. She had rings on every finger, with lots of bracelets on her wrists. Black platform boots, dark eyeliner and lipstick completed the ensemble. She was the polar opposite of what you would expect a jock's best friend would look like.

"So, you and Ray are best friends?" I asked.

"Since high school."

"You went to Lincoln?"

"Yes."

From what I could see on her face she was telling the truth. Plus, there was no exposed private skin to throw me off, as with Ariela.

"I know you don't believe me. Most people don't when I tell them."

"Actually, I do. Though it does seem you two are different in a lot of ways."

"Yes, we are. Probably wouldn't have been friends if it wasn't for him speaking up for me with some boys who were bullying me at school."

"At Lincoln?"

She nodded her head.

"You became friends?"

"Yes. We've been close ever since and we talk almost every day."

"But not lately, I'm guessing."

"No. He's been distant since his last concussion. I've tried to reach out to help him, but I haven't had much luck. I think he has been getting himself into some trouble. I know he was hanging out at a strip joint with a couple of bad dudes. He wouldn't give me any details because he felt he could handle it. I think he was into something he couldn't get out of."

"Do you know their names?"

"No. He never told me. I wouldn't be caught dead in that hell-hole, as they demean women."

"When did you last talk with him?"

"About a week ago, and only via text. He's been avoiding me lately. I think he was mad I was on his case. I was worried he was going to get hurt. I care a great deal for him."

"So, no ideas on where he might be now?"

"There was a dancer he'd been seeing."

"Yeah, she ended it with him. Said there was no future. What about the cheerleader, Shawna?"

"I doubt it. She was pretty hung up on him, but he didn't love her."

"And you do?"

She stopped in her tracks and turned to me, her eyes looking at her boots. I'd hit a nerve and she acted uncomfortable at the suggestion. After a minute her eyes met mine.

"What makes you think I love him?"

"A hunch. Little clues that make me wonder. The look on your face when you talk about him. Body mannerisms when you say his name. Part of the skill of being a detective. Actually, more of a wild guess, to tell the truth."

"OK, yes, I love him. Though nothing will ever come of it."

"Because of the differences between you?"

"Yes. He is my best friend, but I know we'll never be a couple. His dad would never approve, and his approval is important, even though Ray would never admit it."

"Have you ever met his dad?"

"Yes, but he didn't like me. Bill didn't want Ray and me to be friends. He believed his son could do better."

This really surprised me about Bill. I thought he was a little more progressive about things like interracial relations. Maybe it was because it was his kid. Or he had a hidden side to him I'd never witnessed before. Not surprising, since he wasn't exactly an open book.

"Here is my card," I said. "Call me if you hear from him."

"Please call me, too; I need to know if he is OK."

She gave me her number and I placed it into my phone. Her real name was Constance, but she liked to be called Raven.

"It's good he has a friend like you," I said. "I'll be sure to let you know if I learn anything after I call his parents. Can I walk you to your next class?"

"Sure," she said, and we talked the whole way. I found her interesting and quite smart.

Once we said our goodbyes I headed towards the athletic center again to try and find Shawna. The maze of people I conversed with so far had led me to few new facts on Ray. No one seemed to have any idea where he was right now, which wasn't a good thing. His closest friend didn't know much and was worried. Now I needed to see if the girlfriend knew anything that would shed some light. It hadn't been this hard to track him down the first time. I was growing concerned there was more involved.

Arriving at the building I asked for directions to where the cheerleaders practiced. The lady at the front counter stared at me strangely like I was a pervert. Showing her my license, I told her I was searching for a missing student and that one of the cheerleaders was his girlfriend. She seemed relieved, and pointed me in the right direction. I went through the hallways until I found the gym. Inside there were several female and male students working their routines. An older woman approached me, telling me this was a closed practice. I again showed my ID and asked to talk with Shawna.

"She is busy, can this wait?" she stated with a growl.

"Her boyfriend is missing, so I'm sure she can spare a few minutes from saving the world." It was my shot at what I thought of cheerleading in general. I doubted it helped much to place it on your resume.

She grumbled but called out to Shawna to come over, and with a jog she joined us.

"This man needs to speak with you," she said. "She can spare ten minutes then she must get back to work. Our routine is in the toilet and we need to fix it quickly."

"Shawna, my name is Jarvis Mann and I'm a private detective. Can we go for a walk and speak some?"

"I don't think Coach would be pleased if I left," she replied.

"It makes it easier to talk and frankly, 'your routine in the toilet' is not a major crisis in my book. If she gives you any grief, I can shoot her if you'd like."

She gave me a big smile. "Sure, I guess it would be OK."

We stepped out of the gym and made our way down the hall. I figured it was always best for people to open up without prying eyes and ears nearby.

31

"I'm looking for Ray," I said. "His parents are worried. He appears to be missing. I understand you two are seeing each other, so I'm wondering if you know where he might be."

She stopped in her tracks. "Missing?"

"Yes, for a little over a week now. Have you seen him recently?"

"No. We broke up about ten days ago. He called a couple of times, but I didn't want to talk with him."

"Why did you break up?"

"Because he was seeing that slut! Banging her instead of making love to me. I don't stay with two-timing guys."

"Who was he, uh, banging?"

"Some dancer at a strip joint. I didn't know her name."

"When did you find out?"

"Shortly before I left him. I could smell her on him. I didn't want to get VD. Who knows who else the whore had slept with? Probably screws guys as part of her living."

From talking with Ariela, this appeared likely.

"How did you find out?"

"I got suspicious, so I followed him to the club he'd been going to. He was there with her and those two mean friends of his. I met them once and didn't care for them, either. They were eyeballing me, whispering to each other and imagining what it would be like to screw me. They were creepy."

"Do you know their names?"

She stopped to think for a minute. "Grady and Mack, I believe. Grady was black and Mack was white. They dressed well but they were thugs. I didn't like Ray being with them, but they made him feel special, especially after the injuries had knocked him down a peg or two. He needed some masculine building-up and they were providing it. I also think they were spotting him cash."

"Was it a lot of money?"

"I don't know, but I warned him he could lose his eligibility. The NCAA doesn't look kindly upon those things."

"Did you tell anyone this?"

"No. I cared too much for him to squeal. Please don't tell on him. Even though I think he is a pig for cheating on me, I still don't want him to lose his scholarship. It would only make it worse for him. Football is his life."

"How long had you been seeing each other?"

"We started dating earlier in the year."

"Was your relationship exclusive?"

She threw her head back and sighed.

"It was for me. I knew he played around some, being a big-shot athlete. Girls were always coming on to him. I looked the other way for a while but the way I felt about him…as time went on, I sensed he didn't feel the same for me."

"When did it go completely off the rails?"

"He was having issues after the first concussion, although it was much worse after the second one. It really threw him, and it changed him in a lot of ways. His concentration was off and he had real trouble sleeping. In bed together it wasn't the same, if you know what I mean. I did my best to understand and help, but he was too proud to admit to having problems. The macho athlete code got in the way. He was drifting, and I knew I'd lost him and wasn't getting him back."

"Do you have any idea where he'd be now?"

"If he isn't home then he'd be with those two creeps or with the slut. Check out the club and you might find him. It had been his fortress of solitude the last few weeks before I broke up with him."

"Shawna," sounded the booming voice of her coach from down the hall. "It's time to get back to work. No more dilly-dallying."

"I've got to go. Mother is calling."

"I can still shoot her if you want. A little flesh wound to change her attitude."

She smiled again, though a few tears filled her eyes. "Thanks. Save your bullets. I do hope you find Ray. I don't want anything bad to happen to him. I did love the guy, but I had to move on."

I handed her my card, with the same line as all the others. The way I was handing them out, I'd need to order a new supply. Hopefully they would yield some results, as I was killing a lot of trees.

Chapter 8

I decided to get a bite to eat at a local Subway in an effort to drop a few pounds. In the commercials they claimed all I had to do was eat there every day and off it would come. Since Madison Avenue never lied, I'd be slimmer and trimmer in no time.

I enjoyed the meal in my car while checking out the location of The Hustle. It wasn't a long drive but took me to the other side of town, east of the campus. It was already dark when I arrived short of 7 p.m. The day had flown by but still I hadn't a clue where Ray was. I was hoping to strike gold here and finally learn something that would lead me to him.

It was early yet so the parking lot was mostly empty. I navigated the potholes and found a place up front. The outside appeared shabby and I didn't have high hopes for the inside. I decided I'd better have my gun with me, as it didn't appear this was a family-friendly environment. I slipped on my shoulder holster and strapped in my Berretta, making sure it was loaded and the safety was on, all concealed under my jacket. As I reached the front door, a large black man asked me for some ID.

"Members only," he bellowed.

I pulled out a couple of twenties and handed it to him. "Will this cover me for one night?"

He pocketed it without hesitation while letting me in. "Enjoy yourself."

Once I stepped inside I saw the place wasn't a total dump, but it wasn't Vegas either. It was very warm and the sound was ear-shatteringly loud, with modern dance music I didn't care for. There were about ten patrons in the place, all men, most of whom were in suits. They were enjoying the show on the stage, where the mostly naked woman were doing their best to dance. Their G-strings barely covering their lower bodies, the chests completely exposed and wiggling to their gyrations. Many places like this didn't allow the patrons to touch the dancers but here it appeared to be encouraged, as two of the men were getting rubbed down by one dancer, while she bounced back and forth between the two. The more money they flashed the more she would do. If I wasn't so real world–hardened I'd probably be blushing, not that anyone could see it in this dim lighting. I sat down at a table and a waitress, slightly more clothed, wearing spandex bottoms but still topless, came up asking me what my pleasure was, her chest pointed straight at me.

"I'm sure many men here answer your question in a naughty way," I said to her.

"Yes, most do. We are trained to say it, make it sound sexy. Gets them riled up. Good for business."

"Good to know they don't skimp on training the staff," I said. "I'll do my best to control myself. I'll take a draft light beer if you have it, and run a tab."

She wiggled away, also part of the training, and I had to admit I enjoyed the skin she was showing, though I'd say Melissa's was more to my liking. She returned quickly, setting the suds and bill on the table.

Surveying the room, I saw two guys who fit the description of Grady and Mack, though it was hard to tell since the lighting was so bad. The stage strobe flashed in rhythm with the music, doing little to brighten the place and only blinded you. They were sitting at a large table near the front, each with a woman cradled on their laps whispering in their ears. When the sound stopped, the two women left and went backstage. About ten minutes passed and the music started again and a new pair of dancers hit the stage, one of whom was Ariela. She had on a biker outfit, chaps, spiked leather boots, a black leather bra with tassels, and a skull cap covering her hair. The other dancer was dressed nearly the same and both began to dance to "Bad to the Bone." This brought hoots and hollers from the men in the crowd as they gyrated around, doing their best to tease the men and slowly disrobe.

I decided to move closer and made eye contact with her. She had now removed her bra and was slowly stripping out of her chaps. I pulled out some cash and began waving it at her. She stepped down off the stage and came over to me, snuggling up against me with her sweaty body. I took a couple of bills and placed them into her G-string, and she came around and straddled me, rubbing her crotch against mine. It wasn't entirely unpleasant, and I was playing a part, looking like someone enjoying themselves. She put her mouth to my ear and began nibbling.

"It's the two at the big table on the right," she said above a whisper, so I could hear over the music."

35

Running my mouth now across her ear, I answered, "Thanks. It's what I suspected."

"We need to keep this up a while longer. Grab my ass."

Doing as I was told, she gave me a full-mouthed kiss with lots of tongue. Again, it was not unpleasant, but I was trying to control myself. She began licking my face and putting her hand on my crotch. Now it was getting more difficult to not get aroused.

"You actually are pretty cute," she murmured. "If you're ever lonely, you know where I live. Stop by for an enjoyable time. I even have a female friend who will join in. We like touching each other while you watch and then…" She whispered some graphic details in my ear, leaving little to the imagination.

She crawled off me and I placed some more cash into her G-string. The next song started playing and she moved onto another patron. I got myself back under control, enjoying the show until it ended and stepped over to the bar. There was no one at it other than the bartender. I asked for a refill and handed him my tab.

"Quite a place here," I stated. "The ladies are very friendly, more so than most places."

"Part of the service," he answered while placing the fresh beer in front of me. "People pay big bucks to come in here and get their rocks off. If the girls aren't in your face and crawling all over you they don't work here long, if you know what I mean."

"Yeah, I can tell. The one on my lap nearly had me busting through my zipper. A few more minutes…"

"Ariela is a hot one. She keeps them coming back for more, if you get my drift. Don't think I've seen you here before."

"Possible new member; I'm here on a trial basis. What does it cost per month?"

He gave me an answer and I whistled.

"Damn, that is a lot of dough, though worth it for the perks."

"You are only seeing the appetizer. The four-course meal and dessert is in the back. Anything a man would wish for and desire."

I took a long draw on my beer. It tasted watered-down, which was fine with me. No need to get drunk, but I wanted to look like any another customer in the bar. Intoxication would be my disguise.

"Hey, a friend of mine told me to stop by and see him here," I asked. "Comes here often and said I'd have a joyous time. But I don't see him here."

"What's his name?"

"Ray Malone."

His friendly face turned south when I said the name. "I never heard of him." I could tell he was lying.

"Really, are you sure? Said he was a regular and is good friends with two other guys who come here a lot. I figured you'd know them."

"Sorry, buddy, I haven't worked here too long. Excuse me, I need to get some more peanuts from the back."

Sitting in front of me, the peanut bowl was full. Stepping away, I knew he was going to warn someone. I turned to face the show and the place got loud again, being time for the next show. I was watching the table and saw Grady grab his cell phone to check something, a text message probably pointing me out. He glanced over my way and slapped Mack on the back to draw his attention away from the dancers. Both were eyeballing me now, and I raised my beer glass to drink the rest. Slowly they got out of their chairs and walked towards me, neither one looking pleased. They approached and I stood straight up, smiling a happy drunk expression. I wanted them to think I was just another wasted patron—an Academy Award presentation.

"We understand you're inquiring about someone," said Grady, loud enough so I could hear him over the music.

"Yeah," I stated trying to slur my words. "A buddy of mine, Ray Malone. Do you guys know him?"

"Why you asking about him?" said Mack.

"Like I said he is a friend. Told me to stop by sometime and he'd show me the time of my life. Says the ladies here give the best head."

"I don't think you're a member," said Grady. "How'd you get in here?"

"Money talks. Ray said for forty bucks I could get a preview of the place. If I like it, I could buy a membership and join."

"We don't have any membership openings right now," stated Mack. "It would be best if you leave before we throw you out."

"Oh, come on, guys, I ain't hurting nobody. I'm trying to have some fun. Get a little action. You have some hot girls here and I'm raring to stick it to them."

"I think you've had enough to drink," said Grady. "Let us call you a cab so you can go home and sleep it off."

"But what about Ray? I wanted to say hi and thank him."

"He don't come around anymore and isn't welcome here either," said Mack "And neither are his friends. Now move."

Mack put his hand on my shoulder and I slumped down pretending I couldn't stand. He shoved me to the floor, his strength pushing me about ten feet away. In the process I reached into my coat and pulled out my gun, pointing it straight at the two of them. In their defense, neither of them blinked or showed any fear, but still respected it.

"Now, I came here to find Ray," I said loudly while getting to my feet. "You were friends with him from what I learned, so I figure you know where he may be."

"We told you," answered Grady. "He don't come around here anymore and isn't welcome."

"You guys have a falling-out?" I asked.

No response from either. Their faces remained stoic and weren't giving much away.

"He's missing and I figure you two may be involved. I want some answers."

"You're digging yourself a hole, friend," said Mack. "Might be your grave, so if I were you I'd back out and walk away. This isn't something you want to mess with."

"And what if I put a bullet in one of you? Will this loosen your tongues?"

Both glanced at each other and started to laugh. Apparently, I didn't scare them any, my bluff not called.

"You want to fire, go right ahead," answered Grady. "But if you do, it will only guarantee your own death."

It looked like we had a standoff and I didn't care to shoot the place up. I figured leaving my card this time and asking them to call if they saw Ray wouldn't work with this bunch. I needed to ease my way out.

"OK, I'll walk out of here. But to make sure you don't plug me in the back, ask your man at the door to come in here so I can back my way out."

Mack called out to the man at the door and he ambled in slowly while I kept my gun pointed. If they all rushed me at once I could shoot one or two, but not all three. It was getting time to leave. I stepped carefully to the door keeping an eye in front and another behind. Reaching it, I stepped through when I saw a person and turned. It was the bartender and he tried to grab me, so I punched him with my free hand in the nose as hard as I could. It didn't stop him and he tackled me to the ground, my gun skidding away. I rolled to push him off me and got to my feet, when another set of arms bear-hugged me, nearly crushing the wind out of me. I stepped down hard on his left foot with my heel and pulled loose, only to be slugged in the face by the bartender, which sent me reeling to the ground. The other person was the doorman; he picked me up and I tried to punch him in the stomach, but couldn't get enough on it. He used a right-left body combo, knocking the wind out of me this time, dropping me to my knees. Another shot to the side of my jaw laid me out on the cold cement. I was seeing stars but also hearing sirens, or was it angels calling me home to Heaven? I was done and there was nothing to keep them from finishing me off.

"What's going on?" spoke an amplified voice.

"Nothing, sir," said someone else. "We were persuading this gentleman to leave. He isn't welcome and was causing a disturbance."

"OK, back inside, I'll take it from here," said the voice.

A door slammed, followed by footsteps. Someone knelt beside me and slapped my face to clear my head.

"You OK, buddy," he asked.

My eyes opened and I saw him there in his pretty dark-blue uniform.

I cleared my throat to speak, but I'm not sure if he heard me before I put my head back down to sleep. "Who says there is never a cop around when you need one?"

Chapter 9

I woke up on a gurney in an ambulance taking me to the hospital. My head was aching, as was a good portion of my body. I tried to sit up and found my muscles were extremely stiff. I looked and saw a paramedic sitting there, watching me. He seemed to be enjoying my attempt to move.

"Nothing broken," he stated. "But definitely bruised. You took a good beating. I don't think you should try to get up until the doctors look at you. Besides, you're strapped down."

"I don't like doctors," I replied while noticing for the first time the strap across my waist. "Not thrilled with hospitals, either. Where are you taking me?"

"North Colorado Medical Center. We should be there shortly."

"I don't suppose you can let me off here and I can walk home?"

He chuckled.

"No, sorry. From what the officer said home is Denver, which would be a long stroll."

Once at the hospital, doctors and nurses did a lot of poking and prodding, asking all the time if this hurt or that hurt. My distaste for the entire process was obvious. I argued to be released so I could go home and sleep. Finally, after much badgering, I succeeded, but I first had to give a statement to the cop who saved my ass. They needed to make sure I wasn't going to return to shoot the place up. The thought had crossed my mind.

The officer, by his badge, had a last name of Olsen and was a little less than six feet, with a military crew cut, and biceps and triceps straining at his shirtsleeves. When he walked in his face was serious, his eyes looking me up and down trying to figure me out. He had a clipboard with several documents to fill out. Paperwork was a policeman's least favorite activity.

"From your ID we see you're a detective from Denver," he stated. "Why were you in town causing trouble?"

"Looking for a missing person," I replied. "Ray Malone, who goes to UNC. His father is a Denver cop who hired me to find him."

"Why look for him at The Hustle?"

"Several people with information led me there. I follow the clues until it leads you to another clue."

"And why the confrontation?"

"They didn't like me asking questions. I figured they might be involved in his disappearance, or at least know where he was."

"They claim you pulled a weapon. One of the bouncers inside brought it to me."

"It was to even the odds. It was four against one, and a gun helps in a case like this."

"I guess it didn't help keep you from getting your ass kicked."

"It would have been much worse without the gun and you arriving when you did."

"We got a call claiming there was trouble and I was nearby. A female inside the building, from what we can tell, calling from a cell phone. She saved you."

"I think I know who it was but would rather not give her away being a source. It would put her in jeopardy."

"Not a problem. We don't need her for this. They aren't pressing charges, so you are free to go."

I slowly got to my feet to make sure I could stand. They had given me some pain medicine that hadn't kicked in yet. Acting brave and tough was something a PI needed to exhibit. In reality, I wanted to lie down and take a nap, but not here. *What does a hotel in Greeley cost?*

'What about my car?" I asked. "It was sitting in their parking lot."

"Yeah, we found it and had it towed to the station. It's all yours, once you pay the towing fee."

"Swell."

"It's better than letting them have it. Since they didn't get to finish beating you, they might have taken it out on your car. Hate to see a classic beaten to a pulp."

He was probably right. "Thanks. Can I get a ride over to retrieve it? And can I get my gun back?"

"If you think you can walk, you can follow me and we'll get them to release you. I'm sure they'll be happy to be rid of you. You weren't the best patient from what they told me."

"I hate doctors and hospitals. I only care for nurses when my girlfriend dresses up like one."

He let out a short laugh. "Amazing the fantasies we men enjoy. I'll have to suggest it to the wife."

Once I was cleared he drove me over to the station. I filled out more paperwork and paid a hefty fee for the tow. I asked Olsen about someplace to get a bite to eat to boost my metabolism while allowing the meds to kick in and he offered to join me. I decided the company would be good, so I accepted, and we went to a small nearby fifties-style diner.

When we strolled in the waitress behind the counter called out "Hey, Trey." He waved back and we took an open booth near the front door. She walked over and put down menus. "What will it be, boys?" she asked.

"I'll take a Cherry Coke, Maggie," responded Trey.

"How are your shakes," I asked.

"Fresh-spun and killer," replied Maggie.

"I'll take a chocolate one, as large as you make them."

"If you like breakfast for dinner, this is the place," said Trey after she walked away. "Excellent pancakes."

Breakfast food sounded pretty good. I wasn't real hungry but needed some calories to stay awake on the drive home. I didn't want to spend the night at a cheap hotel and longed for my own bed. Maggie returned with our drinks, and we both ordered some pancakes and bacon. Trey also added some scrambled eggs.

"Some free information off the record if you care to listen," stated Trey.

"Sure, I always welcome information from the police, especially one who pulled my butt out of the fire."

"This place, The Hustle, is run by a slick guy: not the meanest guy in town, but certainly not a saint. If the kid you were looking for was at his place or working for him, then he is probably in trouble."

"What can you tell me?"

"His name is Marquis Melott. He dresses well and runs this gentleman's club with one intention, to make money. He lures in men with the promise of pretty woman and something many of them can't get at home—wild and kinky sex."

"That would make him a pimp?"

"Never call him a pimp to his face, but in a way, yes, only classier. He sells these men a membership to the club. Brings them in, shows them a pleasurable time, and gets his girls to get them hot and bothered. Over a period of time with temptation they get a little more than a lap dance. Maybe a quickie in the bathroom or one of the rooms he has in back. If they are into it, a three-way with a couple of gals. All of this discreetly gets recorded and used to keep them members with the veiled threat it will get posted on the Web. He doesn't rake them over the coals, just keeps a steady income coming in. If they don't come across with the cash they are warned, simply at first, but later, the videos are leaked on the Internet or an email is sent to a family member with the link to view. Normally, the face is blocked out and the message gets him to pay."

"Subtle," I said. "The wife tells him of the message and the link with the dirty movie. She doesn't know it's him, but he knows what it's about. I'm sure if he doesn't pay the next one his face isn't hidden."

"Correct. And here is the best part, he then sells him on something even kinkier, lure him in even more. Maybe some wild fantasy he can live out. Maybe he wants to do it with a guy or an orgy. He'll fork over even more for this and, of course, it's recorded. He is on the hook and can never be free."

"Why haven't you arrested him?" I asked.

"Well, he hasn't done anything illegal, at least not that we can prove. Even if we could get him on extortion, no one will testify. There have been a couple of people murdered we think he may have been involved with, but no evidence. He has a proper license for the business and brings lots of money into the city coffers, with the taxes he collects and pays."

"So, a sweet deal for him and the city."

"Yep."

Maggie brought us our food. The shake was large, cold and thick, as advertised. The stack of pancakes was filling and tasty, though the syrup was a little runny for my taste. I downed the chow carefully, my body still sore from the beating.

"I forgot to mention I talked with Officer Malone," said Trey in between bites. "He verified your story and told me he needed to talk with you. It was important."

I pulled out my phone, which had survived the melee, and contacted Bill. He answered on the second ring.

"I hear you ran into some trouble," he said, knowing it was me. "A Greeley cop called and said you were in the hospital."

"I'm out now and I'll live," I replied. "He said you needed to talk with me."

"Ray showed up at home about an hour ago," said Bill. "He is a little out of sorts and hasn't said much, but seems to be OK."

"Glad to hear it. I wished he'd gotten home a little sooner!"

"Sorry. Did it at least get you any information on where he's been?"

"Maybe. We can talk about it tomorrow after I'm done following my landlord's husband. I'll call when I'm finished and we'll get together."

"Good and thanks," said Bill.

"Looks like his son showed up a while ago," I said to Trey. "Not sure where he'd been but he is at least alive."

"Good to hear. I need to get back to my shift. You need any other info, you can contact the station and they can get ahold of me. I'll assist if I can."

"Thanks," I stated. "I'll take care of the check."

"Is this a bribe?"

"Call it the price of good intel, and I can expense it!"

Chapter 10

The next morning, I woke up in my bed, body aching as if I'd been through a war. Wall-to-wall pain would be the order of the day. I did sleep once I made the long trek back home, but it took several Advil and some strong booze to knock me out. Now, sitting under the shower for as long as the hot water lasted, it felt good Ray was home but bad that I'd taken a beating in the process. Once dressed I called Constance, or Raven as she liked to be known, to let her know her best friend was OK. There was relief in her voice, but I couldn't tell her any news other than he was home. With no desire to cook I grabbed some water, a whole bottle of pain pills and headed to the local McDonalds for an on-the-go breakfast.

I was back in front of Kate's waiting for her husband to leave. He promptly exited around the same time, and we were off on almost the same track. We were up and down the various major streets, Broadway, Federal and Santa Fe, north and south, and Evans, Hampton and Belleview, east and west. He stopped several times to collect or to drop off. I wrote down locations and shot numerous photos, though none were completely revealing. Money was often exchanged, and small plastic bags of some substance were handed out. He had to get tough with two different people today and even punched one of them. After driving all over, we ended up at the same bar again. This time I would wait outside to see who went in, but first I went up the street to a Subway to grab some lunch and use their restroom. Now loaded with plenty of supplies, I found a good parking spot where I could view the front entrance and enjoy my turkey sub.

While waiting, I made a quick call to Bill. "How is Ray doing?"

"Still sleeping," he replied with his normal monotone voice. "We had to give him something to help him get some rest. He was all wound up when he got home. Our plan is to get him to see a doctor again about his concussion."

"Several facts I learned in Greeley to fill you in on. Do you want to do it over the phone or should I stop by later?"

"How about dinner?" he asked. "Rachael is a helluva cook. I'm sure she won't mind."

"What time?"

"We usually eat around six."

"So, did you ever run down the plate I gave you?"

"No, I didn't have time and I'm taking another personal day. Call down to the station and ask for Officer April Rainn. Last name spelled with two N's. She is the one I delegate your requests to. Drop my name and she'll be happy to help."

"Can do. See you at six."

My eyes stayed on the front entrance and forty-five minutes after I arrived, the BMW from the day before showed up. The same two men climbed out and entered Eddie's. It was a little warmer today, so they weren't wearing heavy coats, and I could easily see the bulges under their jackets, signaling they were armed.

After a couple of bites of my sandwich I called and got hold of April.

"Bill Malone said I should drop his name and you'd help," I stated when she came on the line.

"Yep, I'm his personal gopher," she joked. "What are you needing?"

"I got a plate number I need run down," I said. "Any info would be helpful: owner's name, any criminal record, street address, any parking tickets—the works." I rattled off the digits.

"How fast?"

"Today, if possible. I normally buy Bill a beer, so I guess I owe you for all these years."

"OK, I should be able to have it for you by end of my shift. As for the beer, I may take you up on it sometime. Is this the number I call you back on?" She read off the caller ID on her phone.

"Yep. Thanks, April."

I finished up my lunch and rolled down the window; the sun was warming things up. Like the day before, the two goons in the BMW came out about an hour later and left. I had an urge to follow them but decided to sit still. I needed to find out if Jack's ride showed up again today.

Passing the time was already hard when staking someone out. I tuned into the classic rock I streamed from my mp3 to the car stereo. The wonder of technology: where you can carry your entire music collection with you wherever you go, with the cheap cost of gigabytes of storage. I ran through Led Zeppelin, The Stones, the Beatles and the Doobie Brothers before the white Mercedes I'd seen

Jack leave in two days earlier arrived. The window was down and I could see the driver, a longhaired redhead with big, round sunglasses hiding her face. I took snapshots and got her plate number. Jack ran out the front and jumped in, and I got other shots of them hugging and kissing. They sped off south on Broadway and I quickly pulled out, as she was moving at a fast clip.

Now, like the day before, she cut off other drivers, and weaved in and out of traffic. Fortunately, this stretch had quite a few lights, so I was able to keep up but had to be more aggressive in driving than I cared to, as I didn't want to lose them. We continued south for several miles, reaching Dry Creek Road. With a squealing of tires, she turned left and now was heading east at a pretty good clip. I pushed the pedal and kept up the best I could. She reached University, turned right and quickly turned into the parking lot of some condominiums. I lost her and couldn't see her once I entered. Up and down I steered until I finally found the car. I slowly drove past and saw them walking arm-in-arm up some stairs, his hand firmly patting her ass. I stopped and took the best pictures I could and pulled into the first open spot. I waited until 4 p.m., but they never came out. There was little doubt Jack had himself a girlfriend. The digital shots would easily get Kate the divorce and freedom she was looking for.

The day wound down, so I left and headed back home. My cell rang and it was April, so I pulled over to take some notes.

"Car is owned by a Dirk Bailey. He has priors including assault, assault with a deadly weapon, attempted murder, aggravated robbery and I could go on and on. Spent a couple years in jail at one stint, and five more later on. Several times the charges didn't stick or were dropped at a later date."

"Sounds like a winner to me," I replied.

"Yes, he is. He generally hangs around with another winner, Merrick Jones. His list of priors is as long, if not longer. Both work for a street hood named Roland Langer. Deals mostly in loan sharking, but dabbles in drugs, gambling and prostitution. Wanted for a couple of murders, but never convicted of anything where he had to do any hard time. Generally, no one lives long enough to testify, if there are any witnesses to start with. He is one nasty person."

"Wow, you made my day!"

"Whatever you're into, I'd say get out, unless you are very tough or very stupid."

"Probably a little of both. I have another plate if you could check on it."

"Bill said you'd ask for the moon."

"I'm guessing you talked with him."

"I wanted to make sure he directed you to me; can't be too careful."

"It's worth another beer?"

"Are you trying to get me drunk?"

"My intentions are nothing but honorable. My girlfriend might object to me taking advantage of an inebriated woman other than her." It was the first time I called Melissa my girlfriend and it had a quality ring to it.

"Too bad, it might have worked. The good ones are always taken. Give me the plate number, but I'll need to get you the info tomorrow as I'm off the clock."

"Tomorrow will be wonderful," I said after giving her the letters and numbers. "I'm still good for the beers. Boone's gives me a volume discount. You name the time, other than tonight, and I'll pay up. I'm having dinner at Bill's house."

"OK, I'll call you late morning with the info once I have it, and we can meet up afterwards."

I agreed and hung up. It was too bad I was seeing someone; I'd always wanted to make it with a female cop. Those handcuffs were a real turn-on. *I wonder what size police uniform fits Melissa.*

Chapter 11

I arrived at Bill's promptly at six for dinner. They live north of the Valley Highway off University Blvd. Their neighborhood was a step-up from mine, living in a two-story brick home with a detached garage and a huge backyard.

His wife, Rachael, whom I had met a few times, greeted me warmly at the door with a friendly hug. Bill had warned me she was a hugger and there was nothing you could do about it, so deal with it. Since I wasn't the most touchy-feely person in the world, I coped. She is a wonderful lady, and there was nothing about the embrace that ever felt phony in any way.

"Jarvis, it's so good to see you," she said. "You're looking pretty good, young man. Have you lost some weight?"

Truth be told, I'd put on a few pounds. But Daddy always said never question a compliment.

"Clean living keeps me fit," I replied. "Most of it is probably much firmer now."

"The curse of being single; no good woman to cook for you."

"Oh, would you quit doting on him, Rachael," stated Bill as he walked into the room. "She does this to everyone who comes over."

Around his wife Bill always seemed like a different person. He was cold and aloof most of the time, but with Rachael he was a happy man. She certainly brought out the best in him.

"Well, I don't get to see him much," she said. "It's always a treat when we have company. Bill doesn't care to socialize. You should be honored he asked you. He must actually like, or at least tolerate, you."

"Probably the latter," I said. "I don't get invited much for dinner, either. Hopefully I can remember my table manners and how to eat with a fork and knife!"

The African American couple laughed, which was the first time I'd made Bill laugh out loud. It was good to see, and I hoped the mood remained after the information I would be sharing with them about Ray.

"Well, I hope you like lasagna because its Ray's favorite," stated Rachael. "I always cook it for him the first night he is back from school."

"Mom, the timer is going off," said a young girl who walked into the room. "I think the bread is done."

"Thanks sweetie. Say hello to Jarvis. I'm not sure if you remember him or not," Rachael said while heading to the kitchen.

"Hi Jarvis," she said shyly, while going over to hug her father.

It had probably been or year or so since I'd seen Monika. She had grown quite a bit and was much taller. She was the spitting image of her mother.

"Hi, Monika. I can't remember the last time I saw you. What are you now, eight or nine years old?"

"She's ten," stated Bill. "I see her every day and I'm amazed how much she has grown. She is quite an athlete, like her mother and brother. Swims, runs track and plays soccer. And is an A-student."

I always remembered her being extremely shy and this hadn't changed, her face turning red from her dad's comments, and she buried her head into his chest from embarrassment. Bragging was the right of every parent.

"Dinner should be ready shortly," called Rachael. "Monika, can you go get your brother? He should be done with his shower by now."

Monika ran off and I followed Bill into the dining room. The living area was wide and expansive and through an arched opening was the table and chairs. The whole room was brightly lit, the place settings glistening from the candelabra that hung over the table. I sat down after Bill pointed to where I should sit. Rachael was bringing in the food and it all smelled superb. It had been a while since I'd had a good home-cooked meal.

Monika walked in and Ray was right behind her. He towered over her and everyone else in the room. Bill was probably close to 6'2", but Ray was two inches taller and all dark-skinned muscle. He was the prototype size for the tight end, with the power and quickness I'd seen when he played in high school. He was dressed in jeans with holes in the knees and a UNC sweatshirt. He pulled the chair out for Monika to sit down and came over to say hi.

"Good to see you again, Jarvis," he said while shaking my hand with a viselike grip.

"Glad to see you too," I replied. "How are you feeling?"

"Pretty good. I had a good night's sleep. Best I've had in a while."

"He slept until almost noon," stated Bill.

"Home is always comforting," I added. "I always slept well any time I stayed at my parents' house back in Iowa."

Ray took his seat next to his sister and the final dishes were brought out. We all sat down holding hands and Monika said grace, thanking God for bringing her brother home safe and for my presence at the table as an honored guest. I think I blushed when I heard it.

Besides lasagna, there was salad, garlic bread and some steamed carrots. The food was passed around and I filled my plate. Ray took a huge slice of lasagna and several pieces of bread. He appeared to be famished. The normal caloric intake for a man his size would have been costly all these years. While eating, the conversation took various paths, Monika talking about school and her homework and a boy at school who was crushing on her. It then turned into Rachael asking about my love life, and I proclaimed I indeed had someone I was seeing, which appeared to please her. But the conversation never turned to Ray, on where he had been or what he'd been doing these past days. The subject would be left for later.

After dinner was finished, there was chocolate cake and ice cream, another of Ray's favorites. Once the meal was done, the dishes were cleared and I was stuffed, we headed back to the living room to talk.

"Ray, why don't you and Monika go downstairs and play some Xbox while we chat," said Bill.

"Come on, Monika," stated Ray. "Let's see if I can finally beat you in Need for Speed."

"You've got no shot," she answered. "I'll race you to the basement." And they dashed off.

"You need anything to drink, Jarvis?" asked Rachael.

"No, I'm good. Thank you for the wonderful meal. A demanding work out tomorrow is needed, I'm stuffed."

I sat in a comfortable black leather recliner while Bill and Rachael took the matching sofa together. I know they were waiting for me to give them an update, but I was trying to figure out where to start.

"What did you learn?" said Bill, breaking the silence.

"Ray is maybe mixed up with some less than honest people," I said pointedly. "The girl I found him with the last time, Ariela, is a dancer at a club called The Hustle. Ray is involved with them somehow and they might be leveraging him for money. I won't know for sure before we talk with him."

"And why would they want money from him?" asked Bill.

"It's a gentleman's club. The exotic dancers do a little more than dance for the customers. The owner, according to the Greeley policeman I talked with, draws men in with memberships with benefits, does some digital recording of their actions with the female staff, and squeezes them for more money. Blackmail, pure and simple."

"I find it hard to believe Ray would be involved with this," said Rachael. "We raised him better than this."

"I don't know this for certain, but it is the game these people play. He was a hotshot college football player, simple to manipulate. Remember he is a young man on his own for the first time. The lure of sex with pretty girls is easy to use on a man his age."

"But he told us he was dating someone," said Rachael.

"Not anymore. I talked with her and they broke up over his affair with Ariela." I left out the part about him sleeping around. No reason to shatter a mother's vision of her son completely.

"He is seeing Ariela now instead?" asked Rachael.

"No. I visited her too, and she was there with some other guy. She hadn't seen Ray for a while. It appeared to be strictly a sexual relationship, and possibly a way to blackmail him."

"Oh my," gasped Rachael. "Are you certain of this?"

"Enough that we need to confront him. I went to the club and when I started asking around, I got bounced out on my ear. I took a pounding from two of the thugs Ray had been hanging out with. They said they didn't want him around there anymore, but I doubt what they said was completely the truth."

"I saw the bruise around your eye, so I was wondering," said Rachael.

"I've got a few more you can't see. Lucky for me the police arrived, or it would have been much worse."

Rachael grabbed Bill's hand and closed her eyes. It wasn't easy for her to hear this about her son. I wasn't thrilled with telling it either, but I was used to giving unwelcome news in my business.

"I talked with his roommate, other teammates and a coach. They all tell me he's been having a tough time with this latest round of concussions. Poor concentration, can't sleep, followed by terrible headaches and exhaustion. When he does manage to sleep, he has crazy dreams, making for a restless night. The coaching staff is encouraging him to get medical help, but he's been resistant. Concussions are nothing to fool with and could lead to long-term issues. He requires proper treatment before it gets any worse."

"We'll get him whatever he needs," said Bill. "We'll spare no expense."

"I know you will. But keep in mind he may not be able to play football anymore, depending on the extent of the injury. Facing the facts won't be easy for him."

"First is treatment and getting him healthy; it's all we care about," said Bill.

"First, we need to see what he is into and get this resolved," I said. "I think it would be best if Bill and I talk with him, Rachael. I don't think he will be real forthcoming discussing this type of sexual dalliance around his mother."

"But I need to be there for him," stated Rachael.

"You will be, only not during this step. He must admit to the problem before we can figure out how to fix it."

"He's right, honey. Why don't you head to the basement and send him up here?"

Rachael resisted, but then gave in. She walked out of the room, and within a few minutes Ray came upstairs. His father told him to sit down and we needed to talk.

"Son," began Bill. "Jarvis has learned some things we need to get cleared up. He believes you may be involved with some people who don't have your best interest at heart."

"Really?" he replied. "And who would that be?"

"Mack and Grady, to start with," I said.

"They are guys I hang out with from time to time. Show me a good time."

"Bad guys who carry guns and bounced me out on my ear when I asked about you."

"They don't like cops."

"They didn't know I was a private cop."

"They can tell. They deal with them all the time."

"Men who deal with cops all the time generally deal with them for a reason."

53

"They hassle them because they are viewed as pimps. But they aren't. They are providing a basic service for their paying customers."

"And are you one of their customers?" asked Bill.

"They comped me because I'm a football star. I didn't have to pay."

"What about money? Did they loan you any?" I asked.

Ray was getting uneasy, his hands clenched.

"I needed a little to pay for some things. You know how it is for college athletes, they don't give us any money to live off of."

"And did they ask you to pay it back?" said Bill. "Did they threaten you if you didn't?"

He didn't answer, his face displaying anger or embarrassment.

"And what about Ariela, or any of the other girls? Were they free or was the money to cover sleeping with them?" I asked.

"If we slept together, it's because I'm a stud football star. Ray don't pay for sex. I can get it whenever I want it."

"And did they record it and try to use it against you?"

Ray gave me a cold stare and didn't reply to the question.

"Did they, son?" asked Bill.

This time, Ray turned his frosty expression onto his father. He got up from the sofa and left the room, running up the stairs to his bedroom, a door slamming behind him.

"I think we got our answer," I said to Bill. It was what I'd feared.

Chapter 12

We gave it time, but Ray never returned, so I headed home, leaving Bill to deal with it. He and Rachael would continue to try and get through to him. It was a thick wall to break down. I told him to contact me when he was ready, so we could figure out our next move. I didn't sleep well and called Melissa, even though it was late. I required an ear to chew on.

"I was asleep," she said when answering the phone. "Are you OK?"

"I had a tough couple of days and needed to hear your voice. I miss seeing you."

It was a hard confession to make, as I rarely in my life missed anyone.

"I miss you, too. Once this legal proceeding is over we can be together; it's kept me busy in court. Hopefully it will wrap up Friday afternoon and you can take me to dinner and vent on me sexually."

I wanted to see her, to touch and smell her. Lying lost in her arms would be a five-star relief.

"I can come over and vent now."

"Well, buddy, the most you're going to get from me is phone sex; I'm whipped and need my sleep for tomorrow. What type of dirty words do you need?"

Her saying it made me feel better. I would have loved to heat up the airwaves, but wanted to save my best for Friday night.

"No, I can wait. Hearing your voice helped. Can I tell you what's been going on these last couple of days?"

Though you could hear the exhaustion in her voice, she said yes. I gave her all the details on both cases but left out the part about me getting my ass kicked. I told her they tossed me out but nothing about the beating I took. No reason to trouble her with worrisome information.

"You think Ray is mixed up with them?" she asked.

"I think so, but he won't come clean. He is a football star and it's hard to admit someone takes advantage of you. He wants to trust they are his friends for the proper reason."

"But they aren't and he can't see it."

"No, he can't."

"What can you do if he doesn't want help?"

"Not much, but his dad and mom won't give up on him. I'll assist however I can. But I don't believe Mack and Grady will let him off the hook easily. It's their job to bring in revenue. There is more to this than we know right now."

"Even though he is the son of a cop?"

"I'm not certain they realize, and even so it won't matter. Cops don't scare these guys."

"Well, sweetie, it doesn't sound good, but I know you will make it right," she said. "I have nothing but faith in your ability."

I was glad she had faith in me, because sometimes I doubted it myself. I would muddle through and persevere to find a solution.

"What about your current trial?" I asked. "What can you tell me about it?"

"Today the prosecution tried to sneak in a surprise witness. Well, the judge reamed him for it..." She continued for about another fifteen minutes giving me details of her last couple of days, including a plea bargain deal they were considering for their client. It all sounded so dramatic, but I knew legal wrangling rarely was. At times it was long and tedious, as both sides attempted to get the upper hand on the other.

"Well, my dear, I think I've kept you up long enough," I said. "I will let you dream of judges' gavels banging on the bench."

"I'd rather dream of something more pleasurable."

"And what would be more pleasurable?" I asked, a bit out of breath anticipating where this was leading.

"You may not want any dirty talk but I'm going to give you a few choice words to help you doze off," she stated. "Graphic details to tide you over until we can be together again."

She proceeded to describe an arousing oral sexual act, which sent the blood racing from one head to another, before hanging up. The teasing image rolled through my body, though strangely enough it did help me sleep after a bracing cold shower eased the stiffness.

Chapter 13

After my good night's sleep, with visions of Melissa's narrative graphically playing in my head, I awoke to the alarm at 6 a.m., eager to begin my day. I hadn't worked out in several days, so I was off to the gym with my usual running, lifting and punching routine. Always good for working out anger, sexual and body stiffness from the beating I took. A good hour later with the heart racing at a comfortable pace, sore muscles feeling better, I went home and showered, ready for one more day of gathering evidence for Kate. As I reached the car my phone rang. It was April with news on the last plate I'd given her.

"Her name is Dona Wiggins," said April. "No arrest history other than some juvenile arrests that are sealed and I can't access. She does have lots of speeding and hazardous driving tickets. License is suspended, so she shouldn't even be behind the wheel."

"Yes, I witnessed her automobile skills," I said. "Worse than a man and with reckless abandon."

"Probably sexually frustrated."

"I don't think so. The person I'm tailing gave her a long, passionate kiss when she picked him up and they walked into her condo with his hand on her butt. Never saw them leave after several hours. I assume they were getting it on."

"Slut!"

I had to laugh. "What else did you get?"

"Lives down in Highlands Ranch in Douglas County." She gave me the street and number.

"Not the address I followed her to. I doubt her lover is fronting the place; doesn't have the money."

"Married and enjoying a little on the side," said April.

"It does appear so. And he comes back to his home late each night."

"Glad someone is getting some action!" stated April. "Wife hired you to tail him?"

"Yep. His old lady is tired of him and wants him out."

"Good to know I'm not the only one who gets involved with losers. So, do I get my beers tonight?"

"And sparkling conversation. What time shall I meet you at

Boone's?"

"Around 4 p.m."

"How will I recognize you?"

"I'll be the single girl in the booth packing a sidearm!"

"I can't wait."

I had pretty much all I needed for Kate's lawyers, but wanted a little more before sending it off. My agenda today was to pick someone Jack collected from and see what information I could get out of them. It would be icing on the cake. The question was how I was going to approach them. I had two options—either as a customer or a detective. My plan was to play it by ear, but I dressed the part of someone a little bit down on his luck, with raggedy clothing, to appear more like someone who's street-weary. I didn't have to dig very deep in my closet for the role.

After Jack left home he made two stops, the last of which I decided would be my target. He stopped at the corner of Broadway and Alameda in the parking lot of an Auto Parts Store to meet with two men he'd hooked up with before. I took several pictures of him pushing them both pretty hard to get what he wanted, and I could tell they weren't thrilled to see him. They might not have much of an issue rolling over on him if I played this right. After he left, they walked heading north on Broadway at a slow pace, so I got out of my car and started following them and caught up quickly.

"Hey, guys," I called out.

They each turned and I got a good look at them. The first was Caucasian about 5'9" and famine-skinny, with dirty jeans hanging so low the waist was closer to the ground than to his mid-section. Ratty canvas high-top sneakers laced up his ankles, while he wore a blue fabric coat with a hood covering his rumpled hair and long enough to cover his ass since his jeans didn't. The other appeared to be Asian, a hair taller and plumper, beige dungarees hanging low, but not as low as his friend's, black boots and tattered black leather jacket, his uncovered shaved head shining in the cold November sun. As I approached they both smelled like they hadn't showered in days, acting cautious to what I wanted. The white guy kept his hands in his pocket and I was on the lookout for a weapon. I was armed today with my .38, hoping to keep it holstered. I decided to play the detective part and see if I could coerce or buy knowledge from them.

"What?" said the Asian man, his hands now also in his coat

pocket.

"I need some information," I stated. "I'm wondering if you're in a sharing mood." I pulled out my license and showed it to them.

"You a cop?" said the Caucasian.

"Private."

"We done nothing wrong."

"I'm not here to roust you. Only want some answers to simple questions."

"What's in it for us?" said the Asian man. I could see his hand twitching in his coat pocket. The small bulge had to be a knife, not large enough for a gun.

"You walk away without me calling the cops down here and even get paid for your trouble. Money appears to be something you can use."

They both glared back and forth then back at me again, and each from their pocket flashed a knife blade at me as a warning. I wasn't too worried; they had cowered when Jack pushed them. I showed my revolver to make sure they understood I was armed, the weapons disappearing into pockets, knowing they were out-classed.

"Again, I don't want trouble," I said to balance the gun flashing. "Answer a few questions and I can give you each twenty bucks. If one doesn't want to talk they can walk away and the money goes to the other. If neither is interested, I'll ease on down the road not to bother you again."

"Ask the question and we'll see if it's worth it," the Asian said.

"I want to know what Jack collects from you when he stops by," I asked. "Seen him a couple of times pushing you around."

"You know Jack?" the Asian said, rubbing his nose.

"Yes. We are acquainted."

"Why?" they both said simultaneously.

"Let's say I have a client gathering intel and we'll leave it there."

"Jack is connected," stated the Caucasian. "Going against him can be harmful to our health."

"It's nothing about his connection, strictly on a personal matter. It won't even get him arrested."

"Getting him busted might get him off our back," said the Asian man. "Wouldn't be all bad for us. Of course, someone else would take his place. Would only delay it a day or so."

"How about forty each," stated the Caucasian.

"If the information is good, sure," I answered.

"Let's see the green," said the Caucasian.

I pulled out the four twenties. "They're all yours."

They each grabbed the cash quickly and pocketed it. I was prepared for them to run, but they stayed put. I doubted I'd shoot them over eighty dollars, but then again…

"Roland Langer," said the Asian. "Jack works for him. He is a loan shark and all-around mean guy. Jack is his collector, well, one of his collectors. We are into Langer for money we can't get out of."

"Let me guess, interest rates above the legal limit."

"Stupid of us, but banks don't loan to guys like us," said the Caucasian. "Jack is angry, aggressive and doesn't like it when we can't pay. We must scrounge every day to come up with something, or else. Unless we win the lottery we'll never get out from under him."

"Is Langer into anything else?" I asked.

"We hear he does take bets on games and runs some illegal gambling parlors," said the Caucasian. "Cheap and expensive pussy if you want it. Drugs here and there. Nothing we are a part of."

"Does he have two other men working for him? Big guys, linebacker size."

"Couldn't tell you," said the Asian. "Jack is all we've dealt with, which is bad enough. He did mention he could bring some tough dudes down on us if he wanted to. Always made it sound like he was doing us a favor."

"Do you think the money ever gets back to Langer?" I asked.

Again, the back and forth, followed by a dumb stare of who-the-hell-knows.

"The balance never seems to change much," said the Asian while rubbing his bald head. "He could be skimming but not much we can do about it. Our knives are no match for his six-shooter. We can scare old ladies and fags on the street but not him. And we got no money to purchase a gun."

"Be cool if you can get him out of our hair," said the Caucasian. "Might be worth the eighty you gave us."

I wanted to tell them to use the cash to buy some soap and deodorant, but resisted.

"We'll see," I said. "You may get your wish in time. Thanks for the information. Of course, I never talked with you."

"Jack is a mean SOB. I'd be careful of him"

"I appreciate the advice," I replied. "I won't take him lightly."

Once back in my car I had the connections I needed, confirmed by the two men on the street. Jack was a collector for a loan shark and all-around bad man. Kate had a right to know, to get him out of the house and out of her life. She deserved better. I gathered all the data together and carefully organized it and sent it off to her lawyers electronically to process when I returned home. The upload meter took its time, the Internet running slowly, though it never seemed fast enough no matter what I was doing. I verified they had received the information, then called up to see if Kate was at work so I could give her the news personally. She was down knocking on the door about thirty minutes later. When I let her in she sat down, and I gave her all the details I'd discovered. It was a relief, but also a burden.

"Bastard!" she said angrily. "I want him out of my home."

"It will take a couple of days to get the paperwork filed for the divorce and restraining order," I said. "By early next week we can bounce him out on his ear."

"I don't think I can handle him in my home anymore. Can't you throw him out?"

"Not legally. Let's wait for your lawyers to come through. Once they have the paperwork we'll serve him and toss him out. Get a locksmith scheduled to change all the locks on your home and business. I mean, it's not like he doesn't have a place to stay, from what I can see."

My words were said insensitively, and Kate began to cry. Even though she was mad, she was hurt. Anytime someone you loved and shared children with betrays you, it stings. I came and put my arm around her and she cried into my shoulder for several minutes. I hate with a passion women crying and cringe when I see it, but I persevered.

"I'm sorry to have lost it," she said, composing herself. "I don't know how I'm going to make it through these next few days with him in the house each night. I'm scared for my kids. Is he dangerous?"

"Possibly. He is dealing with dangerous people. But I've seen no reason for his world to collide with yours." It wasn't necessarily true, but I didn't want to add to her pain.

"I don't want to chance it. If something happened, I'd never forgive myself."

"Take them on a trip somewhere. Colorado has many marvelous things to do. Go to Colorado Springs and stay in a hotel until Monday. I'm sure the kids would be happy to get away on a mini-vacation. Could even pull them out of school for a few days and leave tonight. Every kid loves getting extra time off. Think of it as a snow day."

"I hate to abandon the business."

"Close up for a family emergency, or let one of the other ladies handle things. I know they like their boss and would do anything for you. I can check in on them and even stop by the house and make sure it's OK. Do it for your sanity as well as your kids. I'm certain they are stressed about this too."

She would think on it and used the bathroom to clean up her face before going back to work, telling me she would let me know what she decided. I never liked giving people bad news, but it was part of the job and I was handing it out to client's times two. I wanted to call Melissa, but I knew she was in court. It was too late for lunch, so I would save my stomach for Boone's and my meeting with April. I had an hour to kill, so I checked what was on the TV and found nothing of interest. Even the sports channels were disappointing, so I called to check up on Bill and see if there was any progress with Ray.

"He has pretty much shut us out," he stated. "I think if he had somewhere else to go, he would. He did tell us he plans to go back to school after Thanksgiving break. For now, he seems to be spending lots of time sleeping, gaming or on the Web. We are lucky to even get a 'hi' out of him."

"He ever say where he was the last few days?"

"No. For all I know he was sleeping in his truck."

"Hopefully he'll open up. Are you working today?"

"Yes. I'm trying to make up the time I lost. I have to work all weekend."

"You or Rachael call if you need anything. My newest case has pretty much wrapped up, other than serving papers on the husband. I'm available to help."

"Thanks," he said and then hung up. Bill's gratitude was often bare bones.

As 4 p.m. arrived I made my way to Boone's and entered to the smile and wave from Nick the bartender, who seemed to always be working there. Stepping in, I searched around the bar until I saw her in a booth. I made my way over and smiled as she stood up. She was about my height, with short dark hair parted in the middle and a fresh face. She was a bit on the heavy side, but appeared to be firm with lots of muscle tone. I shook her hand and it was strong for a woman. She had the uniform on, with sidearm, mace and handcuffs. I tried not to drool too much from the handcuff fantasy I'd had for many years.

"You must be Jarvis," she said while sitting down.

"April. Nice to meet you," I replied. "I see you haven't ordered anything yet. I'm famished and I'd be thrilled if you'd join me for dinner if you didn't have other plans—a down-payment on future research."

She smiled. "I can eat and no, I don't have plans. Some spicy chicken wings would hit the spot."

I wasn't much into the spicy ones, because of heartburn, but I'd manage thanks to the wonders of modern medicine.

"Sounds good."

The waitress was promptly there, and we ordered some chicken wings, fries, two beers and a glass of ice water to take an antacid pill. It was the all-American bar meal.

"What is it like being a lady cop on the Denver Police force?" I asked.

"Fair," she replied. "Still hard to get past the prejudices; some handle it better than others. But you have to pay your dues to break through."

"How is Bill to deal with?"

"He's pretty good. Not the worst but not the best either. But I think he sees me as a cop first."

The waitress brought our drinks and April drank half the beer in one gulp. I imagined she could drink me under the table. I felt like an old man having to take my OTC drug, although I didn't care to be up half the night with searing heartburn from the hot wings.

"How about the politics?" I asked.

"Like any job, it's there. I'm biding my time. I'll be on the street eventually. Bill says it will happen. I'll be a good cop if I'm patient."

"You look like you can handle yourself," I said. "Definitely not a wilting flower, the way you chug a beer."

63

"I had three older brothers, so I had to be tough," she said. "In time I could kick their asses. I was certainly a tomboy who did everything the boys did. I didn't dress up in pretty dresses or put on lots of makeup. I wore jeans and a T-shirt while getting in the dirt, grease and mud. It's what I love and still do."

The waitress was on top of things and brought a second beer for both of us, though mine was still mostly full. The place was starting to fill up with the evening crowd. A couple of ladies stopped by to say hi to April. She introduced me as a friend, though they didn't buy it and gave me the once-over, followed by a nod of approval to April.

"They think you're hot," stated April.

"You could tell from a simple head nod?" I replied.

"I'm trained in catching other women's signals. The heat was smoldering off their ample bosoms."

"Can you teach me, because I can never tell for certain until the clothes come off? If I'm lucky enough to reach clothing removal."

April laughed loudly, which increased her attractiveness. A female friend would be good for me to have, to test my resolve. Of course, Melissa might argue the point.

With more food, we dug in. April ate the chicken wings and fries quickly, though I swallowed the fiery meat more slowly. She had a good appetite and a second batch was ordered. I directed the conversation toward what it was like for a female cop to build long-term relationships.

"Not easy," she said. "The hours make it difficult and some men are threatened by a strong woman. They want to screw us, but not stay with us. Heaven forbid I'd have an opinion to share. I'm fine for now since my career is what's important. But the day will come when I want more. There are always battery-operated devices to fill the void."

I was smiling and blushing; the frank talk surprised me some, though deep down I enjoyed hearing it.

"Now I know what to get you for Christmas if you don't find him," I stated.

She laughed at the banter, not embarrassed the least bit.

"Plenty of time," I said. "He'll be out there somewhere. Maybe you'll arrest him and it will be love at first sight."

"It's the handcuffs, right?" she asked.

"Every man's fantasy come true," I replied.

My secret was out, so we sat and talked for two more hours, enjoying a stress-free meal together, exchanging R-rated innuendo as if it were a Judd Apatow movie.

Chapter 14

I made it to Friday and was happy the weekend was near. Feeling good, I was off and running after a good night's sleep, at the gym pushing hard, the last vestiges of the beating's soreness and bruises gone from my body. Tonight, I would be meeting up with Melissa after a week apart, with dinner, a movie and, with luck, passion on the agenda. My heart was racing, and it wasn't from riding the elliptical.

This day was for me. No more following Jack and no dealing with Ray's problems. I did need to check on the salon, since Kate had decided to leave town until Monday. The ladies were all smiles as we chatted for a few minutes and everything was running smoothly. This left me with some time to run errands and get myself prepared for tonight.

One stop I did need to make was to Lincoln High School down the street to visit with a former client and now friend. I texted Dennis Gash to see if he had some time to talk as I wanted to get a football player's perspective on some things. At 2:30 today with the weather being pleasant for November, he planned on running around the track at the school a few times and throwing the ball around with Terence and the team quarterback named Deion.

With my errands done, I swung by Kate's house and found all was good. No sign of Jack, which wasn't surprising; he was probably shacked up with his girlfriend for the afternoon, after a day of pushing around bums and addicts. From there I headed over to Lincoln High School. I strolled over to the football field and saw Dennis with his two friends, running. I took a seat in the bleachers and waited for them to finish.

Dennis had filled out and even grown some since the bubble gum card case. He was now about an inch shorter than I was and a muscular 195 pounds. He'd grown his Afro out and walked with a sturdy confidence beyond the shy boy he was when we first met. It had been a good year at running back for him, though the team itself only won three games. He was a solid player now and continued to get better with one more football season in front of him. I suspected he would get some type of scholarship, maybe even at UNC like Ray, as they actively recruited in the area.

As they finished up on the last lap, they raced to the finish line, with Dennis winning, Deion second, and Terence bringing up the rear, but only by a few feet. This wasn't bad for a man his size. He'd also filled out some and was now a senior. He played both football and basketball, and could be a two-sport college student. Though still a few months away, the offers would start coming in.

"Jarvis, good to see you," said Dennis.

I took his hand, the grip firm but not overpowering.

"How are you? You don't look like you've lost any of your speed."

"I'm faster and stronger now," he replied. "You remember Terence."

"Hello, Jarvis," stated Terence.

"How's the family doing?" I asked.

"Great. My dad's working steady again and even Mom has full-time employment. Money is still tight, but we're together."

I was happy to hear this. Terence was a good kid who'd made a dumb mistake to help his family out of a financial jam. The reasoning and motive was correct but via the wrong execution.

"Jarvis, this is Deion," said Dennis. "He is our quarterback."

"Good to meet you," said Deion. "Dennis mentioned you're a private detective. Sounds like a cool job."

"It's not bad. I don't get all the girls like a QB does, but it has its rewards."

Deion was your quintessential high school quarterback. He was tall and lean, probably 6'2" and 180 pounds, and could run fast and throw OK. Since it was the wishbone offense, being a runner was key, and passing being second. He was not your classic NFL QB, but for college he had potential to be pretty good. Some small institution would likely take a flyer on him.

"You said you wanted to ask me something?" said Dennis.

"I can ask all of you. Have any of you had your bell rung on the field? Suffered a concussion?"

"I have," replied Terence. "It was this year in the first game; head-to-head with another team's running back. I saw some major stars."

"Did you keep playing?"

"Yes. I don't remember much of what happened until the third quarter."

"They didn't pull you?"

"No. I did a good job of hiding it. You know, soldier on and play with pain. I got up and went back to the huddle. Good thing I don't call the defensive plays, or everyone would have known. A couple of the guys said I was speaking gibberish."

"Any problems since?"

"No, I've been fine. Headaches for a few days, is all."

"But you should have been pulled?"

"Probably. This is high school and they don't provide the medical staff like in college or the pros to catch things like this."

"What about either of you?" I asked of Dennis and Deion.

"No," replied Deion. "But I've seen guys go down like they've been shot—knocked out cold. It's pretty scary when you see it. Your joints and ligaments can be repaired, but your brain—that's a different story."

"I've been a little dizzy after a few hits before," said Dennis. "Like Terence says, you soldier on and play with it. It's how we are taught."

"Why are you asking?" stated Terence.

"Do any of you know Ray Malone?"

'Sure," said Dennis. "He is a legend in the area. One great high school player until he blew out his knee."

"He's suffered two major concussions this year," I said. "He doesn't seem right and I think it's affecting him in his decision-making process. I've had a couple myself through the years, but not from head-to-head bighorn-type collisions. Of course, I wasn't back out there banging heads again a week later."

"Is his football career over?" asked Deion.

"He is done playing for this year," I replied. "But with the decisions he's making, I'm more worried about his life in general. He's making mistakes I'm uncertain he'd make otherwise."

"Wow, what a shame," said Dennis. "I wish we could help."

"Nothing you can do. I appreciate the feedback. It's always good to hear from others, especially football players who've been through it."

"We're going to toss around the ball," said Dennis. "Would you care to join us?"

"I'd love to, but I have a date to get ready for, so I don't want to get all hot and sweaty."

"At least not until later," kidded Deion as we all laughed.

I said my goodbyes and left them to their football. It was good to see the young men growing up and enjoying themselves. They were all well-grounded with solid families to guide them correctly.

When I reached my parking spot at home I noticed a familiar Silver Acura RL parked out front. Melissa had a key, so I figured she was waiting inside. It was earlier than I expected but the more time with her, the better. I walked in, but she was nowhere to be found.

"Melissa, are you here?" I called out.

At the bedroom door she stood wearing a see-through teddy, leaving little to the imagination. Her beautiful body enticed me, with a come-hither look on her face. My heart started racing at the thought of what lay ahead.

"We wrapped up the trial early with a plea bargain," she stated. "I couldn't wait to see you."

I walked over to her to get a closer view, enjoying the titillating sight.

"I can tell," I replied.

"Ever since I described the wonderful sex act to you over the phone I could think of nothing but doing it."

She grabbed me by the shirt, pulled me into the bedroom, stripped me down and turned fantasy into a reality.

Chapter 15

No dinner or movie out, we stayed in bed enjoying each other's company and pleasure, having food delivered. After a good night's sleep, we were up and showered and ready for a day together.

"You got away with dinner in last night," said Melissa. "But you are taking me to breakfast. I need some calories to replenish my body."

"It was your idea for the seduction over dinner out," I stated. "Not that I'm complaining. Where would you like to have breakfast?"

"You know the area, you decide. Something with eggs and pancakes would be great. But not Denny's! I'm not a grand slam, thank you ma'am kind of lady."

I smiled and decided to take her to Rosemary's Café, which was down the road on Sheridan. It was a quaint café with good breakfast at a decent price and good service. We arrived and had to wait about fifteen minutes for a seat during the Saturday morning rush. Once we sat down, we promptly ordered eggs, hash browns and pancakes. I chose milk to drink while Melissa wanted orange juice. I spent most of the time waiting, staring into Melissa's green eyes, enjoying every line and mark on her face. It was a face I was getting familiar with very quickly. It wasn't long before the food arrived and we ate quietly, and with each bite gazing at each other. It was a quiet meal, and after finishing Melissa had the look of someone who wanted to ask me something, but seemed leery of saying it.

"What do you want to ask me?" I said.

"Is it that obvious?" she stated.

"Pretty much. You probably are bad at poker too," I replied with a smile.

"I'm wondering what you would think about me going back to school?"

I was a caught off guard by the question.

"School for what?"

"Law school. I'd like to be a lawyer."

"Wow. Will you be going full time?"

"No. It will be nights and then weekends studying. I actually started a few years back but had to stop for personal reasons. But I think it's time to finish what I started."

"You can afford this?"

"Bristol & Bristol will pay for some of it. I have money to cover the rest."

"How will this affect us?"

"Well, it won't happen until after the first of the year. Nothing will affect us at first. But it won't be easy; I will be very busy. But I don't want to be a legal assistant the rest of my life. And with a little luck, I could be a partner in the firm someday."

"Bristol, Bristol & Diaz."

"My name part of the brand would be cool. My mother was a lawyer and partner in her own firm, though she is mostly retired now."

"I think it's great. If it's something you really want, I'll support you. I might grumble some, but in the end, I want what is best for you. You need to make me a promise, though."

"Sure. What is it?"

"That you hire me when you need detective services done for your clients. I can always use the work."

She reached out her hand and placed it on mine.

"Sleeping with the boss might give you a leg-up on the competition. But you'll need to submit a resume and be interviewed."

"I promise to do whatever it takes to satisfy the requirements for the position."

She smiled her bright smile and we left the café arm-in-arm after paying. The morning sun was now blanketed with clouds, the threat of rain and snow creeping over the foothills. We reached the car and she turned to me and hugged me for a long time, the warm feeling seeping into my whole body.

"Wow, you rocked my world," I stated. "Do we go back to my place and continue this?"

"No, I need to do some shopping first to limber up before jumping you again. I want to walk around Cherry Creek and see what new outfits I can find for work and school. Not the mall, but the shopping center up and down 2nd and 3rd streets. Lots of cool places a lady can swipe her credit card in."

No need to argue, since I knew it would get her juices flowing. We headed on down Evans to University, traveling north. I knew construction was messing up much of the area around Cherry Creek, but we weren't in any rush. As we got closer my mobile phone rang and it was Bill calling.

"Where are you at?" he said sounding panicked.

"Heading to do some shopping," I answered. "What's wrong?"

"I got a call from Rachael and someone is trying to break into the house. I had her on the line, but lost her. When I dialed back there is no answer. I'm on the other side of town on patrol and can't get there right away. Can you get over there and see what is going on?"

"Sure. Can't you get another unit to stop by?"

"We are shorthanded and there is no one in the area, and you are close. Too many sports events: college hockey, NBA and college football. I need to make sure she is safe. It will take me thirty minutes to drive over."

"I'll get there as soon as I can," I answered and then hung up.

I did a quick, illegal U-turn in the middle of University and headed back the way we came. Bill's house was only a couple blocks away.

"What's wrong?" said Melissa, startled by my abrupt direction change.

"Shopping has to wait. Bill's wife maybe in trouble."

"He's the Denver cop you've been helping?"

"Yes. And with his son mixed up with some bad people, they may be looking for him. Rachael called him and said someone is trying to break in, and then he lost her."

I pulled up a block short of his house, as I didn't want to put Melissa in the line of fire. I unlocked the glove box but remembered I didn't have my gun with me. I wasn't expecting to do battle today. A rain-snow mix had started to fall and was beginning to cover the grass. I handed Melissa the keys to the car and kissed her quickly.

"Stay here. Get behind the wheel when I leave, and if anyone approaches who isn't me or the police, drive off. I promise to return once I know all is safe."

She looked dumbfounded when I left, with no words to say, doing what she was told. I ran up the street to the front of the house, my hands in my coat to keep them warm. Seeing the front door ajar was not a good sign and I could hear a man yelling and a woman crying. Peeking around the door jam, I could see two men, one standing with his back to the door, his arms crossed, the other on top of Rachael on the sofa holding her down. It was the two men from The Hustle I'd

72

encountered before, Mack and Grady.

"Tell me where Ray is, woman, or I'm going to make this very painful for you!" said Mack, while slapping her across the face.

"I don't know where he is," Rachael answered through the sobs. "He left and didn't tell me. He is a grown man who doesn't check in with his mother. Honestly, I don't know."

"Could be true, but here is the deal. He owes us and if we don't collect we are going to get it another way as a message to him. And I don't think you'll like what we have in mind, will she, Grady?"

"Nope. But we'll like it quite a bit," Grady replied with a hideous laugh.

Mack started to pull at Rachael's shirt. To her credit she fought him the best she could, but he was too heavy and big for her to handle. I had no time to contemplate my move, so I reacted. Lunging into the room, I punched Grady as hard as I could in the nose. He went backwards and fell over an end table crushing it in the process, his face now covered in blood, his nose obviously broken. My hand was stinging from the punch, but my adrenaline was flowing, so I wouldn't feel the effect until later.

"Get off her," I said with a growl. "Let's see if you can collect from me, asshole!"

It was a stupid thing to say, but I was trying to sound tough and the endorphins were flowing.

Now Mack's best advantage against me was Rachael, but he gave it up once he recognized me. He stood up and jumped over the coffee table, landing a few feet in front of me, an impressive feat for a big guy. I had my hands up in a fighting stance and began jabbing him, left, right and left once more. But he was pretty good and blocked each of punches. He followed with a combo of his own and I did my best to block them, though one got through and struck me in the chest. I countered with some body shots, but he was solid, and didn't even wince. He came at me again and I did my best rope-a-dope, but a solid wall doesn't work as well as the ropes in a boxing ring. I blocked every hit, so he went low and got me in the ribs and I was down. Before he could follow up, the sounds of sirens in the distance spooked him. He pulled the bloody Grady off the floor and headed out the back way.

Standing up, I went over to console the crying Rachael. Her top was torn up and I took her in my arms to cover her up. Two officers came storming in with guns pulled. I identified myself, and luckily, one of them was April, who happened to be out on patrol today for some reason.

"Is she OK?" she asked.

"Call for some paramedics," I said. "They were beating her pretty good."

"Anything else?"

"No. I stopped them before they could go any further."

I held onto her until Bill arrived. His look was of shock at what had happened, and he took my place holding her.

"I'm here, baby," he said while rubbing her head.

"They wanted Ray," she said through the crying. "Said they were going to take it out on me if he didn't pay them."

Bill looked up at me and I nodded my head. "That's what they said."

"Did they get away?" asked Bill.

"Went out the back. I gave April a description, but they appear to be gone. Didn't see a car but I know who they are. They work at the club where Ray had been hanging out. I know them as Mack and Grady. Greeley police should have more info."

The paramedics arrived and took Rachael to the side to check her over. She was bruised and battered, but didn't appear to have anything broken. My ribs were stinging. So were my hands and arms. I would be sore for several days. Another beating my body would have to overcome.

"Sir," said one of the officers at the door to me. "There is a lady here saying she knows you."

"Damn," I stated.

I'd forgotten about Melissa. I went over to the door, and she was standing there with a look of anger on her face. I stepped outside and took her in my arms.

"You said you'd be back. When I saw all the cars but not you, I feared the worst."

"I'm sorry," I answered. "I'm OK. I needed to help Rachael and time got away from me."

"Damn you!"

"It's what I am. It's what I do. I hope you understand."

She pulled away and punched me in the arm as hard as she could, adding to my bruise total. I knew the dangers of my job had crept into our relationship for the first time.

"I'm likely going to be here for a while. Did you want to wait or you can take my car and drive to my place. I can have someone here drop me off when I'm done and we can go have lunch and shop. OK?"

"Promise?"

"Scout's honor."

The anger subsided some from the look in her eyes. "I'll go back to your place. Call me if it's going to be real long, please."

"I will," I said while kissing her on the forehead. "Officer, would you walk her to our car, please?"

As I returned to the front of the house I saw Ray walking up, wondering what was going on. An officer stopped him, but I motioned he was OK to enter. Ray looked at me inquisitively.

"Your mother was attacked," I said. "She is OK but a little beaten up and scared."

"Why," he asked.

"They were looking for you."

Ray couldn't speak. He appeared to be in shock. He walked in and saw them working on his mother. She looked up, saw him and waved him over. He wasn't sure what to do, finally walking over to her.

"Are you OK, Mom?" he asked.

She tried to smile but couldn't because her face was swollen, so she nodded.

"I'm so sorry, Mom."

"It's because of you this happened to your mother," said an angry Bill. "Lucky your sister was at volleyball or it could have been her, too."

"Bill, probably not the time," I said.

He gave me a mean look but decided I was right. Now it was important to tend to Rachael.

"I think we should take her in for a few tests," said one of the paramedics. "Need to be certain there is no internal bleeding or any bones are broken. Doctors will probably give her some pain medicine. She'll be quite sore for a while. Bill, I'm sure you'll want to go with her."

"Yes."

"Can I go too," said Ray.

"No," answered Bill. "I'll call Monika and see if she can stay with her volleyball teammates, who drove her to practice, until we get home. Can you watch over him, Jarvis? I don't want him alone right now."

"Sure. Are you hungry, Ray?"

"I can eat something"

"If someone can drive me to my place, we can get Melissa and have some lunch."

"I'll drive you," said April.

"Lucky you came along when you did," I said to her. "Glad to see you out from behind a desk!"

"I was at the precinct, but Bill called and told me what was going on. No one was in the area, so I commandeered a car and drove over as fast as I could."

"You mean you stole a police car?"

"Strong words, though we'll see what my shift supervisor says. I doubt he'll be happy I left my post."

"I'll write you a note," I stated. "They love me down there."

She started laughing, either at my joke or at the unlikely fact people at the precinct liked me.

Chapter 16

April dropped Ray and me at my place, where Melissa no longer appeared to be angry. She was sparkling and joyful when I introduced her to Ray.

"We're taking Ray to lunch," I said.

"It seems like only a short time ago we had breakfast," she answered.

"Well, believe it or not, it's been three hours since breakfast. Time flies when you're fighting crime. What shall we eat?"

"The Cherry Creek Grill OK with you, Ray?" asked Melissa.

Ray gave a quick nod, though you would have missed it if you weren't watching for it. He'd been deathly quiet in the police car and on the drive to Cherry Creek. We decided to take Melissa's car because it had four doors and Ray was tall, so climbing in the back of my Mustang would be challenging. Parking a couple blocks away from the restaurant, as spaces on the street were scarce, I fed a sufficient amount of coins into the meter to cover us for a couple of hours. The rain-snow mix had turned to all white flakes and we moved swiftly to get inside. It was maybe a ten-minute wait before we sat and ordered our drinks. Ray finally spoke but it was only for ordering a soda. I knew I needed to work on getting him to tell me what was going on, but his stubbornness would be challenging. I was hoping with what happened to his mother he'd give us the whole story. I had whispered to Melissa on the walk over to make small talk with him to put him at ease. It wouldn't hurt a pretty woman asking the questions either.

"No cross-examinations, though," I stated to her. "He's not a witness at a trial and we need to get him to converse freely about what is going on."

"He'll never know he's being grilled for information," she answered.

He was looking over the menu, doing his best not to look at us. The waiter delivered the drinks and we all ordered. Ray had a burger with the works, Melissa went with a salad, while I chose a turkey sandwich. The place was somewhat noisy, but not so much we couldn't talk. Melissa started off with a simple question.

"So, Ray," she said. "I understand you go to school in Greeley.

What are you majoring in?"

"Football," replied Ray

"I'm sure you have a college major requiring you to go to class. Something for when you're retired from football."

"Journalism for now, but I'm falling behind, being out of class. Physical Education is my minor."

"You planning for employment in the media afterwards?"

"Yes. I find it fascinating those who work in TV, radio, newspapers, magazines; even writers on the Web. Working in Public Relations would be cool."

"Glad to hear you speak of a passion for something other than football."

"I still want to make it to the next level," he stated. "Football is much of what I am, and has been for many years now. I know I'm good enough to play in the NFL. But my body is failing me right now and it's frustrating."

"It's a hard game," I added. "No guarantees."

"No, there aren't."

The food was delivered, hot and cooked properly. Seconds on drinks were served. I decided to nibble on my sandwich, as I wanted to keep the conversation going. Something about talking over a meal seemed to get people to put their guard down. Our seats were by a window, and I could see the large snowflakes starting to stick on the cars outside

"Tell me about the injuries you suffered," asked Melissa.

Ray had finished about half his burger already. A man his size was a calorie animal.

"I tore my ACL my senior year. I was set to go to CU but they stopped calling. The big college schools always have their pick of the best, so there is always someone in line after you. UNC contacted me, but with no guarantees, but did give me a scholarship. I would redshirt for a season, get healthy, get my grades where they needed to be and I had a real shot at starting, being they were thin at tight end. They run a pro-style offense, which would get me the ball. It was the best I could hope for and I liked being close to home."

"Then what happened?"

"I'd already caught six passes and no one could cover me. I took a throw over the middle, lowered my head and lights out. I woke up on the grass but didn't know where I was and then was pulled from the game."

"The new rules came into play," I added.

"Yes. After it's ruled a concussion you can't come back in. I had to pass all kinds of tests before I could go back on the field. When I was cleared to play I picked right up where I left off. Can't remember how many passes I caught in those remaining games, but it was a lot, with several touchdowns. Then I got popped again and this one really hurt. I was totally out of it for a day or so. Still getting headaches from time-to-time. It's a little scary."

"Trouble sleeping?" I asked.

"Yes. How did you know?"

"I talked with a couple of your female friends."

"Damn mouthy women!"

"I'm sure they were concerned," stated Melissa.

Ray finished up his burger and polished off his fries. Melissa was halfway done with her salad and I continued the slow pace on my sandwich. We were making progress.

"You've been seeing a doctor, a specialist?" asked Melissa.

"I was, but no more."

"Why not?"

"Because I'm fine. They weren't helping me anyway."

"Why were you skipping school?" I asked. "Disappearing for prolonged periods of time. Surely you know you were worrying your family and friends."

Ray hesitated. He didn't care to answer. He was searching around for the waiter.

"Can I get some dessert?" Ray asked when he arrived. "Maybe some chocolate cake and some vanilla ice cream."

"Come on, Ray. There must be a reason," said Melissa. "You seem like a smart guy. You know school is your ticket to a good career after football."

"The pressures were getting to me," he finally answered after a long pause. "I needed to unwind."

"You started going to The Hustle," I said. "Or likely they recruited you."

"I don't want to talk about it."

"You know Mack and Grady are using you."

"No. They are my friends."

"They came to your house today looking for money. Money, you owe them."

Ray shook his head some more, denying it all, when his dessert arrived.

"They are the ones who assaulted your mother. No friend would attack your mother."

He buried his thoughts in his cake and ice cream. He wouldn't speak another word at the table. I'd pushed him too far but still did learn a few things. I paid the check and we strolled in silence while Melissa power-shopped for clothes. I smiled and gave her my opinions of her choices, all the while my body aching from my latest beating. After an hour or so, Bill called to say they were back home, so we drove and dropped him off. Ray jogged straight in without speaking and went to his bedroom. Bill was obviously frustrated.

"Damn," said Bill. "I guess no progress on him opening up."

"A little," I replied. "I believe he is coming to terms to the pickle he's in but can't admit it."

"Do you think they'll be back?"

"It's a possibility. I doubt they will up and forget this. Men like them don't let dollars walk away. I'm sure we'll be hearing from them again. The question is how to get him off the hook with them."

"Do you think money will do it?" asked Bill.

"I don't know. They'll want more than he owes because they like to blackmail their clientele. A onetime buyout may not be good enough."

All Bill could say was "Crap!"

"How is your wife?" Melissa asked, changing the subject.

"Sleeping. They gave her some pills to knock her out. I'll need to take another day off tomorrow to stay with her. Good thing I have a fair amount of time saved up. Not sure what to do about Ray."

"I'll help all I can," I said. "Whatever you need. Keep working on him. Once he comes to terms with what they did to his mother, he might see the light of day. Then we'll have some leverage. Be alert on what they might do next. As a parent, it may not be pretty to see."

Bill shook his head and saw us to the door. Melissa and I walked back to her car and she grabbed my arm.

"Do you think he's prepared?" she asked.

"For the storm approaching?" I responded. "Most parents wouldn't be."

Chapter 17

Sunday was a quiet and uneventful day for Melissa and me. We spent the entire day together conversing, doing a little more shopping, watching a movie and making love when the mood struck us. With her, even shopping was bearable. She slept over both nights and it was wonderful having her to balance out the craziness in my life. She left Monday morning off for a short week of work, with Thursday and Friday off for the Thanksgiving holiday, and with plans to get together Thursday night after she had dinner with her parents.

Word had come down from Bill on Sunday the Greeley Police had picked up Mack and Grady, but they were out on bail in a few hours. The DA didn't think they had much of a case. There were many witnesses placing them at The Hustle, including several of the dancers. Grady even had a witness claiming to have punched him in the nose, explaining the damage done. It was their statements against ours, so there was little chance of prosecuting them. Bill had decided to take some leave from work to try and get things straightened out at home. For now, he wanted to handle it on his own. So, I was released from working on it.

Kate had returned to town Monday morning, letting me know her lawyers had gotten the restraining order. Paperwork would arrive late in the day, and we could toss her husband out on his ear early the next morning before he left. I would be there to handle escorting him out, as I'd often served papers on people. She would arrange for a locksmith to be there Tuesday to change all the locks at home and at work. The relief in her voice the end was near filled the phone lines.

Feeling refreshed with a day to myself, I paid bills, ran a few errands to pick up some household items, started the wash and did a hard workout. Today after running, punching and lifting, I did several laps around the pool. Other than the latest round of bruising from my fight with Mack and Grady, I felt good physically.

Thinking it would be a stress-free afternoon, my cell rang and it was Bill. He explained Rachael had an ominous call to go to a website to check out a video. They told her it was important to the safety of her family. If they didn't view it and contact them within seven days, it would be posted for all to see. When they viewed it, they were shocked by what they saw.

"I need you over here right now," stated Bill.

I headed straight through the fall air, and entered the house, absolutely fearing the worst. I was ushered into a small office with a notebook computer sitting at a nice oak desk, both Rachael and Bill looking stunned. On the screen was a frozen image. Bill used the mouse and clicked play. He had the sound turned down, but it wasn't necessary to hear what was going on. The picture said it all.

On the LCD with his face digitally removed, lay an African American man on a bed, completely naked. His hands were roped to the bedpost, but this wasn't something where he was forced to be tied up; this was a sexual game. Soon a white woman came into the room dressed in leather garters and cami top, her face also blacked out. She was holding a leather whip with long strands of soft cowskin, running it up and down the man's body, arousing him. It was gentle domination, but still the fetish behavior was hard to watch. From the physical size of the man and the shape he was in I was certain who it was. The scar on his knee was a dead giveaway, the final clue. The woman began to undress when Bill hit the pause button.

"It's Ray, isn't it?" I asked, even though I knew the answer.

Both glared at me and nodded their heads, shock still filling their eyes.

"I'll move this ahead and turn up the volume," said Bill. "There is a message at the end you need to hear."

The speakers popped, the voice obviously digitized.

"By now you probably know who the young man on the screen before you is. He has a debt he needs to settle. The amount is one thousand dollars, to be paid immediately, with monthly installments going forward of five hundred dollars. If these payments are not made, the video without the face blacked out will be put on the Internet. Text messages will be sent to students and faculty at UNC with links to view the footage. As you are aware other students will send the link around like wildfire. Once this happens, there is no stopping it and his life will be ruined, including his chance at ever playing football again. This version will only be on this site for four hours and will be taken down. If in seven days the payment is not made, the unedited file of this video will be turned loose for all to

82

view. You will receive a text message with a PayPal email account you can upload the money to. Any aggressive attempts to retrieve this footage will mean the immediate release of it for the world to view."

"Oh crap," said Rachael. "My baby in a sex tape. How could he?"

"I doubt he knew he was being filmed," I answered.

"What are we going to do?" said Bill. "We can't afford this every month."

"You may need to pay the initial thousand dollars if we can't come up with anything first. Has Ray seen this?"

"No," stated Bill forcefully. "Do you think we should show him?"

"Not yet. I'm afraid he might do something stupid like go up there and confront them. He's not equipped to handle these people."

"We are," stated Bill forcefully. "Maybe we should go up and deal with this. I'm inclined to shoot them both."

I was a little surprised by the statement.

"Wouldn't do any good, for Mack and Grady are merely muscle. The owner of the club is the man calling the shots. We need to think this through and come up with some options. How much longer do we have before they pull this from the Internet?"

"I got the message about an hour and thirty minutes ago. Why?"

"With your permission I'd like to get the web address. I need to see the whole video and search for anything to help us. I will do this at home. You don't need to watch any more of this."

"What do you think you'll find?" asked Rachael.

"It's hard to say, maybe nothing. Part of the job is going over things again and again searching for clues of any kind. It's too unpleasant to do yourselves, so it's up to me. Right now, it's all we've got. Believe me, I won't enjoy it, but it must be done. We need to find something to use."

Bill reluctantly wrote down the web address. Once I got home I ran the video from the beginning, looking for any signs to tell me where it was filmed and who else was in it. The total length was about twenty minutes minus the warning message at the end. It starts out as before with Ray and the white girl, who after disrobing, started providing various manual and oral pleasures. After about ten minutes she straddled him and began to grind away. Shortly after another woman came into the picture wearing a pink see-through negligee. Her face was blacked out, but soon she was naked, joining the festivities, also climbing on top at a different angle. The quality of the video was a bit grainy, though good enough to see details. The whole scene climaxed with lots of wailing moans of ecstasy, with bodies slumping down to the bed, exhausted. There was something there I missed the first time, I couldn't put my finger on it. I watched again and saw it the second time, pausing the scene for a better view. The brown skinned girl had a butterfly tattoo on her right thigh. I'd seen it on the leg of Ariela when I visited her. She had been involved in the video. I checked it again, discovering the walls were exactly like the ugly gray stucco ones in her apartment. The footage had been filmed at her place. *Could she have been in on this whole scam from the beginning?* She had even propositioned me in the club. Could she have been trying to lure me in to be recorded?

There was only one way to find out. I needed to go back to Greeley to see her and find out where it led.

Chapter 18

The trip back to Greeley took me the normal hour plus, so I hoped it would be worth it. I didn't tell Bill of my plan. I was certain he would want to tag along and my scheme didn't call for two people. Before leaving I called The Hustle to see if Ariela was working but they said it was her night off. This worked perfectly for what I had in mind. Going into the club again would only cause me trouble with their goon squad. I needed to have her at her place.

When I arrived, I knocked on the door. After a couple of minutes, she answered, dressed in tight blue jeans and a tank top. She looked somewhat surprised to see me, but let me in. She smelled of flowered perfume and her black hair was cut shorter than when I last saw her. She smiled warmly while sitting down on her old brown sofa.

"You looking for Ray again?" she asked.

"No," I answered. "I was looking for you. After your stimulating lap dance, I thought I'd stop by and see if you were available for some fun. I believe you offered the next time I was in the neighborhood."

She was coy with her response, having been trained well not to be entrapped.

"What offer are you referring to?"

"It was a little hard to hear in there and the warmth of your crotch on mine was distracting, but you stated I was cute and I should stop by sometime and we could have some fun."

"Really. What type of fun would you like to have?"

"Well, you mentioned you had a female friend who would join us. I've always wanted to have a three-way. If you and she are willing, I think I'm up for the challenge."

Ariela ran her tongue along her lip, a seductive move which probably lured them all in. For me it was a game, an end to a means.

"Anything else you'd like?" she purred. "There is little we won't do for a cute guy like you."

"Well, I'm not sure how to put this," I stated while hesitating.

"Come on now, don't be shy," she said while sliding her hands up and down her thighs trying to encourage me.

"I love girls in leather. Those chaps you wore the other night were hot. Nothing better than a woman taking charge and running the show, making me do what you want!"

"Well, you are in luck; we aim to please. Let me contact my friend. She lives close by and can usually be here within an hour."

Ariela got up and came over and kissed me hard on the mouth, grabbing my rear, pulling me tight to her. Walking away she made her phone call, speaking obscene comments into the mouthpiece. She had gotten the answer she wanted and strolled back over to me.

"It's your lucky day, stud. Leather is ready and willing. She'll be here in about thirty minutes. Would you care for a drink?"

"Sure. I'll take a beer if you have one."

"Always," she said while leaving the room.

I scanned the room trying to see any signs of cameras. From what I could tell there were none in the main room. I moved to get a glimpse down the hall and saw three doors, one straight down looking like a bathroom, and one on each side. It appeared this was a two-bedroom apartment, with only one person living in it. The other room might have been a study or work room, but I bet it might be something else.

Ariela returned with the beer poured into a glass. I thanked her and took a fake sip, for fear she might have added something to it. I needed to have my full faculties. Any type of drugging would have put me in jeopardy of being able to resist them. I didn't care to see myself on the Internet screwing these women.

"Sit down next to me," said Ariela from the sofa. "We can warm things up a bit."

I did as I was told and soon she was rubbing her hands up and down my body, kissing me at the same time. It was difficult not to get aroused, and since I was playing the part it was best to let the blood flow. I ran my hands all over her, feeling her body react to each touch. I knew I was good, but I wasn't this good. Her performance was over the top, but I went with it.

In a short while her friend walked in the door, with a full-length leather coat. She slammed it shut and opened the jacket to reveal the same leather outfit I'd seen in Ray's video, with knee-high black boots with spiked heels. She was probably in her late thirties, with long blonde hair flowing all the way to her rear end. She was tall, about my height, well built in all the right areas and wore bright red lipstick, dark eye shadow and big hoop earrings. This was obviously the same woman in the video. She was a smoking hot woman of the age I would take in a heartbeat if I wasn't on the job. Few men could ever resist her.

"What do we have here," she stated loudly. "Are you playing with my woman, mister? Don't you know only I get to touch her down there!"

"I'm sorry, I didn't know," I answered still in character. "What are you going to do to me?"

She pulled out her whip and snapped it against her palm.

"Get your hands off her pussy and stand up! My name is Leather and I'm here to straighten you out."

Following her orders, she walked over and slapped me softly with the whip on the rear end. Her face two inches from mine, growling like an animal. She grabbed my hands and pressed them against her breasts. She nibbled on my ear and whispered.

"She is good, but I'm better," she said. "Come with me and I'll show you how a dominant woman fucks a man. She can watch and learn."

She walked me backwards into the bedroom on the right, pulling me in tightly, licking my neck. Ariela followed us but turned left through the other door. The room was laid out exactly as it was in Ray's video. A brass four-poster bed, with leather straps on each post for tying someone down. Leather clawed at me, my hands touching her. While looking around I spotted where I suspected the camera was. It was well hidden up in the corner, but some exposed wires gave it away. I figured the recording had already started when she pushed me away from her.

"Don't touch me," she yelled out. "You are mine and you'll do what you're told. Take off your clothes so I can see you."

I stripped down but left my briefs on. The room was cold and I had lost my arousal from earlier. I wasn't going to go much further but needed to make sure the action had started. Leather was not happy I was still wearing shorts.

"All of it, buster," she stated. "I want to see your hard man cock."

"Where is Ariela?" I asked.

"What?" she answered.

"Where is Ariela? If I'm going to drop my briefs I want her here too. I plan on sticking it in both of you."

Still in character, Leather shouted, "Ariela, get in here, bitch!"

She walked in, dressed only in lingerie. She was smaller than Leather but still sexy, standing beside her, looking puzzled.

"Come on, you two, I want to see you groping each other?" I said.

"I thought you wanted us to dominate you?" said Ariela.

"Oh yes, but first I need you embracing and kissing with lots of tongue to get me revved up again. There is nothing hotter!"

Hesitating, they glanced at each other, and shrugged, as if to say whatever the man wanted. They turned and started kissing softly. I stepped over, leaned against them and pushed them together over onto the bed and walked out of the room.

Across the hall and into the other bedroom I found what I was looking for: computer equipment recording all the happenings in the room. I closed the door and locked it, sat down and begin looking through files. She hadn't password-protected it before leaving and I had total access. If the data was stored locally, I might be able to find what I was looking for. Under the video folders there were lots of them. I sorted by date and opened each one around the time it would have been recorded. On the fifth file I double-clicked there was the one of Ray unedited and without the face hidden.

"Hey, what the hell are you doing?" yelled Ariela while pounding on the door.

Ignoring her I found many more videos, all in raw format, plus an edited version. I could delete them all but figured I would take all the storage hardware with me. Since it was a desktop computer I powered it down, opened it up and removed the hard drive. There might have been other copies, but I would take it and any devices I found. There were a couple of flash drives and one other external USB hard drive. I gathered them up and placed them in a pillowcase I found in the room. I unlocked the door, pushed my way past Ariela and went across to the other room to get my clothes.

"What the hell!" Ariela said. "Are you robbing me?"

"Actually, I'm keeping you from ruining Ray's life and a few others you had on the computer. This game of yours needs to end."

"Wait now. We are only doing what we are told to do by our boss."

"Sure, lure men in and make their fantasies come true. A couple of sexy women acting out their kinky bidding—then recording it. Maybe even drug them with a drink. I can call the cops right now and have them come in and see the setup you have; maybe test the

88

beer you gave me. You'd be in a lot of trouble blackmailing people. How much they pay you for each performance?"

Both women appeared to be in shock. Neither could muster up an answer. Their best leverage was sex, but they knew it wouldn't work. They were stuck and knew it.

"Not sure how you'll explain this to your boss, but too bad. All the lives you ruined, I'd say it's time to find new employment."

"Please don't," said Leather, now crying. "They will kill us, or worse."

She tried to grab for the bag, but I slapped her, knocking her back on the bed. I had finished dressing and headed towards the living room.

"I have no sympathy for you both. You better get out of town. Pack up now and go. You should have time to get away. I'm not going to tell on you."

"Please. I saved your ass by calling the cops," said Ariela.

"Did you really? I'm not so certain, because why would you help me and now attempt to record me screwing you both? Was it part of the plan? I think you've been in on this from the start. You called them to keep them from killing a potential customer. You figured you would lure me back in here with the sexy talk you used in the club. Another one on the hook and a piece of the action for you. What are they paying you? A finder's fee or do you get a cut of each monthly membership you bring in? If we dig a little further I bet we find you aren't poor as you appear. Maybe you are even running this whole scam!"

The charade seemed to be over now.

"I'm calling Mack and Grady," Ariela yelled.

I pushed her out of the way, went to the phone and ripped the jack out via the cable.

"Pleasure doing business," I stated, walking out with the pillowcase feeling immensely proud of myself.

Chapter 19

Arriving at Kate's bright and early the next day, fresh off my success from the night before, I was dressed in my best throw-the-bum-out-of-the-house clothing: blue jeans, long-sleeved white shirt, hiking boots and a brown leather coat concealing my .38. Since I'd seen Jack armed when running his errands, I wanted to be prepared for the possibility. Knowing I could take him in a fair fight, I needed to make sure he didn't tip the odds with firepower.

At the front door Kate greeted me with an anxious smile. This was the big day, though she did appear nervous. She was barefoot, with black jeans and black lacy shirt. Her hair was in her signature braded ponytail, her skull covered in a bandana. Leading me in by the arm into the living area, she introduced me to her lawyer, who was sitting down on her sofa with some coffee and a folder of documents he was reviewing. Burt Sanders stood up and gave me the rock-hard handshake all men seem to use to gauge their virility. He was dressed in a nice dark suit and shiny business shoes I couldn't and wouldn't wear if my life depended on it. The gray thinning hair led me to believe he was in his fifties, the slight paunch in his belly further evidence. He handed me the paperwork I needed to serve to Jack, which included the divorce papers and restraining order to leave the house and not come within 500 yards of the home, the salon business, or her and the kids.

"Can I get you anything, Jarvis?" Kate asked.

"No, I'm good. Are we ready to do this?"

Kate glanced over at Burt and he nodded his head.

"Ready as I'll ever be."

"Are your son and daughter in the house?" I asked.

"Yes. They wanted to be here to support me."

"It may not be pleasant for them," I replied. "Are they prepared for what might happen?"

Her two kids walked into the room from the kitchen. I'd not seen them in some time and they were hardly children anymore. The son, Cody, was nearly my size and a little leaner. He had long blond hair, the bangs in his eyes where he had to sweep it away from time to time. Baggy blue jeans and a T-shirt with "Don't Fuck With Me" printed in bold letters on the chest. He was a senior at Lincoln High

School and a math whiz from what Kate had told me, hoping to be a building engineer someday.

Beside him was Darcy, the older of the two and the spitting image of her mother. Same build, hair, face and eyes, in a younger version. She was wearing black jeans, but with large pre-fabricated holes on the thighs showing her tanned legs, a white laced top and was barefoot. She was a sophomore in college going to Denver University, and was a performing arts major. She was a talented dancer and writer, from what Kate had told me, and had the lead role in one of the DU winter productions.

"Cody and Darcy," stated Kate. "Do you remember Mr. Mann?"

"Please call me Jarvis."

Both acknowledged me and Cody gripped my hand, showing how tough he was. Any more viselike hand shaking and I'd be wearing a cast!

"Don't worry, we can handle it," said Cody. "Mom needs us here, so we're here."

"He may be our father," said Darcy. "But she is our mom, and he's treated her like shit for too long. She's done nothing to deserve it."

"Okay, if you say so," I answered. "I hope it's simple with no complications, but I've been through this enough to realize resistance on his part is likely."

Both walked over and put their arms around Kate in a show of solidarity.

"I'm glad you're there for your mother," I said. "Please stay right here while I take care of things. It will be best if you remain out of the way and not say anything. Kate, I need you to lead me to where Jack is sleeping downstairs and come right back up here."

Kate led me down a hall and to the stairwell.

"It's down at the bottom and first room on the right. He normally has the door closed."

I motioned for her to return to the living area and I walked the stairs reaching the basement floor. Straight ahead I could see what appeared to be a bathroom. On the left was a recreation room, with big-screen TV, gaming console and a pool table. The second opening on the right was a laundry room. And sure enough, the first door on the right was closed and was locked. I pounded on it, but kept my body off to the side in case he shot first and asked questions later.

"Jack Tanner, open the door please," I said.

I heard noises as if he was grabbing pants.

"Who the hell is this?" Jack said.

"Official business. Open up now!"

There was a long hesitation before I saw the door handle turn. I pushed my way in, turning him to the side, while handing him the envelope with the legal papers.

"Jack Tanner, you've been served," I stated with a sense of pride. "Please gather your things and vacate the premises."

"Who the hell are you?" Jack said angrily.

I showed him my ID. "Jarvis Mann, Private Detective. If you read the documents you'll see your wife is filing for divorce and has a restraining order for you to leave her house and stay away from her, your kids and her business. I'd advise you get your things together quickly or we'll have to call the police to drag you out."

Jack opened the envelope and began scanning the documents. I checked over the room and found his gun sitting on the nightstand. I grabbed it, removing the clip and made sure the chamber was clear. I popped each of the shells out into my open hand and placed them in my pocket.

"What the hell?" Jack yelled, stepping toward me.

"I wouldn't if I were you," I stated firmly. "I'm making sure you don't do anything stupid. You can have the gun and empty clip after you leave, but I'm keeping the bullets. Besides, I doubt you have a permit for this weapon and could spend a long time in jail for having it in your possession."

"I can have a gun in my own home for protection."

"It's not your home anymore. Now pack up your things or you'll be leaving with what you're wearing. You've got ten minutes."

Stepping back, I watched his reaction and each move he made. He gave me a frigid stare of anger, but I didn't really care. One needed to be cold and unemotional for this kind of work. He packed up his clothes in a duffle bag. I wouldn't let him take anything other than clothing, telling him to put back the clock radio and a picture frame he tried to take.

"Can I at least get my things from the bathroom?" Jack said with a snarl.

"Only essentials, and I'll need to see everything you grab."

Jack gathered up a hair brush, electric razor, toothbrush,

toothpaste and some assorted prescription pills which I verified had his name on them. I checked his coat to make sure it wasn't holding any surprises, gave it to him and followed him up the stairs. Walking into the living room, he stopped and stared at his family.

"You bitch," Jack said bitterly. "Tossing me out of my own home!"

"It's not yours anymore," I said. "Keep moving."

Jack wouldn't budge, still giving the evil stare at Kate. I wanted him out of there before all hell broke loose, but Kate had to have her say too.

"You've done nothing to contribute to this home for years now," Kate said. "I did all I could to save this marriage, this family, with my hard work, sweat and blood. You had to run your little scam and fool around with your trollop. It's over and I hope to never see you again."

The words were harsh, but truthful. She may have felt better by saying it, but it set Jack off. He tried to rush her, but I grabbed him by the coat and flung him against the door. He charged me and I popped him on the side of the jaw throwing him back against the door again. He looked at me hard, deciding what to do.

"Jack don't do this in front of your kids," I stated firmly. "Don't let the last thing they see of you is getting your ass kicked. You are older, out of shape and you will lose. Walk out now and don't come back."

Jack scanned the room, searching, staring at his children trying to find an ally. There wasn't one to be found.

"It's over, Dad," said Cody. "Leave us alone and never come back."

Defeated, Jack turned heading to his truck, peeling rubber out of the neighborhood. I would hang around for a while to make sure he didn't come back, so I chose a chair and sat down.

"Can I get a bag of ice?" I asked, flexing my hand, which was already swelling from the second hard punch I'd thrown in three days. *Maybe I need to get myself a Taser.*

Chapter 20

With no sign of Jack after a few hours, I left to grab some lunch, pick up a special cable and power adapter from a local computer store, and work on my other case. Once home, I retrieved the hard drives from my safe and placed them on my desk. The cable and power supply were designed to activate SATA devices, allowing them to be plugged into a USB port enabling me to retrieve the data off them, so long as they weren't secured.

Once I figured out how the maze of cables worked, I fired it up and bingo: my Windows desktop discovered a new mass storage device assigning it letter F. As I suspected the drive wasn't encrypted, a simple security step most computer users didn't do, so I could see all the data. Doing a basic search for video formats, I found the AVI and MPEG files once again and began combing through them. As before, there were the unedited versions and the edited ones with the altered voice demanding the ransom. I had to look through all the folders, gathering as much information as possible. There was nothing exciting about seeing them, but it was my job. I don't know if I'd ever witnessed so much sex in my life, and of all kinds: male and female, three-way with two females and a male or two males and a female. Even some movies with two men going at it. After all of this I wondered if I could ever make love again for there was nothing joyful about the entire process. It was like watching passionless animals doing it.

As the afternoon turned into evening I'd had enough, but knew I now had leverage against the men running The Hustle. I called Bill to tell him what I had. It may have been good news, but you could tell it didn't make it any easier for him since it didn't erase the image from his mind of what his son had gotten himself into.

"Do you think they have backups of this somewhere," asked Bill.

"Possibly, but I don't think will matter," I said. "Bill, we can use this to get Ray off the hook,"

"How?"

"A couple of ways. First, if this is the only copy, we wait, and they will have nothing to post on the Web. Ray will be free and clear so long as he stays away from them. Of course, this may not stop them from coming after him. The other option is to use what we've found as leverage against the owner of The Hustle, Marquis Melott. They don't release the video of Ray and we don't turn this over to the police. There are some faces on here who are well-known. Some local politicians I recognize, a few TV personalities; all very embarrassing for everyone involved. It would create a stalemate which should keep them clear of him."

The pause on the other end was obviously Bill thinking. He was a cop and his instincts would lead him to want to bring the crooks to justice. But family often trumps this, and he had to know this was the best, and maybe only, option.

"Reluctantly, I must agree with number two," Bill answered. "How do we contact them to let them know what we have?"

"Leave it to me. They'll want proof, which I can provide. I'll make copies of everything and have them kept with my lawyer for safekeeping, if you approve. There'll be some cost involved but I'd say it's worth it."

"You trust your lawyer?"

"Completely."

"Do what you have to do. Money is no object." He hung up the phone.

I got to work putting together my technology shopping list, and after buying everything, worked into the early morning hours making duplicates. It was a slow process, as the files were quite large and my computer wasn't a high-end unit. I confirmed all the data was copied properly and placed a set of copies in my gun safe, another for my lawyer and a copy to show Marquis. Now I hoped all the effort would accomplish what I intended it to do, and fell asleep trying to flush the images of naked bodies from my psyche.

Chapter 21

It was a short night of sleep, but I was pumped, ready for the day ahead. I hoped to conclude all this nasty business with the owner of The Hustle. I tracked down a phone number, made the call, and arranged to meet with him in a public place between Denver and Greeley. We decided on Brighton at a place called Copper Rail Bar and Grill. The agreement was only me and Marquis for a beer and a friendly chat at around noon. Of course, *friendly* might be a slight exaggeration.

I arrived twenty minutes early checking the place out, watching for Mack and Grady, or any of the other frontline employees of The Hustle. There was no sign of anyone I recognized, so I took a booth with an unobstructed view of the front door. This was a sports bar with loads of TVs with a cornucopia of athletics displayed, including a 135-inch projection screen smack-dab in the middle for all to see. There was also a gaming room with pool tables and video games and, of course, a bar, with a few patrons sipping down brews from chilled mugs. It was the Wednesday before Thanksgiving, so the place was quiet. I ordered a draft beer and loaded fries minus the onions, which I hated with a passion. I ate and drank slowly, knowing I needed to be sharp, my eyes searching for my guest. I had a vague description of him I'd received from the Greeley cop, Olsen, who rescued me from them at their club. I wanted to make sure I was meeting with the real man in charge and a fake didn't show up. I saw an expensive Mercedes convertible pull up outside and him getting out. Trey's portrayal had been spot on.

Marquis Melott strolled in dressed like a high-class lawyer. Armani brown suit which matched his deep brown skin, black Florsheim shoes with tassels, diamond-studded earrings in both ears, and a hat to cover his bald head, which was revealed when he removed it. *A well-mannered crook!* His suit was perfectly styled and fit him to a tee, and if he was carrying a gun the bulge couldn't be noticed. He seemed to know who I was, spotting me right away, sitting down across from me without a word. He motioned at the remaining loaded cheese fries and I nodded, so he took a couple and munched them down. The waitress was promptly there and he ordered a microbrew I never heard of and a shot of Jack Daniels. He didn't speak until his drinks arrived and he drank a long sip of beer and followed it with the entire glass of Jack.

"Fries are good," he finally stated. "They could use some onions to perk up the flavor."

I already didn't like him. He was too smug, too stylish and liked onions on his cheese and bacon fries. *If we hadn't been in a public place I might have shot him out of spite!* I held my tongue and let him continue. He got straight to the point. No small talk, which was fine with me.

"I've been told you want to make a deal," Marquis said. "Here, on behalf of the Malone kid. What are you offering?"

"I've come into possession of certain videos," I began. "Videos which can harm others and hurt you."

"What type of videos?" Marquis asked while eating more cheese fries.

"Of a personal nature. People acting out fantasies. Clients of yours."

"Why would I be interested in them?"

"Because they were used to encourage high-paying registration fees at your club. Coerced with embarrassing sexual activities."

"I run a legitimate business. There is no coercion involved. It is all voluntary."

"At the beginning yes, until they are digitally recorded and you blackmail them to pay more money or else you release the video on the Internet. Those videos would be very embarrassing to those photographed. They are doing some pretty kinky things, even in an X-rated world."

Marquis waved for the waitress and ordered another beer, since his was gone, and another round of loaded fries, this time with onions. He stopped and contemplated how to proceed until the drink and food arrived. I didn't need another beer, still having half a glass, but was brought one anyway.

"Even if it were true, why would I care? Why would they care? As you said, it's an X-rated world. No one worries if their dick is on the Internet."

"These people do. Some on these recordings are of politicians, maybe men who do you favors, vote your way to keep their face and so much more off the Web. It would be embarrassing for them and for you, not to mention their careers and personal lives. Their wives would take them for every penny they have in a divorce. Then the police and the Feds get involved and go neck-deep into your business. Then the IRS starts delving into your financials. There is no need for this if you give us what we want."

"And this would be?"

"Release Ray Malone from his financial obligations," I stated. "Leave him and his family alone. If he comes near your club, throw him out. He doesn't belong there and has a possible professional football career ahead if he can stay clean and healthy. Why ruin the kid's dreams? It makes the most sense for him and you."

"I'm to take you at your word you have these videos?"

"No." I pulled out of my pocket a 64-gigabyte thumb drive and slid it to him. "All the proof you need of what I possess. Keep it so you can verify."

"Where did you get this from?"

"Not part of the deal."

"I'm sure I can figure it out."

I shrugged, as if to say so what.

"You have other copies."

"Yes, the originals and several duplicates. Left with lawyers and an angry Denver cop whose son is the young man we've been discussing. They stay hidden if he is freed from his debt, is no longer harassed, and the video showed to his family is never placed on the Web for all to see."

"And if I were to encourage you to give them up?"

"They'll be released to the public and given to the Greeley police and the Feds. Not in your best interest."

"I can come down hard on you."

"It won't matter. They will be out there and you'll have a big mess to deal with. There will always be another paying customer you can replace him with. The world is full of horny men with money to burn."

Marquis stopped again and ate some more fries. There was a powerful sense of danger coming from his mannerisms, a fire inside, an anger he was keeping a lid on. It was there and I could feel it. He could try to scare me all he wanted, but it didn't matter. I was in control and planned to keep it this way.

"It would seem trying to intimidate you won't work, what about buying you? I can throw a lot of money your way. I understand your business isn't a real high profit profession. You generally live from job-to-job, based on the research we've done. I'll give you ten percent of the profits I make off them going forward, tax free, with five hundred dollars up front. Then you can move onto your next divorce case."

"No, thanks," I replied. "The Malones are worth more to me than money."

"We are in a difficult position. I don't like to be told what to do in my business. It makes me look weak and others might exploit it."

"I'm in the business of getting my client out of tough scrapes. It's sensible from a professional standpoint. Chalk it up as a loss and a learning experience. No one else will know. We could care less about what the people in your club do. It's a free country. You keep on going along on your merry way making lots of money, getting the votes you need to advance your cause, and we live down in Denver as if none of this ever happened."

He drank a little more and ate some fries. His cold eyes bore into me and were giving some final thought. I left his fries alone, the onion smells alone killing my appetite.

"Okay," stated Marquis, his voice going softer but frighteningly firm. "Understand one thing, if you or the Malones go back on your word, I will have all of you killed. Starting with the wife and sister, with Mack and Grady having a lot of fun before they die, both the husband and son watching, helpless to do anything. From a business standpoint, this will make the most sense if you double-cross me."

I sat there and met his stare with my best *you don't scare me* expression. I gave him no further response, so he stood up, tossed down a twenty-dollar bill and walked out.

Now, I didn't often get frightened, but the chill from Marquis's last words sent shivers down to my toes after he left. There was little doubt he meant it, and there was little doubt we wouldn't double-cross him. If he kept his end of the deal, there would be no reason to. I finished up my first beer and contemplated my second when a man slid into the seat across from me. In street clothes, Trey Olsen dressed like any another person in the bar and not a Greeley cop. He had offered to provide backup in case things went wrong, after I told him my plan when I called for information on Marquis. It was always good to have a friendly face join you after an evil one left.

"So how did it go?" Trey said.

"Pretty good," I answered. "He accepted the terms but threatened to kill all of us if we reneged. His detail of the killing was graphic and chilling."

"I guess it's his way of telling you he respects you."

"A type of respect I can do without. Shall I buy you lunch?"

"Of course, I'm famished. What's your budget?"

"Sky's the limit," I stated.

He ordered a burger, fries and a light beer. Small price to pay to have him available to keep them from back-shooting me in the parking lot when we left an hour later.

Chapter 22

I survived the holiday weekend with Melissa at her spacious townhome after her Thanksgiving dinner with her family, which I happily avoided. Together, we mixed in a little Black Friday shopping, some bike riding, long walks holding hands in the warmer-than-normal November weather, and some quality time in bed. All good things must come to an end and I left her Sunday morning with a warm embrace and kiss, as I was involved in an intervention for Ray at my home office.

Bill and I discussed the fact that since the threat was likely over, we needed to confront Ray about his problems. Time had come to face up to them and we were going to use the videos to drive home the point that he required help. If this didn't work, I had one other item up my sleeve.

The two of them arrived late morning at my place and I welcomed them in. The weather still was warm, so both came dressed in jeans, a T-shirt and light jacket. Bill had taken the family away for the holiday to visit other relatives in Kansas. They had driven back Saturday night, as planned. Bill and I knew that before Ray returned to school this issue had to be cleared up, or it could start all over again.

With a long HDMI cable, I hooked up my computer to my large-screen TV to view the recordings. There wasn't anything pleasant about this, but a trigger was required to show Ray he was being used, like they were using others at The Hustle. I had videos cued up in a certain order with the volume set loud enough to hear, tested and ready to go. I was letting Bill do the talking until I was needed. You could see Ray was uncomfortable, sensing what was before him.

"Son, we brought you here today to speak with you," stated Bill. "With school starting back up tomorrow, we need to get all the cards on the table. Time to clear the air on what you've been involved with."

The clichés were coming quick and often. Bill had been rehearsing this for some time.

"Since your last concussion, we've encountered some bad men. Two of which came to our house and roughed up your mother. They were about to rape her if Jarvis hadn't intervened."

Ray glanced my way and I nodded.

"They wouldn't have gone through with it, Dad," said Ray.

"How do you know this?"

"Because…" Ray stopped in mid-sentence, trying to find the right words. "They are my friends."

"No, they aren't," answered Bill. "Friends don't break into your home and beat on your mother and threaten to sexually assault her. Those aren't friends; those are evil men. You can't defend what they did."

"I'm not defending. They were mad because I owed them money."

"Why didn't you tell us this?"

Ray shook his head. "You wouldn't understand."

"We understand more than you know. Did you borrow money from them to join their club?"

Ray nodded his head.

"And what happens there?"

"I can't tell you."

"Sure you can, son. Jarvis has been inside and seen the place. He knows the goings-on. Some booze and some pretty women with very little clothing on, dancing for you. Is this where you met Ariela?"

Ray was starting to close down again, his pride in the way of admitting what he'd done.

"Go ahead Jarvis, show him," stated Bill.

I clicked the mouse and the first video started. There was a white overweight man naked and strapped to the bed. Standing beside the bed was the blonde woman I'd encountered at Ariela's with her leather outfit on. She had a crop with leather tassels she was whipping him with. The man was moaning loudly in excitement when Ariela walked in, also dressed in leather, and rubbing the blonde woman with her hands, kissing her on the ear, telling all to hear what she was going to do. The scene started getting more explicit, so I stopped it.

"Recognize the two women?" asked Bill. "Is the one walking in last Ariela? Wasn't she your last girlfriend? Or would sex buddy be a better term?"

"She is doing her job," replied Ray.

"OK, let's go to the same scene, only this time it's edited, and listen to what is stated at the end of it."

102

I started the modified version with the faces blacked out, and an audio track recorded over it. It basically said the same thing as the edited video of Ray, to either pay up the increased fee or the footage would be placed on the Web for all to see, with the man's face no longer covered up.

"Next," said Bill.

This one was of two men and Ariela doing things I had a tough time watching. Once I played some of it I switched to the edited version, which almost word-for word had the same threat. We continued this through two other videos until we came to Ray's.

"Watch this next one closely. I believe you'll know who is in this one."

The video started and Ray saw himself. He closed his eyes, but Bill firmly told him to look. I only played about two minutes of it and switched to the edited version with the included threats. We went straight through to the end. When I turned it off you could see the embarrassment on Ray's face. He tried to get up and walk out but Bill stopped him by grabbing his arm. Ray attempted to pull away, but Bill was strong enough to hold on, until Ray shoved and broke free.

"Leave me alone," yelled Ray. "I can handle this. I don't need your help."

Getting out of my seat I went to block the door. Ray was a big, muscular kid and I didn't want to use force, but I needed to keep him there. He stared me in the eyes with a determination of *get out of my way*, but I told him no. Whatever I needed to do I, would to keep him there.

"Ray, sit the fuck down!" yelled Bill.

Ray appeared shocked at his father's profanity and wasn't sure how to act. He backed away from me and up against my kitchen wall, his head down, chin on his chest. He put both hands on his head in pain. The scene was a bit scary. You wondered if he was losing it, his mouth moving though no words came out. A gentle knock came at the door and he looked up. I opened it and in came Raven, her timing perfect. I had called her and asked if she could join us. She was his best friend and the strongest bet in getting through to him. She walked over and stared straight in his eyes and wrapped her arms around him.

"Constance," said Ray, the one person she would allow to call her by her given name. "What are you doing here?"

"I was about to ask the same thing," stated Bill.

I hadn't told Bill of my plan, uncertain how he'd react to it, since Raven had mentioned he didn't care for her. I motioned for Bill to be quiet and let them converse.

"Come on, you two, take a seat on the sofa," I said. "You have a lot to talk about."

I took her jacket and hung it on the wall with the others. She was dressed all in black, down to the top of her boot-length skirt, a silver chain through the belt loops, a blouse adorned in flowers with burnt orange flames coming out of them. Her black hair with red highlights extended to her shoulders covering half her face, a gold necklace of skulls around her neck, matching earrings sparkling under her hair. She took Ray gently by the hand and they sat down on the sofa. I waved Bill to join me in the kitchen.

"Why didn't you tell me she was coming?" Bill whispered to me.

"You would have said no," I replied. "So, shut up and listen."

His stern glare was met by my own, but he did as he was told.

"Ray, I know how you feel," said Raven, both of her hands holding his. "Your parents are getting on your case about everything and you want to tune them out."

"Yes," Ray responded.

"It's bumming you out, bringing you down."

"If they would leave me alone, I'd handle it."

"Parents sometimes don't get it; won't let us grow up and deal with our own problems and stick their nose into everything we do, as if we are children."

He nodded again, looking our way.

"But they are right this time," Raven stated with a gentle voice. "I've seen what is going on with you, heard what you've been doing, and it's not the man I know, have known for some time now. This is something you can't handle yourself."

Ray glanced down, not wanting to look her in the eyes. She took her hand and softly turned his head up again, so their eyes met.

"They care about you, Ray," she continued. "Love you and want what is best for you. The way you're behaving is not right. I love you too and want to help you, like you helped me years ago with those assholes that were treating me like dirt, all because of the way I appeared to them, the way I dressed. But you knew to dig deeper and see I was a person underneath. Like now, I know deep down you are a good man who has gotten lost, gone down the wrong path. I want to help you like you helped me. Tell me what is going on."

"I don't know for sure what happened," Ray said. "I'm losing what I loved, which is football. I was a big shot on campus and now I'm nothing."

"This isn't true. You are more than football. Don't be some stuck-up jock sticking it wherever he can. A clichéd athlete you hear about every day. This girl you were banging didn't care about you. She was screwing you for money. Hell, I didn't like your girlfriend, Shawna, but at least she wasn't using you and cared for you. And you tossed her aside for a piece of tail or tails, from what I heard, a fantasy moment which will cost you your soul. What is going on in your head? You've got to talk about it."

Ray still was staring into her eyes, trying to find the words.

"Ray, I love you," said Raven boldly. "I've loved you for some time now, but couldn't say it. Love is one of those odd things I wondered if I'd ever feel for someone, but I do for you. More importantly, I want to help you find your way back from this evil world you've gotten yourself into. Please let them aid you, let me guide you."

"It hurts," said Ray finally. "My head aches and I have strange thoughts and don't know what I'm doing at times. I want it to stop, so I do things to take my mind off the pain. I was the man who was going to play in the NFL, be a star, and now I can't find my way. I'm lost and can't seem to get these demons out of my head."

Ray's eyes started to water and soon he was crying. Raven grabbed his head and pulled it to her shoulder, embracing him as he let out all his emotions.

"We'll help you," she said while looking our way. "All of us will bring you home."

"I'll be damned," stated Bill softly.

I knew it was his way of saying thanks.

Chapter 23

The remainder of the intervention went smoothly. After Ray had calmed down, Bill called Rachael, and she and Monika met all of us for lunch, allowing for additional decisions to be debated. It was agreed Ray would opt-out of college for the rest of the semester and get the help necessary with the school doctors and the best specialists in head trauma they could find. Rachael would drive him back and forth wherever he needed to go, and Raven would join them when she could. One could sense the relief in the family for crossing this hurdle, though they knew others would present themselves. It was a marathon and not a sprint.

With my services no longer being required, the next day I prepared an invoice to give to Bill covering my expenses. I was going through finalizing it when my cell phone rang from a number up north. I answered and it was Trey, the Greeley officer who had been helping me.

"A social call, I hope," I said.

"I wish. Farmer found a body in his cornfield, with your business card nearby. County Sheriff looked you up in the Law Enforcement database finding I had connected with you recently and asked me to contact you. They want you to come to the crime scene to see if you can identify and make a statement."

"Am I a suspect?"

"A person of interest for now."

"Male or female?"

"Female."

I was afraid to speculate. "I'll leave right away. Probably take me an hour to get there."

"It's what I told them," replied Trey. "They will be on the scene for a while. Meet me at the station and I'll drive you from there."

The late Monday morning commute was pretty good. Many took the day off as part of the long holiday weekend, so I got there in good time. Trey was there and I jumped into his squad car and we headed north into farmland, outside of town. The area was crawling with County and State units. When we arrived, Trey showed his badge and we were let in. We found the County Sheriff in charge. He was an older, balding man, tall and muscular, with a weather-worn face and crows' feet around his eyes. His shirt ID said Sheriff Aldon and his demeanor was standoffish. Without a word, he walked us over to the covered remains. He removed the sheet and there was the naked body of Ariela looking pale, bruised and very dead.

"Do you know her?" said Aldon.

"Yes," I replied. "Her name is Ariela Martinez. She was a dancer at a club in Greeley, The Hustle."

"Found her with your business card," said Aldon. "Any notion why?"

"I was working a case and gave it to her to call me."

"What type of case?"

"Missing person's. Son of a friend who hired me to find him. He had been staying with her."

"No clothes, no other possessions other than your card. Care to speculate?"

"No idea." No reason to lie but no reason to give the whole story either.

"Something must come to mind? Maybe the son got mad and took it out on her."

"No. He has been with his parents all weekend. I was there for part of it. He has an alibi."

"Still need a name. Need to talk with him."

"Can't give it to you until I discuss it with my client."

"You know I can hold you as a material witness."

"Sure, but my lawyer would get me out pretty quickly. I'll cooperate but I need to speak with them first. Client confidentiality."

He nodded, though not happily. He covered Ariela back up which was a good thing, being I wasn't a fan of dead bodies. Seeing someone so alive, now being so lifeless wasn't pleasant. Though my discomfort didn't do her much good.

"Not a pretty thing. She appears to have been raped, beaten and lastly strangled. Crime guys will be looking for what they can, but I don't like this happening in my area. We plan on catching the bastards who did this. Any reason to believe you were involved?"

"I was with people all weekend who can vouch for me. Do you know the time of death?"

"Not yet but it's been recent. Probably dumped her overnight. The rape, beating and killing likely happened elsewhere. Should we be looking at this club The Hustle?"

"It would be where I'd start."

"We'll do some digging and see what we come up with. But I need to know what you know. If you don't come clean, we'll haul you in. Understand?"

I nodded but didn't figure he could do a whole lot. So long as there was no evidence of my involvement, threats would be all he had, though the business card was connection enough for them to get pushy.

"I'd check out where she lived," I said. "Good place to start. I can take you there if you want. It's in Greeley."

"Since it's in your jurisdiction, Olsen, why don't you take him and see what you can find? Treat it as a crime scene. You discover anything, call me. We'll need to get our guys on it. Try not to trample on the evidence."

Trey and I headed back to town, and with my directions we arrived quickly. We found the manager and she reluctantly agreed to let us in.

"She moved out a couple of days ago. No notice, no nothing. Someone in the building saw people moving stuff out and told me later. Didn't leave a damn thing in there."

"Any description of the men?" asked Trey.

"Who the hell cares? A bunch of big colored guys is all I know."

Letting us in, we saw what she said was true. Other than the dirt and stains on the carpet, the place was empty. No food in the cabinets or fridge, and no clothing or furniture left behind. It had been completely cleaned out.

"At least I get to keep the cleaning deposit," said the manager.

"We'll need to get the rental agreement, payment methods, copies of checks, anything at all," said Trey.

"OK."

"We'll need our crime guys to go over it and see what we can find. Don't let anyone in until we say so. And don't have the place cleaned."

"I can't leave it empty for too long," said the Manager. "I need to collect rent to make a living."

"For now, you'll need to rough it. No one in or out but us. Give me the key, please."

She handed it over and stormed away. There wasn't much they were going to get from the room, but some fibers here and there would confirm she lived there. They might get lucky, but it didn't look good. Trey grabbed some crime scene tape and placed it over the door. He called Aldon and gave him the news. We sat and waited for the CSI unit to arrive.

"Care to spill to me what is going on?" asked Trey.

"As I said, I need to wait until I talk with my client."

"The Denver cop who hired you. The meeting with Melott and the deal you made with him."

"Good memory. Why didn't you tell Aldon?"

"I may in time, but figured I'd give you some leeway. I doubt you're involved, but a woman was killed, and like Aldon, I don't care for it."

"Neither do I," I said.

The question was what I could do about it? Apparently, this case wasn't finished after all.

Chapter 24

The crime scene team arrived and started going over the apartment. Trey had received all the lease information from the Manager. DMV had provided a license plate on a nineties Chevy Malibu Ariela owned, but for now was missing. I was free to head back to Denver to consult with my client, but remain available for further questioning. I had not mentioned Leather to either of them, but I wondered what had become of her. One would think both would have been disposed of, but so far there was only one body. She lived nearby is what Ariela had said. Could she have gotten away or was she more involved than what had appeared? Her crying scene might have been an act. In my anger, I might have missed the charade. I would keep her in the back of my mind and possibly track her down if necessary. Though with the only name I had being Leather I'd doubt it was listed in the Yellow Pages. A trip back to The Hustle asking to see her probably would be a bad idea without the Marines for backup.

I contacted Bill and gave him the scoop. He didn't care Ariela was dead and didn't want to get dragged into this any further. As far as he was concerned, they had broken free and wanted to keep it this way.

"She used my son, so the hell with her," he said bitterly. "And don't go telling Ray. He doesn't need the additional stress."

The client was always right, but I still didn't feel good about this. This wasn't closure, but going against Bill's wishes wasn't an option. Although, I planned to revisit it with him, if necessary. Digging into this further at this time would only lead to Melott coming after all of us. This certainly wasn't on my bucket list of things to do.

Feeling a bit worn, I grabbed workout clothes and swimming trunks and headed for the gym. Vigorous exercise always helped clear the head and I decided to do the full complement today, so I could let go even for a short while. The place was busy with everyone working off the heavy Thanksgiving turkey dinners, the flab index higher than normal. After showering I didn't care to go home, so I called Melissa.

"What are you doing?" I asked.

"Wrapping up my day—how about you?"

"Well, I was feeling like some company. You up for some dinner?"

"Well, I have legal briefs I need to go over. Make me a better offer and I'll weigh my options."

"There is an excellent restaurant up in Morrison I've been dying to take you to. It's got dark lighting, candles and an expensive menu I would only spend on my best gal."

There was a long silence, and I think a little bit of shortness of breath on the other end. Apparently, I'd hit a nerve.

"We can go to Lookout Mountain and look over the city," I added.

"And?"

"Do some necking and a little making out."

"Wow, it's been a while since I went up there. Do people our age neck?"

"If they don't, they should. Time to relive your youth. Does this sound better than doing lawyer work tonight?"

"Absolutely. Do I need to get dressed up?"

"Yep, nice duds, but not too nice. You know my wardrobe is limited."

"What time?"

"Does seven give you enough time to beautify?"

"No extra time needed. My beauty requires little effort to impress you. Pick me up at my place. I'll be waiting."

Limited as my wardrobe was, I still managed to dress well enough for a fancy night out. Black slacks, gray sweater and brown loafers. No tie, as I hated them. I put on my brown suede leather jacket and was off to Lakewood. When I arrived a few minutes before seven, Melissa was there looking radiant. Even in work-in-the-garden clothes she was pretty, but now she was extraordinary. With little effort, she was striking. She had a silver dress with thin black rope as a belt, matching over-the-shoulder purse and short-heeled pumps, with a red button up sweater to keep her warm. I moved forward and kissed her on the lips softly, trying not to mess up her light coating of lipstick. Her face glowed in excitement. She looped her arm in mine and we walked to the Mustang and were off to dinner.

Morrison is up in the foothills west of Denver, a small quiet town.

In November, there would often already be snow on the ground at this elevation, but the warmer than normal weather had melted the little bit that had fallen so far. The crisp air felt good as we got out of the car and walked right in. I had reservations, but the place was quiet and we were seated in a booth, a candle lit to provide a romantic atmosphere in the darkened space. I sat next to Melissa holding her hand. The waiter brought us water and I ordered an extravagant red wine, supporting the mood. After the good and bad of the last few days, I wanted happiness again, and it was right next to me.

The menu was expensive, but I didn't care. We agreed to share a meal and decided on duck with a honey glazing, seasoned potatoes and a salad. Melissa enjoyed the salad, while I had some fresh made bread provided with the dinner. Green was one of my favorite colors, though green food wasn't. I broke off a large piece while staring at her.

"What is the occasion?" Melissa asked. "Getting together during a week night is unusual for us."

"We had a breakthrough yesterday with Ray and I was on cloud nine. After a downer morning I wanted to feel good again, and who better with than you?"

"What was the breakthrough?"

"We got him to admit his problem. I had a brainstorm on getting through to him and it worked..." I explained what all had happened.

"Wow, this is marvelous news. Bill actually said 'I'll be damned!'"

"Yep, might have been as giddy as I'd ever seen him. It was almost orgasmic."

"What was the downer today?"

"I rather not spoil the mood. It would be best to forget it for now."

"Hey, buster, if we are going to be a couple I need to hear the good and the ugly. Keeping it from me won't bring us any closer together."

It was good to hear.

"There was a dead body I had to go identify today..." I explained in vanilla detail what had happened. Though the event was a downer, it felt good to talk with her about the bad along with the good.

"So horrible," Melissa said. "Poor woman. Do you think they'll get her killer?"

"Hard to say. I'm inclined to dig into it further, but would put Bill and his family at risk. I'm afraid it is up to the Sheriff's office and Greeley police to find her murderer. I can't solve all the crime on the front range."

The duck arrived along with the potatoes and it was simply delicious. We ate in silence, each of us looking at the other between bites. She was very stylish while eating, being brought up by her strict, mannerly parents. She lived in a different world than I had: the detective and the lady. I knew I was a lucky man.

After dinner, we decided on a light dessert of ice cream on a chocolate brownie with caramel sauce. I paid the check with plastic and left a super tip while Melissa went to the ladies' room. When she returned, I walked her to the car and hugged her tightly before opening the door. Once inside we glanced at each other and said at the same time "Lookout Mountain" and laughed.

Lookout Mountain sits high above Denver with a wonderful view of the entire city. At night you see the maze of city lights twinkling in an amber grid. It's a fabulous site, and once parked, you can see how large the area and its suburbs are. I found a secluded spot and we sat with the motor turned off gazing off in the distance. It was almost like a clear starry night, littering the landscape below us. No heavenly constellations, though with enough imagination you saw what you wanted. I turned to her in nervous anticipation, putting my arm around her. The bucket seats and stick shift would be an issue. I looked at her with an expression of "what should we do?" She pointed to the backseat where we'd have more room, and crawled back there.

Having some foresight, I had tossed in a blanket to keep us warm in the cool night air. Once situated, I turned into her, gazing into her eyes and sensing sexual tension. I kissed her lips with a heated caress, softly at first and with each touch it became firmer, and we locked in full passion. Her perfume was exciting, as was her persona. Kissing was overwhelmingly sensual with her. She met my aggression with her own. I moved over to ears and her neck, sucking and licking. Her breath became harder, my hands touching her breasts, feeling her chest moving in and out. Grabbing one of my hands, she slid it down her dress and under her skirt, parting her legs, gliding me to her pleasure zone. She was not wearing any panties, so it made it easy to slide my fingers inside her.

"Someone is going commando," I said faintly into her ear.

"I pulled them off in the bathroom," Melissa whispered back. "I was getting so horny thinking about us coming up here after dinner, I was afraid I was going to soak through them as your fingers can tell."

And hot she was. I continued kissing her, sliding one finger and then two, in and out with a smooth rhythm that drove her crazy. She started moaning louder and louder, as I felt her body tense up in excitement. She screamed out in ecstasy over and over, her breath rising and falling with each orgasm. I went faster and faster until she pulled my hand away when she had all she could take. She needed a minute to recapture her oxygen and compose herself.

"Despite my religious upbringing, I'd always wanted a boy to finger me when parked, but would never let them," she admitted. "I would let them kiss me and fondle my breasts, but nothing below the belt, even though deep down I desired it. But Mother's voice always was there, telling me to save myself for the right man."

"I feel lucky you allowed me to be your first," I said with a thousand-watt smile. "Listening to you almost got me off too. Hearing you cry out was so hot. I enjoy giving you whatever pleasure you desire. All you have to do is make a request and you shall receive."

Her eyes lit up with excitement and request was what she did in a naughty tone.

"You know what else I wanted to do with a boy when parked?" Melissa said.

"Tell me."

She leaned over and whispered in my ear a four-letter word I don't believe I'd heard her use before, the expression sending a shudder to my excited body. Her hand reached down slowly and unzipped me, pulling my pants down enough so she could climb on top. While looking me in the eye, a sensual glaze behind her pupils heightened my desire. My arousal in solid state, my eyes meeting hers, I was enjoying the sensation with each up and down motion, sliding me in and out of her, testing the rear suspension of the Mustang. When I whispered to her that I wouldn't hold out much longer, she quickened the pace even more, as she wanted to feel me explode inside her. My body tensed until the full wave of pleasure

114

was released for both of us, our cries echoing within the car, for I, too, experienced a first for me while parked.

Chapter 25

The rest of my week was fairly quiet. I had sent off a bill for both cases and had checks in hand and deposited. I wanted to celebrate, doubting I could eclipse my evening in the car with Melissa. But I'd be damned if I wasn't willing to give it a try. The weekend neared, so my mind wandered over numerous options on what we could do to top it, when I heard some loud noises coming from upstairs in the beauty salon. Sounding unpleasant and what appeared to be a man yelling, something went crashing against a wall, shaking the ceiling. I grabbed my .38 and headed out my door, dreading what I was going to find.

Reaching the stairs to the salon, I kept my gun at my side and out of sight. At the door opening, I peered in through the glass and saw three men inside, two standing and one other in motion threatening Kate. It was her soon-to-be ex, Jack. He was yelling something about wanting money while tipping over a shelf of hair products onto the floor. I saw Kate, two of her co-workers and four female customers up against a mirrored wall, scared to death. I pulled out my cell phone and called 911. I intended to wait for the police when I saw Jack grab Kate by her shirt, pulling her toward him and slapping her in the face twice, with threats to do worse. Waiting now wasn't an option so I walked in, the bells chiming, announcing my arrival. All the parties turned my way and I raised my gun, pointing at the three of them.

"Gentlemen, I suggest none of you move or I'll shoot you," I said firmly.

Jack's eyes focused on me still holding Kate and realized who I was. It was the opening Kate needed; twisting free from his grip, she kicked him in the balls, the metal-tipped biker boots she was wearing unleashed the perfect pain for his groin. He doubled over and dropped to his knees. She kicked him again in the face, breaking his nose, the blood instantly running everywhere.

"You son of a bitch," Kate yelled out. "How dare you lay your hands on me?"

There was a loud "ow" from the other women, and a change from fear to smiles. Jack was down, but was trying to get up.

"Jack, I'd stay down if I were you," I stated, "or she is going to inflict more damage on you which will only bring more glee to the ladies' hearts."

One of the other two men started to move, but I drew back the hammer on the .38.

"Another inch forward will get you shot!" I said. "Both of you on the ground, now!"

Each of them did as they were told, but with a glare of cold, steely eyes. I recognized them as the two muscle-bound men who had met Jack at Eddie's Bar to collect money. Dirk and Merrick, as I'd learned earlier, were dressed in dark jeans, sneakers and leather jackets with weapons underneath I'd leave for the Denver cops to find. I stood there firmly and pulled out my license to show the police as I'd heard their sirens outside. They entered, guns drawn, and I held up the ID, putting my .38 in the air, the hammer no longer cocked.

"My name is Jarvis Mann and I'm a private detective hired by the owner, Kate Tanner, who is standing over the bleeding man on the floor. He and the two others prone were busting up the place when I intervened. They are all armed."

One of the officers knew me and walked over beside me, his gun lowered slightly.

"Jarvis, give me the weapon," he said. "Sit on the ground until we can sort this out."

Soon came in a flood of officers to handle the scene. Ten minutes later I was allowed to get on my feet, once they got information from Kate and handed me back my .38. I stepped over to her to see if she was alright, as she was being attended to by a paramedic for a darkening bruise on her cheek. She gave me a weak smile while holding an ice pack to her face.

"Nice shiner you're going to have," I stated.

"His nose and balls will be worse," Kate replied.

"Two well-placed kicks; I have to say, I'm impressed."

"The bastard had it coming to him. I'd have cut them off if I'd had a knife!"

"He ever hit you before?"

"No. There were a couple of times in the past I thought he might. He always knew I'd give it right back to him. I'd have done it sooner if he didn't have his goons for backup and I was worried they'd hurt the other ladies. You came in, he was distracted, and so I pounced and struck back."

I nodded, happy she had extracted a measure of retaliation. I saw them pulling Jack off the floor in handcuffs, the paramedic now cleaning him up and packing his nose with gauze. Our eyes met, and his cold stare hadn't softened any from his beating. I knew I'd be seeing him again down the road.

"What did he want?" I asked.

"Same old thing—money," Kate answered. "He said he owed someone and needed it fast or he was in trouble."

"How much did he want?"

"Everything I had here. We only keep a little bit in the register, but he knew I stashed cash in the floor safe. He wanted the combination, but I wasn't about to give it to him. I generally have a grand or more in there from the week's receipts before they are picked up by armored truck. He needed all of it or the two men with him were going to take it out of his hide, or so he said."

This wasn't good news for Jack. If he owed them money it meant either he was skimming from collections and they caught him, or he was gambling again and lost more than he could pay back. Might have been why he had been raiding Kate's bank account before she cut him off. No matter, he was desperate for cash and now he was going to get all of them put in jail, which wouldn't help his cause any.

The scene was crowded but through the throng, I saw Detective Mallard heading our way. I had not seen him for a few months, but time always seemed to stand still with him, appearing like he always did. Reaching us, he acknowledged me and spoke to Kate.

"I understand you're the owner," he said to her. "I need to get a statement from you about what happened; from hotshot here as well."

"Good to see you too, Detective," I replied.

"What do you need to know?" said Kate.

"Start at the beginning…"

And she did. From the point where she hired me, the reason why, the evidence I'd acquired, the divorce and restraining order, to today's events. Mallard wrote it all down in his little notebook, her detail so complete there was little to add.

"Is this your handiwork?" Mallard asked of me while pointing at Jack's packed nose.

"No, I did it," replied Kate. "He grabbed and slapped me, with threats to do worse. So, I kicked him in the balls and in the face after Jarvis came in."

"Off the record, since I'm supposed to be impartial, but good for you. I'm assuming you are going to press charges."

"Damn right!"

"You'll be a witness?" Mallard asked of me.

"Yes, sir. I'm sure the other ladies will be thrilled to testify."

"We're getting their statements now, but I'm sure what they say will match what you just told me. This will probably take some time, so get yourself comfortable. Contact your insurance agent. I'm sure you'll want to get working on fixing some of the damages here."

Kate nodded and headed to her office in the back.

"Seems like a helluva lady," stated Mallard. "I hope you aren't sleeping with this client."

It was a shot at me from my previous case, which had turned bad.

"She's my landlord, whom I've known for many years. She is a client and nothing more."

"Good. We don't need a repeat of your last clusterfuck. Who are the two goons with him?"

"Dirk Bailey and Merrick Jones," I replied. "They work for a man named Roland Langer."

"Roland is not a nice guy. Her ex was working for him?"

"Yes, and I suspect into him for money he couldn't pay. He'd been stealing from her and she cut him off. He was trying to get more today when I stopped him. I didn't want to say anything more to her, but I'm certain they'll be back once they hit the streets. Desperation will force him to try again."

"Well, if he works for Langer they will have lawyers bailing them out quickly. She probably needs to close her business for a while. Take a long vacation, because you're right, he'll be back."

"She is tough, so I doubt she'll back down. I'll talk with her and see what she wants to do."

"Can you protect her?"

"I will assist her the best I can since I live downstairs. I can't stay with her 24/7. And she has two kids, too. We both know they can get to her no matter what I do if they try hard enough."

Mallard nodded. This wasn't good and I needed to figure out something.

"Any chance I can chat with Jack before you haul him away?"

"Not a good idea. I doubt he will talk with you anyway. He's been staring at you this whole time. And not with a 'hey, let's be pals and have a beer' expression either."

"Yeah, I know. Give me five minutes. I want to see what he says. You know he won't say diddly to you and once his lawyer arrives he'll be out again. We have a little history and he might slip up and say something stupid."

Mallard glanced over at Jack, walked over and told the paramedic to step away for now. They both gave me some room and I stepped over to him trying to match his frightening glare. I came up close to his face and spoke.

"Your cold glare isn't scaring me off, so listen carefully. Coming around here again is a bad idea. It will get you shot if you show up. If anything happens to Kate or your kids, I will hunt you down. You need money, but you know Kate, and she is tough as nails, so you aren't going to get any from her. Now we can all make nice and go on our merry way or we can do this the difficult way. What's it going to be?"

Jack continued the hard stare and checked around to make sure no one was listening.

"You made a big mistake getting involved. The people I know won't take this lightly."

"You mean your buddies being hauled off to jail, Dirk and Merrick?"

He appeared surprised I had their names.

"They'll be the muscle doing the dirty work, but not the ones calling the shots."

"Yes, I know. You're employed by Roland Langer, and he is a bad guy. From the way I see it, you owe him money, not Kate. The only heat he is going to bring is on you. When you don't get the cash, I think you will be the one to pay. You need to think of some other way to get it and leave her out of it. Because, like I said..." I took my finger, pointed it at him and shot him with it, and stepped away.

I walked past Mallard, mouthed "thanks" and headed back to Kate's office. We needed to talk about what we'd need to do going forward, making arrangements to keep an eye on things to help her out. Providing her protection when I wasn't around was required.

Though I wasn't thrilled about it, a discussion about getting her a gun, a permit and time on the range to learn how to use it was necessary. As tough as she was, I knew she had the fortitude to do what needed to be done. We talked it all out, the day dragging into night.

Chapter 26

As I suspected, Kate wasn't about to back down. She was prepared to do whatever it took to protect her territory. So, over the next couple of days we worked out getting her a weapon, a small snub-nosed .38, a permit to carry it and practice at the gun range. She would have to pass a background check, which would take up to a week, but I used Bill to help speed things along and had her cleared within twenty-four hours. Once at the firing range she was a natural and was shooting with a fair amount of accuracy after a couple of lessons. I was confident she could handle it without hurting herself or anyone innocent, like her children.

"Make sure your kids know about the gun and what it's for," I stated to her. "They are not to play with or use it. If they have an interest and want to learn how, we need to go through the same procedure you are going through. It's not a toy, so make them understand this. Don't hide it and tell them the truth."

From there, I spent my days hanging around the salon. Since I lived downstairs with nothing else going on, staying in the salon all day wasn't much different, other than I had to live with the TV selection of the female staff and clientele. It was heavy on *The View*, a couple of soaps older than me, and Ellen DeGeneres. I was generally the only male in the room, other than the occasional man who stopped in for a haircut. I felt a touch out of place especially when the discussion on the tube, or initiated by the ladies, covered men. When the conversation got angry about some bastard who used someone, I often sensed the eyes on me as if I was the culprit. Occasionally, I'd have to step outside to escape the hostile atmosphere and even look back on my own behavior and question it.

So far there had been no sign of Jack and his two brutes after three days. They had been bailed out within 24 hours, with arraignment dates several weeks away. I knew I couldn't stay here forever, but needed to be sure. I gave Kate my half-price special. I had little on my plate other than the murder in Greeley. There were limits to her funds, but money would do her no good if she was dead. I was looking over my shoulder a great deal. I was a target, too. It was always fun to be popular.

As for Greeley, I was summoned to give a statement. My lawyer,

Barry, came along to protect my rights in case they tried to force me to reveal my client. If they didn't subpoena the information I could withhold it. So far, they were happy to get any info I could give them because they had nothing much to go on. The apartment and any paperwork led them nowhere. All transactions were done via cash so there wasn't any trail to follow. The unaccounted-for Malibu had been located with no usable physical evidence, and was registered in her name only. Talks with the owners of The Hustle revealed nothing but surprise and shock Ariela was dead. They had phoned in a missing person report the morning she was found, saying they were worried she'd not been into work for a couple of days. It was a good alibi and stone-walled the city and county investigators. These were not dumb people.

"There was a friend of Ariela," I said to them during the statement. "I only know her name as Leather. She liked wearing sexy leather outfits at the club. I was aware via my investigation they had some ties and may have socialized outside of The Hustle."

It was a subtle way of putting what they were doing, but I couldn't reveal all I knew. So, I was trying to give them a little more to work on.

"Why didn't you mention this at the scene?" said the county DA.

"Simple oversight," I answered, with a straight lie. "Probably the sight of her dead body caused a brain fart on my part. But I'm telling you now."

"Give us a description."

I did, down to as much detail as I remembered, since I'd seen most of her naked body.

"If she is still working at The Hustle," I added, "she shouldn't be hard to find."

After some other questioning, I was free to go and I was back on the road into town. It seemed I was wearing a groove in the pavement from all the back and forth. I hoped the Mustang was up to the task to handle all the mileage. The tanks of gas I was going through were adding multiple digits to my credit card.

Melissa and I had a quiet weekend together. I was worn out from the latest events and she was tired from her recent case, staying up late several nights to catch up on the night of work she'd lost on our evening out and exploits on Lookout Mountain. She spent the night at my place Saturday, and we actually did sleep in bed, with no sweaty contact other than some tight cuddling. Exhaustion had grabbed us both and sent us off to slumber before any heavy petting got started. The warmth of November was replaced with December winter weather, with several inches of wet snow blanketing the city into the late morning hours. It was dark and dreary, and we slept in until 10 a.m. After awakening, events got a little more heated, and once finished, lunchtime beckoned. After showers, we decided on Chinese delivered and Melissa had to get home, with more legal briefs to finish in preparation of her newest case on Monday.

"I'm sorry I have so much to do," she stated. "I'd love to stay all day, read fortune cookies, watch football and screw your brains out at the same time, but I must get this work done or it's my ass."

"I understand," I answered. "I'm guessing Tony won't accept a note from me saying you are laid up, so to speak."

Melissa laughed and kissed me hard on the lips, tasting the food and beer. She left me alone, but inside and warm, with a football game on TV. The afternoon wore on, the snow had slowed and darkness started to creep over the city when I heard loud noises above. It was a Sunday and the salon was closed. I grabbed my phone and called Kate.

"Where are you right now?" I asked.

"I'm at home with my kids," she answered. "Why?"

"It sounds like someone is upstairs working. Should there be?"

"No," she said firmly.

"Call the police. I will check to see who it is. I doubt it's Santa Claus."

"I'm coming down."

"No, stay home until I summon you. Call them now and tell them someone has broken into your work. Warn them I may be there, so they don't shoot me."

I got up after putting on my boots and a sweatshirt. I heard more noises and two gunshots, followed by louder crashing and what sounded like a smoke alarm going off. I hurried out the door, my .38 at the ready. Turning the corner, I saw two figures coming down the steps. It was dark but via the streetlights they saw me and one of them raised his arm, took aim and fired. I ducked down but felt a burning on my left arm. I stayed down while more bullets ricocheted around me. Clutching at the ache on my bicep, I noticed the blood running, though it wasn't bad, appearing to be a minor flesh wound.

The shots stopped and a loud diesel engine started up. Looking up, I saw them leaving and fired, hitting the tailgate and back window, shattering it into a million pieces. They roared away and were gone before I could fire anymore.

Smelling smoke, I ran up the stairs and opened the door, feeling the heat intensify, the entire room ablaze. I tried to step in but was pushed back by the choking smell and bright red flames, the intense blaze hotter than anything I'd ever experienced, the flammable chemicals from all the hair products feeding it. Moving back out onto the sidewalk, I sat down in the snow and inspected my arm, the blood starting to clot, the pain increasing. I checked myself for any other wounds, but found none. The siren and lights came from all directions and I knew more police statements were in my future. This did not please me in the least bit, and I cursed several times into the darkness.

Chapter 27

The police had arrived first, a female officer doing the questioning. The fire truck showed up next, followed by a paramedic unit. The officer relayed to the firefighting team what she had learned from me. It is amazing watching firefighters working. They arrive on the scene, get whatever data they can get, put on their gear and with a stream of water beating back the flames, run into a burning building. What it takes to do this is quite spectacular. It wasn't long before they had the blaze under control, knocked down all the flames and had it completely out. Only the smoke and a horrid stench remained. I suspected they would find a body inside and about forty-five minutes later this was confirmed. It appeared to be a male, and from what I told them, it appeared he was dead before the blaze started to cover up the murder. With the coroner's technical skills of today, they would have learned the truth eventually.

The paramedic patched up my arm as best they could, but a trip to the hospital was in order. I felt I didn't need to go, but apparently any type of gunshot wound required it. I was arguing with them about this when Kate arrived. It hadn't taken her long to make the trek after my follow-up call. The look on her face when she saw the damage was shocking.

"Oh my," she stated, trudging through the snow in her knee-high black boots. "What the hell happened?"

"Kate, I'm so sorry. They torched the place before I could stop them."

She noticed them working on my arm.

"Were you hurt?" she asked.

"It is but a flesh wound," I stated in an English accent.

"Oh my!"

"Are you the owner?" asked the female officer.

Kate nodded, still with a stunned appearance.

"I'm sorry, too. Jarvis here has given us a statement. He says he rents the place below and is a detective you've hired on a domestic case. Is this correct?"

She nodded again, a few tears now filling her eyes.

"Would someone be working tonight?"

"No. The place was closed."

126

"Not a cleaning crew or anyone else?"

"No, they come later in the afternoon before we close. It seems like we won't be open for a while."

"Any reason why someone would be inside this evening?" asked the officer.

"If someone was in there they broke in. Why do you keep asking this?"

"We wanted to double-check because we have a dead body. It appears they had been shot before the fire was started."

"Jarvis, what the hell is going on?"

"I'm not certain, Kate. After previous events I have my suspicions."

"Jack?"

"Maybe. We won't know for a day or so. I'm wondering if they came to break into your safe and when he couldn't get in..."

Kate appeared as if she was going to fall down. I grabbed her tightly around the waist to keep her upright. I felt the pain surge through my arm. We walked her back to the squad car to sit her down in the back. Her eyes were still moist. But she wasn't crying, although she appeared to be in shock.

"Even though I was angry with him, I wouldn't want him dead. What am I going to tell the kids?"

"Nothing is concrete yet," stated the female officer. "It may be a good theory, but let's wait for the coroner to come back with a positive ID before jumping to conclusions."

"She's right, Kate. We'll see what they say."

"Even so, someone is dead and my salon, my livelihood, is ruined. What am I going to do?"

"Insurance will cover the damage and they can have it fixed up and better than new in no time. You'd be amazed what contractors can do."

She glanced over at me, trying to shake off the shock. "Where are you going to live?"

Good question. It's possible my place wasn't damaged too badly, but still I wouldn't be able to inhabit it for several days. There was certainly smoke and water damage. Plus, it was part of an active crime scene.

"Don't worry about me, I'll be fine. They are saying I must go down to the hospital to get checked out. Why don't you come with me if it is OK, Officer?"

"Sure. She can ride with you and I can follow you down. I still need to get a formal statement from Kate."

I helped her over to the paramedic unit, letting her lay down on the gurney and we rode down to Swedish Medical Center. The ER was a busy place and we had to wait about forty-five minutes before someone saw us. They checked out Kate at my insistence, giving her a mild sedative once the officer had gotten her statement. I was patched up further and given a prescription for an antibiotic to prevent infection. The wound wasn't bad, but bullets had punctured the skin, and it was nothing the medical profession fooled around with. They offered me some strong pain medication, but I declined because I didn't like the way they made me feel. Two hours later we were cleared to leave, and I called a cab to come and take us back to Walgreens for my medicine and back to the salon to get my car. Kate fell asleep in my front seat most of the way and I drove her home, still uncertain where I'd be sleeping tonight. I didn't want to disturb Melissa, as I knew she was busy working. A hotel was where I was going to wind up, and I was trying to think where there was something decent nearby when I pulled into Kate's driveway.

"We're home," I said to her.

She was half awake, her eyes now open fully.

"God, what a weekend!" she stated. "I keep thinking the craziness will end, then something else happens."

"It will get better in time," I said. "Have to get through these rough patches. Let me walk you inside."

We stepped in and her kids were there, hugging her, while she explained everything. She left out the part about the dead body and my theory so as not to worry them. They each had lots of questions, but I was too tired to listen to them.

"Well, I should be going so you can get your rest," I said, reaching for the door.

"Where are you going to go?" asked Kate.

"I'll find a hotel and crash. Tomorrow we can assess the damages and make more permanent arrangements."

"He can sleep downstairs," said Kate's son.

"Yes, the sheets are clean and there is a bathroom," said her daughter.

"Great idea," said Kate. "You shouldn't have to drive out after the

128

day you've had and find a motel. We'll be happy to have you, and I'd feel safer with you around."

"I don't want to impose," I said.

"You won't be and we insist," replied Kate. "It's clean and quiet."

I was too tired to argue with them and agreed. Cody showed me downstairs, even though I'd been there once before. After using the bathroom, I found a comfortable spot in the middle of the bed, on my good side away from my arm wound, and was asleep in a matter of minutes, hoping to flush the weekend's events from my dreams. If it were only so easy...

Chapter 28

After a night of rest, and it was better than one would expect, we made our way over to the salon to assess the damages and get her car. Kate's insurance man met us there and the news was bad. Most of the space would need to be gutted and rebuilt. Everything inside would need to be thrown out and replaced. The roof appeared to be undamaged, but the attic area would need all new insulation. My downstairs living and work quarters had bad smoke and some water damage, requiring repairs her insurance would fix. My insurance would have to cover my personal possessions. Much of my clothing, bedding and towels would require washing to remove the smoke smell and residue. Furniture would need cleaning; all electronics would be checked for damage. Likely, two weeks and I could move back in, although the salon probably was a month or more before it would be operational again. It wasn't what Kate wanted to hear, but she dealt with it as best she could. The lost money and revenue would hit her and her co-workers hard, while my ongoing client bill with her wouldn't be paid right away. For now, I had cash reserves to get by on.

I was allowed to gather up some clothes that weren't too smoky, along with my computer, which after powering on worked, and my Beretta, since the .38 had been taken by the police because of the shooting. I also grabbed any usable perishable food and any other staples I needed. Kate had insisted I continue to stay with them for now, and I accepted. She had even given me a key and the code to their alarm system. It was a relief to have a real home to live in for the next two weeks and not incur the hotel expense.

In my Mustang, I ran over my things to Kate's while she continued to work with her agent. After I dropped everything off, I headed down to the police station to learn the latest. I had put two bullets into the fleeing truck and wanted to know if they had found it. I'd gotten a couple of numbers off the plate and the best description possible in the darkness. With what I had they should have something to go on, and I wanted in on it. Once inside, I tracked down Bill at his desk. I took a seat and got my usual cold greeting, which was warmer than most got from him.

"How is Ray doing?" I asked.

"Pretty good," replied Bill, while shuffling some paperwork. "I believe we've turned a corner and got him on the right track, seeing the right people. The hope is in time, he should be good as new."

"Glad to hear it."

"I doubt you're here for idle chit-chat," he stated while signing off on a sheet and filing it away. "I understand you've gotten yourself into another mess. Is this why you're here?"

"Yes. Who was assigned the murder case? I left for the hospital before anyone arrived."

"Mallard has this one. He'll be thrilled to see you again."

"Pals till the end. Is he in?"

"Yes. You can go on back. I'll stay here and miss the reunion."

I smiled and headed towards his office, the visitor badge allowing me to wander the halls. It had been ages since I'd been to Mallard's office, but still managed to find his door. I knocked and he hollered for me to enter. He was sitting at an old wooden desk in a room the size of many walk-in closets, with one extra chair and the limited floor space, covered with tall file cabinets.

"Good thing you aren't claustrophobic," I said.

"Damn," he stated, ignoring my wit. "Every time I see you it's something bad."

"Good to see you too," I answered. "We can plan dinner with the wife and kids to change things up, but I don't see you as the evening out with friend's type."

Mallard grunted. "I was this close to vacation time and you come along with a body I have to deal with. Do you purposely try to fuck up my life?"

I threw up my hands and smiled.

"I suppose you are looking for info on the fire and the dead body."

"I'd like to help if I can. It happened in my client's place of business and my home office. I have thoughts of what may have transpired. I'm not certain who else was there, but have a fair idea. Any ID on the body yet?"

"No. Coroner says later this morning or this afternoon. It's a male, probably in his late forties or early fifties. From the report you say you have a hunch it might be your client's ex."

"Yes, I'll be surprised if it isn't him."

"Because of the incident at the salon?"

"Correct. He was in debt with Roland, possibly skimming from the collections. He had gone there to get money from Kate and failed. After he was bailed out, I'm guessing he returned to try and break into her safe. When this didn't work, they killed him or something along those lines."

"Did he have the combination?"

"No. She had it changed."

"If he didn't have it, what good would it do?"

"He was desperate. Maybe he thought he could figure it out. Talk or slug his way out of it. No one claimed he was bright. Might be what did him in."

"Can't collect from a dead man."

"No, but it sends a message to others what will happen when you steal from him. Could have been an accident—fought his way out and got shot. Maybe he pulled his gun and they killed him in self-defense. A lot of ways it may have gone. Again, it's only a theory, but I think it's a solid one. What about the truck?"

"We located it a couple miles away, abandoned," Mallard answered while pulling out some photos. "You can see the rear window was shot out and we found lots of blood on the seat, dash and floor. So much so we figured we'd have a body, too. But haven't run across one yet and no hospital has reported anyone coming in for a gunshot wound."

"Head injury?"

"Probably. Must have hit a passenger, since they didn't stop. We figure a corpse will show up eventually."

"Who is the truck registered to?"

"A woman who lives in Highlands Ranch. She called it in as being stolen the night of the fire."

"Do you have a name?"

"Sure, it's here somewhere. Yeah, it was Dona Wiggins."

I recognized the name.

"Holy shit!" I said.

"You know her?"

"Hell, yes. She was Jack's girlfriend, or at least so it appeared. I'd say this is a bona fide clue there, Detective Mallard."

He might have cracked a smile, though he hid it well.

"I do believe you are right. How do you know this?"

I went about letting him know about following Jack and the

132

evidence I had gathered for the divorce case, right down to the little love nest where he and Dona would go after dropping off his daily collections.

"Doing collections for Roland Langer?" stated Mallard. "Damn, he is one mean SOB. He certainly could have been the one who pulled the trigger, if it is Jack who bought the farm. Proving it will be difficult."

"What is the address?" I asked.

Mallard rattled off the number and street, it matching the address I'd gotten earlier.

"We can get him if you let me work on it."

He contemplated for a minute, rocking back in his chair, rubbing his temples and loosening his tie.

"I can certainly use the help. I'm up to my neck in cases right now. Where would you start?"

Mallard's phone rang and he answered it. After a couple of minutes he hung up.

"They identified the body and it's Jack Tanner. They'll be letting the family know here shortly."

Mallard put everything back in the file and tossed it my way.

"Where are you going to start?" he asked again.

"When there is a woman involved, you follow her," I said, while grabbing the folder. "Dona will be a grieving girlfriend and grieving girlfriends can be extra chatty."

"She's all yours," said Mallard. "Be sure to report back what you find."

I think I'd been unofficially deputized, but I don't think he'd be real happy if I asked to be sworn in and given a badge like in the old westerns, so I kept it to myself. *Yippee ki-yay!*

Chapter 29

The information on Dona wasn't much more than what Officer Rainn had supplied me a few weeks back. The address given was in Highlands Ranch, but I saw her going into a condominium north of there with Jack, acting like a couple. People often move and don't update their listing, so this might be the case here. Still I would start with the address given, in the burgeoning suburb south of County Line Road and see what I found.

This whole area had a wide range of homes: expensive sprawling mansions behind secured covenants to smaller, cheaper pre-fab structures built on small lots, crammed together where reaching out a side window and touching the outside wall on your neighbor's home was a possibility. The address I had was the former and I couldn't get in without the owner's permission. I flashed my ID at security, telling him I was conducting police business and to call Denver detective Mallard if he had any questions. Since this was a minimum wage rent-a-cop barely out of his twenties who was easily intimidated, he let me in. He didn't write down my name or take note of my license plate while driving through the open gate. Apparently name-dropping worked, and I'd need to remember to use this in the future.

Each of the homes sat on huge lots, with manicured green grass, fancy landscapes of rocks, bushes, perennials flowers and a small tree here and there. The whole area had once been farm and prairie land, so large trees were nowhere to be found. I drove the winding road, finding my way to the address I had on hand. The home was a red and brown multi-story, wider than a city block, with a three-car garage larger than some of the cheaper homes a mile away. A long curvy driveway twisted up the hill, with a circular parking area for guests in front. Outside sat what appeared to be a white Mercedes, looking a lot like the car I'd seen Dona driving. The notes in the file had stated she was not employed, and no marital status was listed, so if she lived here in this close to a million-dollar home she was either married, seeing someone with money or a rich heiress. The question was why she had been meeting Jack in a lower-class condo several miles north.

The area was so open it was hard to appear inconspicuous, but

134

there didn't appear to be any mobile security driving around, so I waited. I sat outside watching for any sign of her. She had normally picked Jack up at the bar on Broadway around 1 p.m. or so, and it was nearly time. She likely had not heard the news of Jack, since I had only learned it myself, so if the routine held, she would be leaving soon for her afternoon tryst. If not today, then I'd try again tomorrow. My hope was if I could get her alone, she might talk.

I saw her step out, dressed in a short blue skirt, a revealing sheer white blouse under a tan leather jacket and high heels. She got into her car and flashed a lot of sexy leg, which I admired. I pulled ahead of her and took the road to Eddie's Bar, hoping the pattern was followed and I'd beat her there. Traffic was bad, but I stayed in front, which was difficult, since she was an aggressive driver. I saw her back further, but we were on the same path. I matched her insane driving, pulling away, and a couple of red lights slowing her down helped. Finding a spot nearby, I got out of my car and moved to the other side, waiting for her. She pulled up, double parking as she had done the other times, holding up traffic, and I stepped over and hopped into the passenger seat, smiling at her.

"What the fuck!" she yelled.

"Jack sent me to meet with you," I said firmly. "He is tied up, but I'll take you to him."

"I don't know you. How can I trust what you're saying is true?"

I opened my jacket, so she saw my Beretta.

"You see I'm armed to do my job. There is a problem and Jack didn't want to be seen with you here. He asked for me to help so he could meet with you elsewhere. It's why you haven't heard from him today."

I was making this up as I went along. It sounded convincing enough and she seemed to believe it. *Used car sales could have been a career choice!*

"I was wondering why he didn't text me I thought he was busy or something was wrong. We always have a standing appointment on Monday, so I drove down to see if he was here. Where are we off to?"

"Head south on Broadway. I want to make sure we aren't being tailed."

She pulled out per her normal, squealing tires and horns a-blaring. It was amazing she didn't get in more accidents. Either she was extremely ballsy or dumb.

"You should dial it back some," I said. "No reason to call attention to ourselves."

I was fearing for my safety as much as anything.

"Okay," she replied, slowing down to the speed limit. "So, it's a dire situation?"

I kept looking back keeping up impressions someone might be following. Acting might have been a second career if selling used cars had not worked out.

"Yes. He wants to make sure you're safe."

"So, I'm in danger?"

I didn't answer but gave her a yes glare. I continued to stare out the back and check the mirrors. We drove several miles and I had her turn onto Belleview, taking us west. I was looking around for a restaurant to go into. We came to Santa Fe, so I had her go right, knowing there were lots of retail businesses in that direction. I saw a Chili's on the left-hand side and had her get off at Hampden and we back-tracked. Once there, I counted my blessings we had survived the trip, as even at the speed limit she was reckless when changing lanes and taking exits. It appeared she never used a mirror to check for traffic all around her. It was as if she was driving down the streets all alone. I'd left an obvious handprint on the door handle from squeezing it.

Once inside I asked for a booth near the back, so I faced towards the entrance to see anyone coming in. She appeared nervous and a bit scared. Her mood wouldn't get any better once I gave her the news of who I was and what had happened to Jack.

"Where is he?" Dona asked. "Is he meeting us?"

A young lady came and took our drink orders, Dona ordered a beer and I did the same. I waited to speak until the drinks arrived and I asked for more time before ordering.

"Dona, I have some news you won't like," I stated. "Please listen to all I have to say before deciding anything. Believe it or not, I'm here to help you, though you may not accept it when you first hear it."

Her face turned red. "You lied to me. Who are you?"

"My name is Jarvis Mann and I'm a private detective."

She started to get up, but I put my hand out to stop her, so she sat back down.

136

"What do you want?" She took a sip of beer. I was happy I wasn't wearing it.

"I'm investigating a murder. You may have some information which can help me."

"Why me?"

"Because you know the person who was murdered."

Her eyes lit up, her face now with a scared shine.

"Who?"

"Jack. He was shot and killed last night."

Cold and hard, as if ripping off a Band-Aid, I blurted out the news. She glanced out the window, her lip quivering now. Tears started streaming down her face.

"I'm sorry," I said, waiting for her to get it back together.

She turned back to me a few minutes later. "Do you know who?"

"It was someone driving a truck with your name on the registration—the one you reported stolen."

"Oh God, no."

"It wasn't stolen, was it?"

She shook her head no.

"Why did you say it was?"

"He told me to."

"Who told you?"

"Oh God, he knows! He'll kill me!"

"Tell me and I can help you."

She thought about it for a moment, uncertain what to do. Sadness had been replaced with genuine fear. You sensed it; felt it. It was real and shook her whole person.

"Oh my God, Roland knows and he is going to skin me alive!"

"Roland Langer?"

"Yes."

"And his reasoning to do this?"

"Because he owns me. I'm his sex slave!"

Chapter 30

My whole body shook at her statement; her fear transported across the table and grabbed me. There was little doubt her words rang true.

"I know what you're thinking, what she is saying is nuts. But it's the truth. I swear to God."

"I believe you; hard to imagine something like this happening in this day and age."

"It can and it did," Dona answered. "Probably the politically correct term these days would be Indentured Servant with Benefits."

I smiled at the expression, though it didn't seem the politically correct thing to do.

"Can you give me some background on how this came to be?"

Dona paused as the waitress returned to see if we were ready to order. I decided an appetizer was all I needed to feed my appetite and ordered some cheese sticks with sauce and another round of beer for Dona, as she had finished hers. I was nursing mine trying to stay alert.

"Why should I tell you?"

"Because I can assist you. You are in danger and I doubt you can protect yourself."

She glared at me straight on, as I tried to appear reassuring. I was using her, this was for certain, but I could help her, too. At this point how, I wasn't sure.

"I grew up here in Denver, but my parents died when I was very young. I don't remember them at all and there was no extended family to take me in. So, I became a Ward of the Court, part of the foster care system. I moved around a lot; some homes were wonderful to live in and others not so much. Some are in it for the money, but many do care. I didn't stay in one place long, and without guidance I became wild."

She paused when they returned with the cheese sticks and her beer. I devoured one quickly to feed my hunger. She took another long swig from the mug, so far holding off on eating anything. Hard to have an appetite when reliving the past, especially a horrific one.

"When puberty and the hormones hit, and my body developed, I learned how to use it for my own gain. It was my most valuable asset and my only one. I hung out with older boys when I was fourteen or fifteen and they wanted sex and were willing to pay. At first feeling me up, a hand job or a BJ, but after a while they wanted to go all the way. I did, and soon I became pretty good at it and even sometimes enjoyed it. It would depend on the guy. Some were good enough to get me off and even wanted me to enjoy myself, and others were only concerned with themselves. As high school came around, my grades fell and I dropped out. I ran away from my latest foster parents with a nineteen-year-old man I thought I was in love with. We stayed in some dump off Five Points and got by however we could. Pete sold drugs and I used my body like I always did, making money doing what I did best: fucking."

Dona stopped and drank down the remaining beer. I'd eaten half of the cheese sticks; being a gentleman, I would leave her the rest. I listened to her unpleasant words and wondered about the kind of life and what it would be like. It was survival in a difficult world many had to endure. Doing what was needed to pay the rent, put food in your stomach.

"Somehow Pete scored this big gig. He said it was his way in to more money for us, and a better life. It was some party where we'd mingle, make contacts, him with his charm and me with my body. I believed in him for some reason, and cared for the asshole. I was still a child at seventeen, but I was in love and would do anything for him. He was the one, in my eyes…" She paused, seeming to lose her composure. "Seems silly now."

"Love blinds us sometimes."

I was trying to be supportive. I didn't want her to shut down. Information was my friend and I needed more clarity. I waved for them to bring another beer. It was loosening her enough to be free with her words. A couple of twenty-something women walked in the front for a late lunch. Their skin-tight jeans didn't reveal any hidden hardware, so I figured we were safe as they went into the bar area. Their heavy coats might have concealed a machine gun, but I risked it.

"We met many people there, mostly men of varying ages, from young twenty-somethings to those pushing retirement. There were a few other women there, but it seemed they were working gals like me. It was a competition of sorts: who could land the biggest fish. Some of the men were well known, celebrities and politicians.

Others were of questionable stature, Pete told me; men who might advance his pipeline of selling drugs. He needed me to grease the skids, make the rounds as he pointed out a couple of the key people there, introducing me. One stood out and it was Roland. He was older than me, probably around forty at the time, but well-dressed, attractive face, tall and slender, but acceptable. We talked for some time before retiring to another room to get it on. He was forceful, but not above providing me pleasure along with his own. I enjoyed myself, and when we were finished, he asked for my name and number, while giving me a couple of C-notes. It seemed likely we would connect again. Afterwards, Pete talked it up with Roland and it seemed they would do business. When the night ended, Pete was walking on stars. We had hit it big, and it was all he would talk about on the drive home."

With another frosty mug on the table, Dona tasted a cheese stick, which now was cold. She asked if she could order something else, deciding on Caribbean Salad. I ordered a classic turkey toasted sandwich and ice water to round out the appetizer, and beer.

"I'm guessing Pete didn't hit it as big as he hoped," I asked.

"No he didn't. A couple of days and still no calls, as he waited anxiously. Finally, two men were waiting for us when we got home one day. Two large men who once played football, I'd later learn. They were Roland's enforcers, who stopped by to say they wanted to speak to Pete in private. I went inside and after fifteen minutes passed, they came in with Pete, requesting I go with them to see Roland. I looked to him to see what it was all about, but he couldn't look me in the eye. He said I should go. No goodbye or see you later; nothing. I wanted to change clothes, but they said I looked fine and to come with them. I left with my purse and what I was wearing, and we were off."

The food arrived and we both took some bites. The sandwich was good, though not outstanding, filling a hole in my stomach. Dona took down several spoonsful of salad, working around the tomatoes, eating quickly, much like she drove. There was certainly an edge to everything she did.

"They took me to Roland's house," she continued, "a huge place in Highlands Ranch. Beautiful furnishings, expensive art on the walls and fancy entertainment centers in most of the major rooms. The kitchen was all stainless steel, marble and granite, and was immaculate. Upstairs there were more bedrooms than I cared to count, each with their own bathroom, it would seem; a study and library filled with endless books. I got a tour of it all, except for the basement. He would leave it for later. He served me wine and a dinner of shrimp and scallops. He treated me well, and I knew what I was there for. We made love downstairs and upstairs. I was in heaven, so it would seem. I spent the night and the next day when I asked when I would be taken home, he told me, 'You live here now.' I asked for an explanation and he stated, 'He traded you for drugs and cash. I own you. You will do as I beckon. Provide for my every wish and desire, until I deem to set you free'. With those words I was stunned. I asked to speak with Pete, so he said 'I bought you. He no longer cares to see you anymore.' I didn't believe him. He let me call Pete and he basically said to leave him alone; I was Roland's property."

The revelation was raw to the nerves to hear.

"You were seventeen when he sold you?"

"Yes."

"You protested this. Tried to get away?"

"I couldn't. I was never left alone for the next six months or so. If I defied him at all, I was punished."

"In what way?"

"The basement which I had not seen the first night, I learned later was his pleasure and pain room. When I first saw it, I was shocked by what was down there. He warned me I would find out what would happen if I resisted in any way. It scared me so much I did exactly what he told me to do."

"The kind, thoughtful lover was no more?"

"At times he was respectful, but his anger would get the best of him. He was extremely aggressive sexually—to the point of being domineering. Not only did I need to provide him pleasure, but pleasure for his clients."

"How did you react to this?"

"At first I was totally numb. With enough booze, anyone can get through most anything. It became a way of life for me. It wasn't all horrible. Better than fucking in the back of a car or a ten-dollar blowjob in a rat-infested alleyway. I had expensive clothes, fabulous food, met rich and famous people, while enjoying the highlife. I even was given money to spend. In time, I was allowed some freedom to do things on my own. There were worse ways to live, I suppose, and now I was living in a palace. I was better off than with Pete, who was marginally better than the life I had before. I knew nothing else, so I made do. I have no other skills other than fucking. I might as well do it on a grand scale."

"How many years ago was this?"

"Seven, soon to be eight, I believe."

"What happened to Pete?"

"I don't know and I don't care. He obviously didn't love me."

I nodded while finishing my sandwich. I still had one eye on the front. It was the late lunch crowd, so the place wasn't busy. A husband and wife walked in with their toddler daughter. Unless the gun was hidden in the teddy bear she carried, we were safe.

"Wow, spilling out my life story," Dona stated. "I don't think I've ever told anyone this before, other than Jack. No one would ask, since normally they were there to fuck me and be done with it. Roland would farm me out to his cronies when looking for favors. Some were nicer than others, but Jack seemed to care, for some reason. He talked with me at least before and after screwing me. In bed it wasn't wham-bam thank-you-ma'am. He opened up to me and tried to bring some joy to my sex life, give me some satisfaction between the sheets. I found pleasure in our daily romps. Fucking was fun again."

"You met Jack through Roland?"

"Yes. He was one of his bag men. Since he had done a bang-up job bringing in the money I was a bonus one night for him in the dungeon. He had two hours to have his way with me and I started crying after he was too rough. He felt sorry for me afterwards. We talked and seemed to find a commonality. Not sure what it was, since there was a significant age difference, but we discovered it. Maybe I was having a daddy complex and he claimed his wife wasn't wild enough. He liked doing it aggressively, but he wanted me to enjoy it, too. We found a way which worked for both of us, a little dangerous and thrilling."

"So, you two would meet up, then?"

"Yes, a day or two a week after collections. Not so much it would be noticeable. We arranged times in advance. My days were open to do with as I pleased, since Roland would be working at his office in Parker."

I tensed up some when two larger men walked in the door. They weren't the two from Eddie's, and after giving a high-five to the manager, they headed over to the bar to meet some other friends, so the tension eased.

"Where did you go for your trysts?" I knew the answer but wanted to hear it from her.

"I had a female friend's place we would use. She worked during the day and we had our fun for a few hours. I'd clean up and head back to Roland's ready for what a night with him would bring me. Weekends were the worst."

"Roland didn't suspect anything was going on?"

"Not as far as I knew, at least until today. Do you know who killed him?"

"Well, they were driving the truck in your name. They took a couple of shots at me before getting away. It was dark, so I couldn't tell for sure. They were big men and I hit one of them. They found lots of blood all over the inside of the cab."

"Do you know why they killed him? Was it because of me?"

"I'm pretty certain it was because of money he owed or stole from them. Did he ever ask you for money?"

Her eyes revealed the answer before she said it.

"Yes, but I had nothing to give him other than a few bucks here or there. Roland watched my spending closely. Anything other than clothes, toiletries and food and he'd question it. All went on my credit card for him to keep track of."

"Money was a factor in Jack's death. I can't say for certain if they knew about your rendezvous."

"If they killed him, I may be next. I heard talk Roland was looking for someone to replace me. There had been someone before me, and it was only a matter of time. He liked younger women, teens and early twenties. Now I'm twenty-five, making me over the hill in his eyes. If Jack told him about us, it will only hasten my departure and it will likely not be pretty. I was told the girl before was tortured and disposed of in a Waste Management site east of town. Like me, she probably had no one to miss her, so she was never found. I can't go back there."

She was shaking now, the realization of what would happen seeping into her veins. Feeling sorry for her wasn't high on my to-do list, though for some reason I felt obligated and couldn't walk away.

Was it the gorgeous legs? The only question was what to do? No bright ideas were jumping to mind at this moment.

"Was Roland home last night?"

"Yes. He ravaged me three times. He has a voracious sexual appetite."

"If it was his two goons last night I ran into, maybe they hadn't reported to him yet. They likely were trying to collect money from Jack. The shooting might have been an accident and they didn't want to tell Roland what happened. If he learned about the affair last night, do you think he would have handled it himself right then and there?"

"Knowing him, yes."

"He gave no indication of any problem with you last night?"

"Nothing out of the ordinary."

"Does he read the paper or watch the news on TV?"

"He only cares about sports and financial news."

"So, we aren't certain he knows. So, you can go back there and hope or you can stay somewhere else until we can figure something out."

"So, you'll help me?"

"I'll try. Not sure what I can do, but I'll make an effort."

"I have no money to pay you."

"It's OK. I have a client." I still was not revealing who it was.

"I have other ways to compensate you. You aren't bad looking and I can provide pleasure however you want it."

I smiled at the backhanded compliment.

"Thank you, no. I have a girlfriend and I don't think she'd be happy with me."

. "She doesn't have to know. I can be discreet."

She was a pretty woman. The view of her legs earlier had confirmed this. Even though she was in her mid-twenties she looked older than her age. Time had been cruel to her. She had lived a hard life I wouldn't want to dip into even if I wasn't with someone.

"Your offer is generous, but I must decline. Even if she didn't know I'd been unfaithful, I would. I couldn't betray the trust we've built."

She smiled, uncertain what to think. Not many men had turned her down in her life and most took it even if she didn't offer.

"I may be able to buy myself some time," Dona said. "I can hide at my friend's. He doesn't know about her or where she lives, as far as I know. We met where I get my hair done and work out together from time to time. I never told Roland about her. The days are mine to do as I please, so long as I'm home by seven."

"Does she know what type of person Roland is?"

"No. I only told her I was in an unhappy marriage and needed a place to go screw my boyfriend a couple of times a week. She was supportive and lived vicariously through me. She loved to hear about my hot afternoon rendezvous."

"Do you have any cash; clothes to wear?"

"I have a little and a credit card. I keep extra clothes at my friend's."

"You can't use plastic because it's traceable. Will she loan you some money?"

"Yes."

"I'd say hide out there for now until we can come up with something better. If you have a cell phone, get rid of it. You need to disappear completely."

"I have a burner phone I can call with. I always had one for Jack to text me on and we used codes in case someone got ahold of his. I'd change it out every few weeks. What should I do with my main cell?"

"Give it to me and I'll destroy it. And give me your credit cards. It's too tempting to use them. I'll pay the bill here. We'll need to do something about your car, too. Stash it somewhere for now. Does your friend have a garage to put it in?"

"I think so."

"See if you can borrow hers, otherwise we'll need to dump it."

We sat for a while longer going over what to do. I had her repeat things to me, so she'd remember. It wasn't much of a plan, but it was a start. Now it was a matter of getting back to my car in one piece. The three beers in her didn't improve her driving skills any.

Chapter 31

We picked up Dona's new burner cell phone in case they had acquired the old number. I entered the digits in my cell and gave her mine, with instructions to call if she required assistance, but to contact the police if there was immediate danger. I got her main cell phone, removing the battery and the SIM card and pocketed it for now, while shredding her credit cards. She assured me she would stay out of sight, but I knew in time she would get antsy. I had to come up with an answer soon. Driving down the road I was about to call Mallard when he called me.

"Damn, you must be psychic," I stated.

"Where are you?" he said, sounding so serious.

"Cruising down Broadway."

"Do you know where the Broken Tee golf course is?"

"Not right off. Why?"

"We have a body. Need you to come down and see if you can identify it."

He gave me the address, so I turned around and headed where the GPS led me. When I arrived, the place was closed off by cops. After showing my ID I was told to park and was taken by a police car to a point and by cart the rest of the way. Like all golf courses, it was wide open green grass, mostly hidden today by traces of the recent snow, with a few trees lining the fairway. We drove into a more wooded area near Bear Creek that divided the course. Several officers, uniform and plain clothes were mulling around along with Mallard. With little acknowledgement he walked me down to the body. I never liked looking at a corpse, but it was part of the job at times and this was the second one in a week, a new record for me. He uncovered it and it was immediately recognizable as one of Roland's two goons. Blood covered his neck, shoulder and a sizeable amount of his shirt. The ME came over to give his analysis.

"Hit in the neck, most likely by a bullet," he stated. "Severed the carotid artery and bled out quickly. Looks like they tried to put pressure on the wound, but it was too late. I imagine death happened almost instantly."

"He was dumped here?" asked Mallard.

"I would say so. If he died here, there would be more blood on the ground. I'm certain once we get some tests it will match what we found in the truck last night. I understand this may be your handiwork."

Killing was never a fun thing to admit to or to see. But in this case, it was hard to feel too sorry for the body before me.

"Though I couldn't see the faces, I do know this man. He fits the description of one of the two men leaving the salon after setting it ablaze. One of them took a shot at me and I returned fire into the back of the truck while they were driving off. So yes, it would seem this is my doing."

"Who is it?" asked Mallard.

"It's one of Roland's enforcers; either Dirk Bailey or Merrick Jones. I never learned which was which. It's definitely one or the other. Any ID?"

"Nothing. We'll get a match on fingerprints. He certainly will be in the system."

"Any idea why they dumped him here?" I asked.

"None other than the place is closed this time of year. They keep a small staff here in the winter to do maintenance. One of them saw something from a distance and got close enough to see it was a body and called it in."

"Any security cameras?"

"We're checking. If there are, they only cover a small area. Nothing this far out."

I turned around, gauging the range. It was a long ways from the entrance, with no roads other than golf paths.

"They would have had to carry him out here."

"Or they drove a cart. We are verifying if any were accessible and could have been used. Probably won't lead to anything." Mallard pulled out a stick of gum and began chewing. "Art, do you need to do anything else?"

"We are combing the area but likely we won't find much else. We'll be taking him away shortly."

Mallard and I stepped away from the scene. He offered me some gum, which I accepted. It was strawberry flavored and probably was turning my tongue red, while the sugar was boring a hole in my teeth. But the flavor was pretty good.

"I found Dona," I stated once out of earshot of anyone.

"Did you talk with her?"

"Yep."

"And?"

"She lives with Roland, something your file didn't mention. The address you gave me was his house."

"Is she his girlfriend?"

"In a manner of speaking; she is his sex slave. He owns her."

He didn't appear shocked by the news; been out on the mean streets too long to be surprised.

"You believe her?"

"Yes."

"You're certain. You also believed Emily. I recall she used her pussy to persuade you. Any chance this is the case again?"

"Wow, you sleep with one client, have to shoot her and you're branded for life. All we did was talk in Chili's, nothing else. She didn't even offer to do me, which is apparently her only talent. Her words, not mine. No, she is telling the truth."

I lied about the offer part. It seemed I always had to hold something back from Mallard. Stubbornness always won out when dealing with him.

"What else did you find out?"

I spelled out everything to him as we walked across the nearby green. He listened intently to every word I detailed, what she had said, and our plan for now to hide out. He seemed to remember all and wasn't taking notes, wanting to keep my involvement off the record. As I finished up he stopped dead in his tracks, turned and looked at me hard.

"She needs to come in and make a statement?"

"Yes, she does, but for now we need to decide what is required to assist her."

"I'm not in the business of assisting her; I'm in the business of catching a killer. You need to bring her down to headquarters."

"She doesn't know who killed Jack. She isn't going to give you anything you can use. Her statement only exposes her to Roland. I promised I'd help her."

"I don't care. Go get her, or tell me where she is and I'll bring her in."

"Not yet. I need to think through the proper course of action. He will kill her before she can testify."

"Jarvis, not this 'more time' crap again! I went through this with

148

you and the Emily slut previously. I teamed up with you because I thought you'd be helpful, and this isn't. Bring her in by tomorrow morning or I'm going to run you in for obstruction of justice."

Mallard took his finger and poked me in the chest. If he hadn't been a cop, I'd have grabbed his hand, crushed it and knocked him to the ground. My eyes met his, the hard glares on our faces matched in intensity. I hoped he'd take a swing, but he walked away in a huff back towards the dead body. I followed along a few feet behind, wondering if I'd be made to walk all the way back to my car. *Screw him. I'll sing out loud all the way back like I'm enjoying myself!*

Chapter 32

Statements were completed down at the station and I made the trek back home. Force of habit had me starting back to my actual home before remembering I couldn't stay there. I changed directions and headed to Kate's. It was dinnertime and I was tired and hungry. I stepped inside finding the three of them finishing up their meal, pizza from the looks of it. I was eating so much; my pee was beginning to smell like pepperoni.

"I ordered extra," she stated. "Wasn't sure when you'd be back or what you'd like, but plain cheese was always a good choice. Please help yourself."

I thanked her and sat down at the table. There was a pitcher of water and a couple of two-liter sodas. She brought me a glass with ice and I decided on water. The pizza was a little cold, but I didn't care. It was nourishment.

"Didn't feel like cooking," said Kate. "It has been a long hectic and stressful day, and delivery pizza is always thirty minutes away."

"I'm assuming the police contacted you?" I asked.

"Yes, they informed me it was Jack's body," she answered. "Damn him. What had he gotten himself into?"

I didn't want to reveal what I had learned from Dona. It would only add to her anxiety. I did give her a few details I did have.

"You believe he was in debt to his boss and this is what got him killed?"

"Yes, and why he was there on Saturday to get money from you. They returned thinking he could break into your safe."

"Idiot had to know I would have changed the combination. What was he thinking?"

"Probably another stall tactic to buy himself more time. I'm sure he assumed he'd figure a way out one way or another."

"Sounds like Jack," she said, looking at her kids, who nodded. "Always looking to make a bigger score. Damn fool."

"I am sorry about what happened."

"We want the killer caught," Cody said. "He may have been a butthead, but he was our dad."

"Yes, we do," added Darcy. "Can you catch them?"

I looked over at Kate; she was in agreement, sadness in her eyes.

"We are willing to hire you again," she said. "We need closure and catching them will start the healing."

"I will do what I can," I answered. "No guarantees, but I'm working on something right now with the Denver Police which may lead us somewhere."

"Thank you," said Kate and she reached out and placed her hand on mine, squeezing it. "We have confidence in you. Do what it takes."

I smiled back while finishing up the pizza. I was tired and soon excused myself, needing to take a shower. Heading for the basement, I stripped down and was about to head to the bathroom when my cell phone rang. It was Melissa.

"You must have sensed I was naked and called," I said.

"Are you okay?" she asked, with a serious tone verging on anger while ignoring my humor.

"Yes. Why do you ask?"

"Well, we're sitting here eating a late dinner at work, flipped on the TV, and lo and behold I see your name in the news. Someone was killed and the place was torched. Why didn't you contact me?"

I had no excuse. I'd been so busy it hadn't crossed my mind.

"I'm sorry," I said. "So much going on I forgot to call. It's been a hell of a last twenty-four hours."

"They didn't say your name, but they said someone was shot, too. Was it you?"

I didn't want to answer, but didn't want to lie either.

"Yes. Only a minor flesh wound."

"You didn't think I should know?"

"I knew you were busy this week with this big case and I didn't want to worry you."

"Well, it's too late; I'm worried. What the hell is going on?"

I explained some of the details of what happened, but left out a couple of others, like my discussion with Dona. I wasn't lying to her, I told myself—only omitting some key facts.

"Damn you, Jarvis," she said. "Don't do this to me. Shut me out. You did this before and nearly ruined us. I won't go through it again."

"Honestly, I would have called you. There was so much happening. The day flew by."

"So, is your place inhabitable?"

151

"No."

"So where are you sleeping?"

"At Kate's for now; she has a spare bedroom in the basement."

There was a long silence on the other end. I could hear breathing but no words.

"Did I lose you?"

"Sorry, I'm worried about you staying with another woman."

"There is nothing to be concerned about. We have been friends for a long time. Both her kids are here too. Nothing will happen."

"I hate not believing you but after what happened with Emily, I get nervous."

It was my turn to be quiet. I understood her worry since I'd screwed over her trust before. I was still gaining it back.

"What can I say other than I only want to be with *you*."

"I do want to believe, I really do. When I'm with you I feel the connection. Only now that you're staying with her, I'm afraid."

"Trust me!"

"I'm trying but it's hard."

"What do I need to do?"

"I don't know!" Melissa yelled out.

I was in a corner and had to say something.

"Dammit. Don't you know I love you?" I shouted out back to her.

The other end was quiet again. The breathing was more labored now.

"Did you hear me?"

"Yes."

"What do you have to say?"

"I don't know. I'm shocked."

"Well, I planned to tell you in a more romantic setting, but now it seems necessary."

"I'd like to answer you back. But I don't know…I wonder if you aren't saying it only to allay my fears."

"Believe me, I'm not. I've not said it enough in my lifetime to blurt it out blindly. I'm not that devious."

"I need some time to think this over. I need to get back to work."

"I understand. Let's plan to get away when all of this is over—my case, your case. Let's go away for a week or two, somewhere exotic and learn what we are to each other."

Again, there was a long silence.

"Come on, Melissa, you know I mean it. Kate is only a client and a friend."

"Yes. We can go away together. Decide where this is going."

"Thank you."

Melissa hung on the line for a few minutes.

"Jarvis?"

"Yes?"

"I do care for you. Please be careful."

The call went dead, but my heart was racing a hundred miles an hour. I couldn't believe I'd said the words. I'd certainly meant it and had no concern about her not saying it back. Now all I had to do was live up to them. This was what scared me the most.

Chapter 33

After a restless night of sleep, the next morning I called Mallard and had it out with him again about bringing Dona in for questioning. The argument went on for ten minutes. It felt like one of my endless fights with an old girlfriend, which never went anywhere, minus the makeup sex afterwards.

"Detective, she doesn't know anything," I said for the fifth time.

"It is for me to find out," he replied. "I'm the officer on this case and you are a lowly gumshoe who I asked for help. I'm still in charge. If you won't bring her in, tell me where she is and I'll send a car to get her."

"No. For now, no one else will know where she is."

"Jarvis, you are getting my blood pressure up. I'm about to come over there and toss your ass in jail for obstruction."

"I'll bring her in, but she needs representation."

"Fine; a court-appointed one can be provided."

"I want someone with a little more experience. Come on, give me a day to get my lawyer down there with her."

"You're stalling."

"No, I'm not. If he is available today, I'll come on down. I need to contact him and see what his schedule is. I doubt he is sitting around waiting for me to ring him for legal advice. Tomorrow, at the latest."

There was a pause and I could hear his chair squeaking from his agitated rocking while thinking why'd he'd ever asked for my help in the first place. I seemed to be making everyone upset on the phone these days.

"I want a call today from you if she isn't coming in by 5 p.m. tonight. If you don't, I'm putting out an arrest warrant for you."

"You are so kind, o great one."

I don't think he liked my sarcasm as he slammed the receiver down. It wouldn't have been a good day for him to get a physical because he wouldn't pass. I imagined his face red with anger and laughed out loud. Being a pain in his side was enjoyable. I got on the line with my lawyer after a ten-minute wait on hold. Apparently, I wasn't at the top of his hit parade either.

"What do you want?" said Barry Anders.

"Good to hear your voice, too," I replied.

"When you call, my day gets messed up. Let me put it more bluntly; what the fuck do you want?"

Any more venom across the circuits and my phone might burn up!

"Can't an old friend say hello?"

"No."

"So cold, Barry, but of course you are right. How is your schedule today and tomorrow?"

"For you I'm booked. Besides, didn't I already drive up to Greeley to save your ass?"

"It's not for me. It's for a lovely lady who needs someone with your skill looking out for her while Denver Detective Mallard questions her."

"What's in it for me?"

"The opportunity to sit next to her, smell her perfume, look at her pretty legs. She likes the short skirts and has outstanding thighs."

"This won't put food on my table."

"Come on—a little pro bono work for your old friend. She's broke right now and I don't want her to have a green Public Defender in there with her."

"How come everyone you want me to help out is pro bono? I can't remember the last time I got paid by one of your referrals."

"Deductions are good for a man in your tax bracket," I replied. "Besides, you have a good heart and a lecherous one. Who knows, she may be forever in your debt."

"In debt is where I'll end up working for you," Barry said. "Let me check my schedule."

As I sat listening to rotten hold music, I wondered when people said they were checking their schedule if they really did. Or was it more of a ploy to give the impression of being busy.

"I have some time tomorrow after one. How long will you need?"

"Well, you know Mallard, he is pretty thorough. I'd say at least two hours."

"So, the Evans precinct?"

"Yes. I'll tell Mallard sometime between one and two."

"Call me before one so you can let me know what I'm saving her from."

"Deal. Thanks, Barry. You are a swell guy. I owe you an

expensive steak dinner and some beer."

"Yeah, yeah. You always say it and I'm still waiting for you to come through. I have a better chance of your client sucking my pecker!"

After I was done with Barry, I called Mallard and let him know. He wasn't completely happy but at least he had a time when we'd be there. If we didn't show, it was my ass! For now, I'd wait to call Dona. I didn't want her to get spooked.

The rest of the day was open, so I planned on taking advantage of it. A good vigorous workout, maybe sit in the gym hot tub for a while and a nice lunch out. While gathering my duffle bag, the chime on my phone pronouncing I had a text went off. This one was from Raven saying she needed to talk. I texted her back, asking where she was and when she wanted to meet. It always felt strange texting back and forth when a simple call could more quickly provide answers. It was how their generation communicated, so I played along. She was in Denver staying at her parents, so I suggested Boone's. She was anxious and said at 10 a.m., so my workout would have to wait until after.

We arrived at the same time, and my smile cracked her tough exterior. She was dressed all in black: jeans, a T-shirt with the logo of some band I'd never heard of, and a long, smooth leather coat I'd seen her in before. We walked in together and found a booth in a quiet spot, away from any TVs, which wasn't easy, as they hung from the ceiling nearly everywhere. The waitress stopped by and asked us for our orders. Raven only wanted ice water with lemon, while I decided on soda. They didn't have a breakfast menu, so lunch would have to suffice. Seemed like all I did was meet people and eat. Getting on the scale probably would be revealing.

"How are you doing?" I asked.

"I'm good."

"How are things with you and Ray?"

"Better. He knows how I feel, and I believe he is discovering his feelings too. For now, he is trying to get through each day."

"Still feeling the effects of the concussion?"

"Yes. It will take time. Doctor says six months, possibly longer. He may need to sit out another year of football. I will stand by and help, no matter how long."

"Well, I'm glad for you too. You make a good couple."

She may have blushed, though with her makeup one couldn't say for certain. Her eyes looked down as if she was embarrassed.

"Why aren't you in school? It's not Christmas break yet, is it?"

"No. I wanted to be around to help him. I'm an A-plus student so I can afford to miss some time. I'll be back for finals and won't miss a beat. I can read through a text book in a few hours and can almost tell you word for word what was in it."

I wasn't surprised, as she seemed extremely smart. Maybe some of it would rub off on me. I could use some of it these days. *Would she consult on my caseload?*

"Ray may get upset at me for telling you this, but he has been getting some texts from a woman of questionable nature."

"Who would this be?"

"She calls herself Leather."

"How do you know this?"

"This is why he'll be mad, as I was worried. I know his passcode on his phone. I've been snooping and saw them. She's been sending them for several days now, once or twice each day. She includes pictures of her in her leather outfit, which doesn't leave much to the imagination; her face though, is hidden. Occasionally, there is another woman in the same picture barely clothed, both touching each other. Other times it was another woman doing things I'd rather not describe. It was unpleasant seeing them and made me angry."

There seemed a tinge of jealousy in her tone.

"I'm aware of Leather's outfit."

"You know her?"

"Yes, intimately. Well, as intimately as one can be without having physical relations. She is one of the ladies in his sex video. Has he been answering her back?"

"I don't think so. I'm worried because she says some suggestive things, a few of which are threatening."

"Like what?"

"Well, she uses lots of dirty talk. The F-word, P-word, C-word; slang I don't care for. Then she says something like 'if you don't come see me soon, we may have to pay you a visit again.' She also says some nasty things she would do to his mother and sister I can't repeat."

"Do you have the number she is using?"

"Yes, I wrote it down. Here it is."

"Damn, they were supposed to leave him alone. I thought my threat of turning over the videos would have kept them at bay."

"What can we do?"

"Well, for now we can eat some food. Order something—it's my treat."

I waved for Julie to come over.

"After lunch, what will you do?"

"I have no idea," I replied.

Pretty much a normal day for me."

Chapter 34

Lunch was good but didn't reveal any "a-ha" moments after sitting and chatting for ninety minutes. Raven was a sharp girl, but none of her brainpower combined with mine provided any type of breakthrough. We parted and I assured her I'd come up with something. I'm not sure she believed me, but she was pretty good at hiding her emotions. She thanked me for lunch, giving me a hug, and was off doing her thing. I decided to forgo the workout. I needed to see an old friend—or best-described as a reluctant acquaintance. I called and he was available to talk. To the west side of town, I traveled after leaving Boone's.

December had finally started to turn colder, after a warmer than normal November. The trees were bare and the grass dormant. There was a damp chill in the air, and dark clouds were building over the foothills. I turned up the heat in the Mustang as the wind was adding to the cold. I like the feel of winter, as I do the other seasons. Adjusting to the change was challenging, but once it happened, I enjoyed everything about it.

The Sparks Builders primary office stood out on the corner of Union Street, a bastion of modern dull architecture. Brandon Sparks had been an ally from a previous case. He was tough, resourceful, a powerful construction CEO, owner and likely a crime boss. But he had owed me for the work I did to save his stepdaughter from herself. We had forged an uneasy alliance; well, uneasy for me, as I doubted with his strength and confidence anything made him uneasy. His experience and connections in both cases would be useful.

Per usual, I had to go through Brandon's personal assistant, Sue. She was slender and tall in her half-inch heels, with a trim body clothed in a knee-length black skirt and red blouse with enough buttons open to show some cleavage in her average-sized chest. Her hair was in a bun, which was how I'd always seen her. With her hair down, she was probably spectacular. I smiled at her to convey this, but she was all business. She led me to Brandon's office with a happy wiggle in her step that I admired all the way down the hall; a quick over–the-shoulder glance catching my glare caused a stone-cold stare to follow. Once inside, I was alone in the huge corner space looking the same as it always had, spacious and stylish enough for a king. I resisted bowing when he arrived.

"Jarvis, to what do I owe the pleasure?" came his booming voice as he walked in from a side door.

He reached towards me with a viselike grip, a shake which had probably crushed many a palm throughout the years. I matched it, knowing his will was stronger than mine, fingers beginning to numb.

"Well, other than saying hi to sweet and sour Sue," I said, "I needed to get some information about a couple of men you are possibly familiar with."

"Sue is the glue that holds Sparks Builders together. I couldn't run this business without her."

"She appears quite controlled under her sexy business attire. Ever been tempted to make it more than business?"

"She is quite fetching. But no, it's strictly professional between us."

"Already spoken for?"

"Possibly, although this has never stopped me before. She would have no interest in me as she plays for the other side, if I may be clichéd."

"Really."

"Yes, she likes the company of the same sex. I don't pry into my employees' personal lives. I could care less so long as they do their job. It's something I've noticed, part of my observation skills of being able to read people. Being a detective, I'm surprised you didn't deduce this."

"I have a blind spot for women, as you're probably aware in my dealings with your step-daughter." I took a seat in front of his desk. "You should have been a PI with your skill set. Are you reading me now?"

"Sure. I'm reading you need a drink. I know you aren't much of a JD fan from the way you nursed them in the past in this room. The bar is stocked with whatever you desire."

"Well, I already ate lunch so bottled water is good enough."

If he was disappointed in my selection, he didn't show it. He pulled out a plastic container handing it to me, while he made himself his Jack Daniels with some ice. He stood tall and rugged, dressed in a gray tank top and white spandex pants, white brand-new looking Nike Air's, a sweatband covering his forehead. He'd either come from a workout or was headed to one. He swallowed down the shot of whiskey, placing the empty glass on the wet bar.

"Care to join me while I get the heart rate up?" he stated, answering my thoughts.

"Where do you exercise?" I asked.

"The room next door," he answered with a sense of pride. "I have my own gym; one of the perks of being a CEO and owner."

"You are in luck. I have my workout clothes out in the car," I said.

He picked up the phone to summon Sue. She was there in an instant. The wiggle was missing when walking quickly.

"Sue, can you have someone get Jarvis's workout clothes from his yellow and black Mustang. And show him to my private room where he can change."

Sue stepped over and I handed her the keys and summoned me to follow. Down a hall or two she led me to what appeared to be a bedroom. There were dressers, closets and a king-sized bed neatly made in crimson sheets and more pillows than I could count. Above it was a mirror for voyeuristic fun. I was going to comment on it but before speaking she told me to stay put, leaving and then returning shortly with my duffle bag. I smelled her perfume, seeing for the first time up close how pretty she was. I beamed my best sexy smile in her direction.

"Are you going to dress me?" I asked.

She grinned for a split second, pulling it back in again, the cold glare returning.

"Hardly," she answered. "I'm sure a tough man like you can handle dressing himself."

"Actually, it was only the undressing I needed help with," I said with a suggestive smirk.

She spun and walked out of the room as I'd ruffled her feathers once again.

Once dressed, Brandon led me to his workout room. It wasn't quite as large as his office, but was a close second. He had all the best equipment; several Nautilus machines, free weights and benches, Elliptical, exercise bikes and treadmills; even a speed and heavy bag to punch the daylights out of. There were mirrors on the walls and ceiling to watch your muscles ripple and sweat. For a personal gym it was spectacular; another perk of being a CEO and owner.

"We'll start here," he said.

He positioned the weight on the Nautilus at 200 pounds. Lying down, he slowly and evenly did presses, three sets of ten, resting a minute in between. He stood and motioned me to go next. I did the same thing, though I struggled a little bit with the last set, but I wasn't going to let the older man best me. Everything he did, I followed up and did the same. When it came time to jog on the treadmill, I was gasping for air, while he was only lightly sweating—his breathing steady. Not only did he drink me under the table, he could exercise me under as well. *Too much pizza.* If I hadn't been so tired, I'd have been impressed. I took a long swig of water and set the treadmill for walking speed.

"Not too bad," Brandon said. "Most can't keep up and collapse before reaching the running part of my workout. You, at least, are still standing."

"Barely," I said, still getting my breathing under control. "For a man who sits behind a desk a lot, you are in excellent shape."

"I may live behind my desk," he replied. "But I've worked hard all my life. Nothing was given to me; I've had to earn it. No one will out hustle me for anything. I must stay virile to keep up with the young ladies who escort me from time to time. No one is going to best me in bed, either."

Brandon was running in a slow, but steady jog. I increased my pace some, but only to a faster walk. There was no way to keep up with him. To get my mind off my exhaustion I started quizzing him for data.

"What do you know about a Marquis Melott?"

"Are you asking for a favor?" Brandon asked.

"Mostly looking for information, if you know him. He is in your line of work."

"You mean construction?" he said with a smile.

As usual, he was coy with his answers in case someone was listening or recording.

"Yes. Well, at least your kind of construction."

"I do not know a Marquis Melott. Where does he work?"

"He is in Greeley. Runs a club called The Hustle."

"My business interests cover all of Denver and south along the Front Range. I do not have any construction projects in Greeley."

"Any chance of asking around?" I was holding onto the rails of

162

the treadmill to keep myself upright.

"I may be able to see what I can find. What is in it for me?"

"You get the pleasure of my company while you work me to the bone, while keeping me on your Christmas list and not have to send condolences to my friends."

"Sounds bad."

"It is."

"I'll see what I can find. Anything else?"

"What about Roland Langer? He runs in your construction territory. Are you two connected?"

Brandon turned off the treadmill, stopping dead in his tracks. He obviously knew the name, but not favorably. I was relieved he'd finally stopped, as I was about to drop to the floor in a heap. *I should have led with Roland's name!*

"I see by your reaction he may be a competitor," I said, stepping off on wobbly legs and finding a towel to dry the sweat from my face.

"Not a rival but more like a pain in the ass," Brandon said. "What are you mixed up with him about?"

I explained the situation, giving details without naming any names, including my client and Dona.

"Quite a pickle; what are your intentions?"

"I'm not completely sure. I was hoping you would shed some light on him. I have some of the basics about Roland, what the police have gathered. A sterile file they have on him pales in what you may know, being the construction kingpin and all."

Brandon took his own towel, drying off, wrapping it around his neck, taking a drink from his bottle of water. You sensed the gears turning on what all he should bring to light.

"A couple things I can tell you. He kills for the pure joy of it. He has a torture chamber in the basement of his house. Likes to inflict the pain or to watch someone else impose it. He would peel the skin off someone a layer at a time, getting a hard-on from it."

"Wonderful."

"It gets worse. In the process of torturing he uses his hard-on to inflict sexual agony. The more distressed they are, the more pleasure he derives from it. He is a violent sex addict who can never get enough. I've heard stories of weekend-long orgies at his place. He'll bring in young women off the street and screw them any way he can.

If they object, they will be tortured and killed. He has a woman who is his sex slave, to quench his every desire when the mood strikes him. She has been with him for years now, but before her, there was another who didn't last much more than a year, and one before her, and on and on. Don't do as he pleases or get too old, he will have one last glorious show with them and they are never seen again."

"Sounds as if you don't like him?" I stated.

"No, he is a deviant pig."

"You have an alliance?"

He stretched his arms, his muscles rippling with bulging veins.

"Occasionally you dance with the devil even when you prefer to strangle him."

"So why haven't you done anything about it?"

"Because in this line of work you let someone else do the dirty deed whenever possible. Doing it yourself has consequences, a domino-effect screwing up your business model. Make others leery of what you might do to them and soon they come after you. Believe it or not, in the construction profession there are some gentlemanly rules we follow."

"So, no one has wanted to do the dirty work in his case?"

"No one has been brave enough or stupid enough. Could you be?"

I had to think about it. Right now, the mess I was in might push me to be brave and stupid enough. But I was going to need help.

Brandon went over to a phone on the wall and made a call. Within minutes, two young women strolled in carrying folding massage tables. They each set up, unpacked assorted items from their bags and removed their robes to reveal neither had any clothes on underneath. One walked over to Brandon and started undressing him, while the other came to me and did the same.

"Ordered an extra pair of hands for me?" I asked.

"No, both are normally for me. I'm in a sharing mood."

It felt odd being undressed with others around, blushing while the woman peeled off my pants. At least she didn't giggle when seeing my body, paling in comparison to Brandon's.

"Time to work out the sore muscles," stated Brandon, who now stood stark naked, the woman rubbing oil on his body.

"This is marvelous, but I'm seeing someone," I said while getting an intimate rubdown.

"Yes, Melissa," replied Brandon, now lying on the table on his stomach, his masseuse working his legs. "You don't have to do anything you don't want done. At least let her rub you down to relieve the stiffness. Give us a chance to discuss what we are going to do about all of this."

I had little strength to deny the woman's touch and was soon laying down, enjoying the sensation while Brandon chatted about the real-life dangers of the construction business. *I certainly could get used to the CEO life!*

Chapter 35

A workout I'd never forget and would feel in my muscles for days. I was able to leave with my virtue intact, even though I was getting massaged in some intimate places. I left relaxed and flushed with desire to see Melissa. Though I called and texted her, I did not hear back until later in the evening. She was still buried in her current case and couldn't talk right now. I hoped she wasn't avoiding me, but I tried not to fixate on the issue. A long cold shower eased my excitement, with minimal results. Thankfully, exhaustion won out over arousal and I fell asleep, the stiffness in my body receding.

Once I awoke mid-morning I sensed the hard workout and required three Advil to thin the blood and loosen up. Between the exercise and the beatings, my body felt older than its age. I stretched to limber up and pieced together breakfast from the nearly empty fridge and cabinets. I called Dona up first to give her the news of what we had to do today. She was hesitant, but I was able to talk her into it.

"Any question they ask, clear it with Barry before answering," I said to her.

"So, say nothing unless he gives me the OK?" she asked.

"Yes. Also wear a short skirt and revealing top, the sexier the better."

"Will this help?" she asked.

"It won't hurt," I replied, before telling her when I'd be by to pick her up.

Calling Barry, I gave him the scoop of what I was steering him into, with every detail I could recall. He didn't sound pleased, but didn't back out on me either. I pissed away the rest of the morning relaxing my physical ache with an easy stride around the neighborhood before going to get Dona and taking her down to the station. We walked in and I knew my advice on her clothing choices had worked; everyone in the precinct watched her. Her short blue tight skirt covered her shapely rear end, her plunging sheer white blouse revealed her black bra, barely containing her chest. We were escorted back to interview room three, the politically correct name for the interrogation room, and sat on the plastic and metal-framed uncomfortable seats. The room was a deep dirty green in color, with a small table and six chairs and a large one-way mirror on the wall. There was a boom microphone hanging from the ceiling, with a recording management device on the table to stop and start the digital evidence equipment. Barry walked in about three minutes after we did, with Mallard and Detective Cummings showing up behind him, a thick folder in Mallard's hands.

"Before we begin, can I get anyone anything to drink?" asked Mallard.

Dona wanted water, as did I. Cummings went to the door asking an officer standing outside to get five bottles of water. Once we all were equipped with our refreshments Mallard hit the record button.

"Miss Wiggins," began Mallard. "We appreciate you coming down today. We want to make it clear you are not being charged with anything. We need to ask you some questions about the use of your vehicle in the death of Jack Tanner. Do you understand?"

Dona glanced at Barry and he nodded. She shook her head, understanding what he had told her.

"Do you own a dark blue 2008 Dodge Ram pickup?" he asked. He rattled off the plate number.

"No," answered Dona.

"You are saying it isn't your truck?" he asked. "It's registered in your name."

"You asked if I owned it," Dona replied. "I don't own it because I didn't pay for it. It's only in my name. Rarely do I ever drive it."

Mallard and Cummings looked at each other.

"Why is it in your name if you didn't buy it?"

"I don't know. You'll have to ask him. Something to do with taxes or something similar I don't understand."

"Who bought it?"

Grabbing her bottle of water, Dona broke the seal and slowly sipped it. She checked again with Barry as he nodded.

"Roland."

"Can you state his full name please for the record?"

"I don't know his middle name, only his first and last."

Mallard's face was starting to change colors, the responses getting to him.

"Fine."

"Roland Langer."

"What is your connection to Roland Langer?"

"Employer. I also live at his house, though I'm not living there right now."

"What type of work do you do for Roland?"

"Personal. I provide whatever services he needs, no matter how trivial."

"Are you his servant?"

"In a manner of speaking."

Mallard was getting madder. "In what manner?"

She looked again at Barry. This time he spoke for her. He had no notes, but his memory was incredible. I knew he remembered everything I told him about the case-names, places and situations. He was a talented lawyer.

"She is indentured to provide sexual favors for her boss in exchange for room and board."

"She is his whore. His sex slave, so to speak?"

"Crudely put, but basically correct," answered Barry.

"How long have you been associated with Roland?"

"Around seven years," she said.

"How did you come to be in his employ?"

Once she got the green light from Barry, she gave the details as she had given them to me. Neither of the detectives appeared shocked or surprised on hearing her explanation.

"Do you know what Roland does for a living?"

"She does," replied Barry. "But we are uncertain how this pertains to why we are here."

Mallard got up from the table taking his water. He stepped over next the glass frame and drank. It was now Cummings's turn to talk, pulling out three of photos from the folder before him and placed them side by side for Dona to see.

"Please look at these," he said.

Dona gasped at the pictures. One was of the truck, its back window shot out. The second was of the front seat with all the blood on it. The third a picture of the deceased body found at the golf course.

"Do you know the dead man?" asked Cummings

"Yes."

"Name, please."

"Merrick. I think his last name was Smith or Jones, something common."

"Yes, it's Merrick Jones," stated Cummings. "He works for Roland?"

"Yes."

"What does he do for Roland?"

Over she glanced again at Barry for confirmation, which he provided.

"Protection. He was a bodyguard, a security person."

"He was shot by Jarvis here escaping the scene where a pair of felonies had been committed. Do you know anything about these crimes? Are you involved in anyway?"

After another drink of water, she shook her head no. Turning sideways she crossed her legs, switching sides, revealing copious amounts of tanned thigh. Not sure she understood the effect it had on men, but I certainly enjoyed it.

"What about these photos," Cummings said.

After putting away the first three, he pulled out two more.

"Oh my," yelled Dona at the first photo.

It was of the burned body of Jack. Even though I'd seen pictures like this before, it still put a knot in my stomach.

"Is this necessary, Detective?" stated Barry. "Do we need to see all these crime scene photos? They are extremely graphic and are upsetting my client."

"Honestly, Counselor, yes," he replied. "Your client may not have anything to do with this felony, but she is connected to the people who committed it, and this dead body. Dona, tell me who is the person in the second picture?"

"It's hard to tell from the photo. It's so yucky."

"Come now. Something should seem familiar."

"I can guess because of what Jarvis told me."

Cummings waited for an answer, drumming his fingers on the table.

"It might be Jack."

"Full name again please."

"Jack Tanner."

"And you know Jack?"

Looking at Barry she nodded yes.

"Knew him intimately?"

She checked and again nodded. Almost like a puppet on a string.

"You were involved with Jack and asked Roland to kill him."

"No!" she yelled.

"Detective, you are barking up the wrong tree. If anything, my client cared for Jack. She was shocked when hearing of his death."

"So why was he killed?"

"She doesn't know," replied Barry.

"Miss Wiggins?" asked Cummings.

"Honestly, I don't know."

"Did Roland find out about your relationship with Jack and murder him?"

"I don't know. Maybe, but…"

"He was mad you were fucking Jack, had him shot and then torched his body to a crisp!"

"It's all speculation on your part and ours," stated Barry. "My client doesn't know and wasn't involved in the crime. If you have no plan to charge her, we are leaving. We've had enough of your badgering."

Barry stood up, gently pulling Dona to her feet. Cummings rose up, knocking the chair over. He walked around the table, looking like he was coming at Barry. I made a beeline in front to block him. He was bigger than I was, but I wouldn't flinch.

"What are you going to do, hit me?" I asked. "I'd say her lawyer made it clear she is here cooperating, but the cooperation has ended. Charge her or let us walk."

Cummings face was red, and I hoped he'd take a swing at me. I'd seen him press the stop button on the recording when getting up, but it didn't matter; there were enough witnesses. Mallard stepped over and pulled Cummings back away. Neither said anything else, so Barry led Dona out by the arm, while I followed.

"Well, this was fun," said Barry once we were outside. "I may not get paid, but it's never boring when you're involved."

"I do my best to make it interesting."

Barry handed Dona his card and told her to call if she needed anything. She gave him a long embrace before I helped her into the car and drove her back to her friend's place. Being cautious, I had one eye on the road and the other in the mirror. There were no tails from what I saw, either from the bad guys or the police. When we arrived, I escorted her up to the condo, following her in to make sure she was safe. Once inside, I saw she was shaking. I came over and put my arm around her, wondering if she was having a breakdown.

She turned herself into my body and started crying. I let it play out, though I hated tears from a woman. But I couldn't leave her alone in this condition. It was several minutes before she stopped, my coat stained with her sobs.

"I'm sorry. They were so mean," she said sniffling.

"First time you've been interrogated by the police?" I asked.

"Yes. I can't say I enjoyed it."

"It's why I wanted Barry there to protect you."

"It was nice of him. There is no way I can pay him."

"Come visit him at his office wearing this outfit should be payment enough."

She gave me a big smile, her body still pressed up against mine. I was trying to remain calm. Coolness was never one of my strong suits in these situations. Staring out the window I saw the chill in the air and wished I could open it to cool the torridness I was experiencing.

"What would you have done to the officer if he'd pressed anymore?"

"Well, another step and I might have shoved him back. He and I have a little bit of history. He doesn't care for me much, and the feeling is mutual. But I wasn't going to let him push Barry or you around. Intimidation is part of the questioning process for the police."

"Normally a cop pulls me over in my car, I bat my eyes at him, flirt some, show a little cleavage and they let me off with a warning."

"No surprise that works." I said with a lump in my throat.

She placed her hand on my chest, my heart pounding against her palm.

"You weren't intimidated?"

I swallowed first before answering, sensing my voice cracking.

"No, I wasn't."

She looked up at me. I sensed she wanted to kiss me, but I resisted the urge to lock lips. All my manly hormones were fighting me, though.

"Excuse me," she said. "I need to go clean up my makeup."

She walked out of the room and I did my best not to leer at her rear end in her short, skin-tight skirt. I continued to stand there, not sure what to do. I should hightail it out of there while possible. I wasn't certain I could trust myself. But I didn't want to be rude, or that was my excuse to stay.

A few minutes passed and I heard her coming. I looked up and she walked in stark naked, except for the high heels she was wearing. I think I gasped when I saw her. For all she had been through, the life she had led being a sex toy to who knows how many men, her body still was in marvelous shape. Her breasts were D-cup firm, her legs shapely like a man would want wrapped around him, and there wasn't a hair on her body anywhere except for the red hair on her head. She came over and moved back into the same spot she had earlier, both hands on my chest, her solidly against me. I swallowed hard again to clear my throat.

"Do you like what you see?" she said in a deep, sexy tone.

I wanted to scream out *hell, yeah*, but resisted.

"Beautiful."

"Do you want me?"

"I do."

"I'm yours. Take me however you want me."

"I can't."

"Why not? I can tell you're excited," she said while running her hand over the front of my pants.

"I am. It's difficult not to be, seeing all your naked beauty. But it wouldn't be right."

"Is it because of my past, all the men I've been with?"

"No. It's because I'm with someone else right now and I want to be faithful to her."

"She wouldn't have to know. I won't tell."

There was a sense of déjà vu, as it was the same conversation we had at the restaurant.

"I know you won't. But I'll know. I cheated on her once before and nearly lost her. I don't want to take a chance again only to get my rocks off, no matter how much I want to."

"Come now, I can be supremely persuasive."

She rose up on her heels and kissed me. It was an A-rated kiss, with all the saliva and tongue a man would want. I obliged by lightly kissing back, but quickly pulled my lips away. I put my arms around her and hugged her. It was all I would do.

"You don't need to fuck me for me to help you," I said in her ear. "I know it is how your life has been. Sex was how you got what you

172

wanted, how men with you got what they wanted. I don't want to use you. I will assist you and expect nothing in return, no matter how much I want to."

As I held onto her I felt her crying again. Hopefully, it was a good cry this time. My suede leather jacket wouldn't be able to handle much more of this. Staring down at her naked backside I saw marks and bruises which were healing; evidence of the hard life she led. It was hard to imagine the pain she had endured all these years.

"I'm sorry," she said. "Might be the nicest thing any man has ever said to me."

"You need to know there is more to life than sex," I said. "Well, not much more, but at least sex with someone you care about for the right reasons."

I think I made her laugh this time, the shaking not sounding like tears.

"Yes, fucking has been all I've ever had or done. It's all I've ever been good at. The question is, what do I do instead?"

"Everyone has a talent or a skill they can fall back on. Something you want to do and enjoy. You must discover what it is. It's a passion in your heart you seek, where you don't need to open your legs and submit to anyone you don't want to submit to. Spend some time thinking about it. I'll help however I can."

Dona pulled away from me and kissed me on the cheek.

"Thank you, Jarvis. I will think it over and search, like you said."

"I'd better be going before I change my mind. Stay put and I'll call you when I know what our next move will be."

She walked me to the door, and, once outside, I took in a deep breath of the cold, damp December air, hoping it would reach all the way down and ease the pressure on my kindled loins. Much more of this and I'd need zipper repair work done!

Chapter 36

I made it through another night, but barely. I needed to stay away from sexy women wanting me, unless it was Melissa, or I might have to take it upon myself to bring relief. After my hard workout with Brandon, today I was going to go jogging with Ray. Raven told me he jogged most every morning at around seven if it wasn't snowing. It was a frigid but snow-free day, so I stopped by his house and waited for him to come out, joining him in a slow jog down the sidewalk. He turned and saw me, nervous at first until he recognized me.

"Jarvis, what are you doing here?" he asked.

"I wanted to see how you were, so I thought I'd join you."

We kept an easy pace.

"How did you know I'd be running?"

"A little birdie told me."

He smiled at my pun.

"How are you two doing?" I asked.

"Good. We have gotten very close. She has helped me immensely."

"She is quite a lady. I like her a lot. You make a wonderful couple."

"Not sure Dad sees it."

"It's not his life or his choice. I know he'll come around. I bet his parents didn't like your mom at first either."

We took a right turn and found a bike path to continue on. There weren't many people out today as the air was cold, the temps in the teens. I could see my breath as we continued the easy pace. The older guy Brandon had worked me into the ground, so I wasn't going to let the young athlete leave me in his dust. He ran easily, his muscles straining against his tight sweatshirt, his honed football body gracefully moving forward.

"Keeping in shape, I can see." I asked.

"I'm in OK shape but not football shape," he answered. "That only happens when practicing, hitting someone and getting hit. I have a way to go before I'm ready for contact."

"It will come. It takes time and patience. Rushing back too fast will set you back longer, possibly permanently."

A couple of young ladies jogging the other way passed us. Both smiled at us as I gave them a nod. Each was attractive in their spandex pants and tops. Not sure how they were staying warm on this frigid day with so little on, but was grateful for the eyeful. So long as the view was at a distance, I was safe. Ray picked up the pace slightly. I continued to hold my own.

"What have you been doing to pass the time?" I asked.

"Medical appointments and some school work. They are allowing me to take some classes from home, so I don't get too far behind. Constance is assisting me. Of course, I'm working out per the doctor's orders; not too much but enough keep the heart pumping."

"How about your family?" I said, now finding I was becoming a bit winded.

"Everyone is doing well. All are supportive and assisting the best they can. Mom has been driving me everywhere I need to go. She's been babying me more than I like, but I understand. Sometimes I don't mind it."

"She is being a mother," I said. "And your dad?"

"What can I say, he is Dad. He is checking up, seeing how I'm doing, talking to me about sports or politics and even his work. Hell, he even asked me about Constance a couple of times. He is there for me."

"He always will be," I added. "He is a hard man, but he cares about you, wants the best for you. Whatever you decide on any matter, he'll be there. He may not always agree or like it, but he'll fight for you. I know and I've seen it."

It was getting a little harder for me to talk. I hadn't run much the last couple of months, other than on a treadmill, so I was not in prime running shape. I was holding my own, but would have to back off some soon. We went another five minutes without talking and I had to slow down.

"Can we walk for a while?" I asked, coming to a halt. "I don't want to push you too hard."

Ray had pulled ahead, stopped and came back to me. I was bent over trying to pull in oxygen. Stretching out helped some but I was no match for him running. His breathing was labored some, but controlled.

"Time to turn around and walk back," he said, making it sound like his plan all along.

"Thanks for being easy on me," I stated. "It will be easier to talk this way."

"Sure. It's cool you coming over to check on me and all. I'm guessing there is a point to all this chit-chat."

I straightened up and was walking better now. I had to stay loose in the frigid air. I pulled out a water bottle I had buckled to me and took a long drink.

"Have you heard from anyone at The Hustle since we made the deal?"

Ray stared off into the distance and didn't seem to want to answer.

"If you have, we need to know," I added. "Our leverage needs to be exerted against them. If they reneged, we need to act. It could put you, your family and even Raven in danger."

Ray remained silent, his hands on his hips.

"I'm here to help. Don't shut me out. It didn't work for you in the past."

"I know, Jarvis. I was hoping it would go away if I ignored it. They keep coming at me more and more, putting the pressure on. I don't know what to do."

"How are they communicating?" I asked, even though I knew the answer.

"Text messages. She sends pictures of herself and other girls."

"Who is it?"

"A girl named Leather."

"How long?"

"About a week now. Yesterday they sent me four."

"Can I see them?"

He pulled out his phone, unlocked and handed it to me. I found all of them under the number Raven had given me. Pictures ranged from single shots of Leather in her bondage outfit, to varying degrees of undress of her and two other girls, to complete nudity of them performing various acts on each other. Every picture had a graphic description of what they were doing or what they were going to do. Like Raven said, there was mention of Ray's mother and sister, which got me angry.

"We have to do something, Ray," I said. "We need to let your father and mother know. All of you are in danger again. We must hash it out and come at them directly. Do you understand?"

He nodded his head.

"I feel so stupid I got myself into this," Ray said. "Now everyone I love is involved. I wish it would all go away."

"It will be alright," I answered. "Youthful indiscretions will come back to haunt you. We all make them and live with them. We still can fix this. We have weapons we can use."

I patted him on the shoulder, trying to reassure him. I don't know why I thought it would help, but it's what my father used to do when I was in trouble and he was cleaning up my youthful indiscretions.

"I thought we had them, but still they keep coming back at you," I stated. "I wish I knew why they won't leave you alone. There is something we are missing."

Ray looked up to the sky and let out a deep breath.

"What is it, Ray?"

"I'm so sorry," Ray said. "I left something out I should have told you. When they first took me there, they spotted me the fee for the club. There was a condition, though, which foolishly I agreed to."

"Go on."

"I would bring in a few fellow male athletes and friends to The Hustle. They would get a free week's trial to see all it had to offer. I brought a couple of wide receivers with me and one got lured into one of the den rooms by one of the ladies after a little too much to drink. He was religious and a virgin. I felt guilty about bringing him, and pulled him out of there forcefully before he went too far. Mack and Grady were mad at me, but I promised to bring other players in."

"Did you?"

"No, I never did, finally coming to my senses and knowing what I was doing was wrong. I wasn't thinking straight, my mind all a jumble. I wanted to be important again. I came to understand I was only a means to an end for them to recruit others and ruin their lives."

It became clear even with the videos we had, they weren't going to let him go. More drastic measures would be needed.

"Let's do a slow jog back and see what we can come up with," I said. "Get Mom and Dad to pay for lunch."

With an easy pace we headed back to his house, my thought process struggling to figure out what the hell to do. Nearing the house, I saw a car idling; I'd seen it when I parked, and it was still there, down the street from his house. An expensive black Cadillac with dark, tinted windows, preventing me from seeing who was inside. I could see the license plate and made a mental note. Still jogging, the car pulled away and came towards us. I wasn't armed, but I moved myself between it and Ray instinctively. The window went down and I could see Grady's face and a gun in his hand. I pushed Ray to the ground, with me on top, but heard no gunfire only the laughter coming from the car, driving away slowly. It was meant to scare, not to shoot or kill.

"What the hell, Jarvis!" shouted Ray.

I got off him and grabbed his hand to help him up. We were both covered in day-old snow and mud.

"Sorry, it was Mack and Grady," I said. "Grady was aiming a gun at us as they drove by."

"Shit!" said Ray. "Were they trying to kill me? Did they miss?"

"No, they didn't fire. They were attempting to scare you—a warning."

I was looking over in all directions to make sure they weren't coming back. I didn't expect they were, but I didn't want to chance it.

"Well, it worked. What are we going to do?"

"I have no idea," I replied.

Maybe this should be the new slogan on my business card.

Chapter 37

Bill and I were sitting in his black Malibu in Greeley waiting, a box of donuts and several bottles of juice sitting between us to help pass the time. He seemed a little nervous, but it was to be expected. I was, too.

"Do you think this will work?" he asked.

"Don't know but it's the best we came up with," I answered. "All I know for sure is the problem is not going away."

"You can trust this Sparks person?"

"I don't know if trust is the right word, but his intel should be good. He came up with a few tidbits about Melott I didn't know."

Bill nodded, his eyes alert to the street in front of us, while holding his half-devoured donut.

"The biggest thing is the silent partner. Apparently Melott is not the main chief like we thought. There is an unknown person running the business, well, at least co-running. It seems to be a closely guarded secret. Something we need to keep in mind when dealing with any of them."

I had mowed through two donuts myself and was on a third. *The perfect crime-fighting food.* I had been lucky they hadn't connected to my midsection through the years. *The right metabolism for donut eating.*

"We know they are greedy, attempting to build more revenue," I continued. "We need to find a bigger fish, a wealthier client for them to replace Ray. It is where our plan begins, the fear of the sex tapes being leaked apparently wasn't threat enough to keep them at bay."

"Seems risky," said Bill.

"It is. There are a lot of parts needing to go right for it to work. Step one will tell us if the next step has a shot. If not, we'll need a new remedy."

"Go up and shoot them all?" stated Bill.

"Let's leave the OK Corral scenario for when we have no other choice."

We were on the lookout for Mack and Grady. We had Ray send a text to Leather saying he was willing to meet her to discuss her offers. With an address in hand we were there two hours ahead of schedule and waiting, giving us time to converse. Well, at least I would do most of the conversing.

"Ray appears to be doing much better," I asked.

"Yes, he is."

"Getting all the care he needs. He looks good and seems to be making substantial progress."

Bill nodded.

"How is Rachael handling all of this?"

"Fine."

"Is she healing OK from the attack?"

"Yes."

"Not traumatized from it?"

"A little trouble sleeping at first, but pills help."

"Keep talking with her. Don't let her hold back how she feels."

Barely a nod.

"Sounds like she and Ray have been spending a lot of time together. Getting closer."

Bill mouthed yes.

"Do you have a limit on how many words you can speak in a day," I asked. "A moratorium on verbiage? Because I feel like I'm sitting here with a mannequin, though a mildly animated one."

"I'm not a small-talk kind of guy, Jarvis," he answered. "You've been around me enough to know."

"Well, we've got lots of time to kill. So, unless you've got some rocking stakeout music to play, talking is all I've got to work with. Believe it or not, I'm interested in you and your family. I do feel like we are friends to some degree."

Bill checked off into the distance, eyeing the road ahead, watching any car driving down the neighborhood street. He found another donut and took a bite.

"I do appreciate all you've done for Ray, for all of us. I am grateful."

"It's part of the job."

"I'm certain you don't go to this extent for all your clients."

"Normally only the pretty female ones, but this time I'm making an exception. In the right light and a little makeup, I might consider jumping you."

Bill cracked a smile, which was seismic for him, but barely noticeable on others. It was the most I could expect, even with my top-notch witticisms.

"Speaking of pretty females, I really do like Raven," I stated. "I think she and Ray make a marvelous couple."

Bill turned and bore into me with his eyes. If I wasn't so brave, I might have wet my pants and jumped out of the car, running away.

"Come on Bill, she is wonderful. What is it you don't like about her?"

"I don't know."

"Is it her attire, her appearance and dress?"

He didn't answer.

"Is it because she is white?"

Again, no reply, his stare had turned back onto the road ahead.

"All of the above?"

"I don't know what it is. I can't see her with him. They don't match up in my eyes."

"Well, you should get used to it. She loves him and I think he loves her. Maybe it won't work, but if it fails I hope it isn't because of you. Raven is pretty, smarter than both of us combined, and the best thing for him right now. Remember, she got him to admit his problem. She also told us about Leather contacting him again. Without her, I don't know where he'd be right now."

I heard a long sigh from him.

"I do understand we wouldn't be anywhere without her. Something about her bugs me. I want to get past it, but I can't. Not completely and not yet. Rachael is on me about it, too. He's never dated a white girl before, and certainly not one of her style. I don't want to be prejudiced about her, but I am. I'm trying to be tolerant. Right now, it's the best I can do."

"Do you want him to be happy?"

"Of course."

"Have you talked with him about it? Told him how you feel."

"He is older now—old enough to make his own decisions. He doesn't want to hear what I have to think."

"Baloney, and you know it. It is important to him. Maybe he won't agree, but still he'll listen if you do it the correct way. He loves you; I can see clearly, he does. Though I hope he learns to express himself better than his father does."

Bill nodded his head while drinking his juice.

"I love him too—want the best for him."

"When was the last time you told him this?"

181

Bill again glanced off in the distance. From his reaction, it had been some time.

"He may not be a kid anymore, but he still needs to hear it. I'm sure Rachael says it all the time. It's tough for men to say it to another man. Telling your son shouldn't be hard to do. I know my old man said it plenty of times and I didn't always understand why, but I miss it now he's gone."

"The last time was when he was about ten," stated Bill. "No doubt, too damn long. I'll get around to it."

"Fair enough. Don't let more time slip away."

We exhausted our discussion quota and Bill turned on the stereo to a station that played old R&B. The music was enjoyable enough that time passed quickly and soon the black Cadillac of Mack and Grady pulled up outside. Bill and I looked at each other, took a deep breath and put the next step into play. I grabbed my cell phone and made a call. Trey answered on the second ring.

"Jarvis," he said. "Are we a go?"

"Yes, they are here. Black Cadillac with plates I gave you."

"We will roll and be there shortly."

I hung up and we waited. It didn't take more than five minutes before two police cars came in silently together, blocking the Cadillac, getting out and asking the two men to step out of the car, both officers their guns at the ready. The doors opened and Mack and Grady stepped out, hands in the air, each lying on the ground as they were told. Weapons were confiscated, they were handcuffed, escorted to one of the vehicles and locked in the backseat. One car pulled away with them, while the other waited, which was Trey. He walked over to us and handed me the two cell phones taken from them. He hung out until the tow truck arrived fifteen minutes later to haul their car away. We were left alone for our next step.

"Good thing we put a BOLO out on them for their fake drive-by," I stated to Bill, "They'll lose them in the system for a day. Should keep them out of our way for now."

Parking in front of the house, we reached the front door and leaned on the doorbell. We weren't certain what we'd get, but we were about to find out. The door opened a crack and we pushed our way in, our guns handy.

"What the fuck!" said the lady at the door. "What do you think you're doing?"

Bill told her to hush and forced her to the sofa. I did a room-to-room to see what I found. It was only a ranch home, with living area, kitchen and three bedrooms. Much of the furnishings were familiar. I located one other woman who was still in her pajamas, lying in bed. I told her to go to the living area and to be quiet. I searched and discovered no one else; the basement was unfinished with only a simple laundry room. When I returned upstairs Bill was eyeballing the two ladies.

"We in the right place?" Bill asked.

"Yep. Both of them I recognized from The Hustle. Some of the furnishings are from Ariela's place. One of the bedrooms has a computer setup and I spotted a camera in the other. Also, some sex paraphernalia. This is their new house of fun."

"Not sure what you're talking about," said the first girl, who was white with curly blonde hair, pleasant figure showing through her Wyoming Cowboys sweater and sweats.

"Ladies, let's not beat around the bush," I stated. "We know what this place is and we know you had a visitor coming today. Someone you knew or have been with before. You need to tell us what we want to know or the father of said son here is likely not to treat you so well. He is in no mood to screw around. You can help us get what we want."

The second lady looked at the first, with fear on her face. She was wearing flannel pink PJ's, barely containing her robust chest. She had brown hair cut short and parted down the middle. Both women appeared to be college-aged, in their early twenties. The curly-haired one mouthed for the other to be quiet.

"Not smart," stated Bill. He leaned down giving his patented evil stare, grabbing her curly hair and whispered in her ear something which frightened her.

"Ladies, let me tell you something," I said. "No one is coming to save you. Mack and Grady are now in police custody. We are not leaving without what we want. We can start by your names and go from there."

"I'm Serena and this is Elaine," said the brown haired one. "We don't know what you want. We were supposed to let someone in when he arrived and keep him occupied. When Mack and Grady showed up they were going to take him away."

"You work at The Hustle?" I asked.

"Yeah. We are both dancers."

"Do you entertain clients here?"

They glanced at each other. Elaine glanced back at Bill.

"Yes," they said at the same time.

"Elaine, you were in some pictures sent to Ray, posing with Leather. We want you to get in touch with her."

"Why?"

"We need to talk with her—come to an understanding."

"She'll be mad at us. So, will Mack and Grady."

"You didn't do anything wrong. We have guns and you were forced, in fear for your lives. We want you to call or text her and say Ray is here, but Mack and Grady never showed up. He wants her here to perform for him, like she promised."

"I'm not good at lying," said Elaine.

"I'll do it," said Serena. "I lie all the time in bed with a man. How is this any different?"

"Call or text?"

"Call."

"This is what you will say. Don't make a mistake or Bill here will take it out on you."

I gave her exactly what to say, while I listened. Leather was questioning what she heard and said she'd call back. The phone in my pocket started ringing as she was trying to find Mack and Grady. After she rang both numbers she called Serena back saying she'd be over in about fifteen minutes.

I waited outside out of sight until she arrived. I wanted to make sure she didn't have reinforcements with her. Pulling in, she appeared to be alone. She went in the front door and I was a couple steps behind her. I placed my gun in her back and told her to join the others. Her first look when she saw me was of anger, but turned on a dime to fear. I wasn't sure if she was acting or not, but I didn't take any chances. I removed her long coat to make sure she wasn't carrying anything. Underneath, she wore skin-tight leather pants with openings on the rear to show her butt cheeks and the crotch area. Her leather top was open below the navel and at the chest, revealing her firm breasts. Apparently, she came ready for action, if necessary.

"I know you," she said, looking at me. "Who is this?"

"I'm Ray's father."

"Yeah, I see the resemblance. I wonder if you are as good as he is in the sack!"

"Lady you'll never know!" Bill grabbed a blanket sitting on one of the chairs and tossed it to her. "Cover up. I've seen enough of you naked and I don't need to see anymore."

"Leather, we've come to make a proposition," I said.

"OK."

"What will it take to leave Ray alone?"

"Not my decision."

"Surely you have some idea. You seem to be the go-to girl in all of the extortion shenanigans."

"The boss wants his money. Let someone walk and it gives the others hope. He is going to have to pay up."

"Not an option."

"Then he is screwed!"

"What if we release the videos we have?"

"What do we care?"

It was interesting she said "we."

"What if we replace Ray with someone else? He stated The Hustle was searching for more clients. How about finding someone with deeper pockets, with a sexual appetite to match. Would this be a fair exchange?"

She hesitated, not certain how to answer.

"I don't think the girls should hear this."

"Ladies, why don't you head to the bathroom while we talk? Don't come out or Bill here is likely to shoot."

He led them to the room down the hall and closed the door. He stood at the end, so he could still see them while listening to our conversation.

"What do you propose?" Leather asked.

"I have someone who is looking for young ladies, twenty-five or younger. Experienced in the ways of the world and who will provide him all the pleasure he desires; and he requires a great deal. We can arrange to have him come by your club for a private demo, where he can check them over and get a taste, so he can make a decision. With the right girls he would jump at the chance to be member, and he has other clients he may bring at a later date to entertain. He would be a much better prize than Ray—a possible revenue goldmine for The Hustle."

"Tempting for certain. What is in it for you?"

"All we want is Ray to be free. Isn't that correct, Bill?"

Bill nodded.

"And if the boss says no?"

"Bill here is likely to kill all of you and walk away, sending him a message. Mack and Grady will do some hard time. They are in jail right now, soon to be charged with several counts. Your boss won't have much of a business left. Hell, Bill here might even go in and burn the place to the ground. You've messed with his family and he doesn't take kindly to it."

She turned to look at Bill. Again, he nodded showing his gun for her to see, the barrel pointed at her mid-section. He was playing a part right now, but it wasn't too far removed from the truth. He was at the point where he would do anything to make this go away. He was no longer a cop and would step outside the law, if necessary.

"What will you need from us?"

"Pictures of your girls for me to show the prospect—the sexier and more explicit, the better. I will take it to him and let you know in a couple of days if he is interested."

"And if he's not?"

"Let's hope he is."

She waited for a minute, thinking over her options.

"I'll have to call and see what he says."

"Please do. No funny business, though. Bill is not the most patient man."

"My cell is in my jacket."

I grabbed it and handed it to her. She pulled up the number and dialed. I listened closely to the conversation. It didn't reveal much other than the person on the other end seemed upset. Leather did her best to convince them and after several minutes they agreed.

"When do you want the photos?" she asked.

"Now; I have a flash drive and you have a computer. I'm sure there is something on there you can use. If not, I'm sure you can get to it."

We both walked back to the second room and she searched for various pictures and a couple of videos. She showed them to me and they were highly explicit, so much so I probably was blushing when viewing them. She copied the files and we left them, with a warning to stay away from Ray or all hell would break loose. Once in the car

186

we headed back to Denver.

"Came out OK," said Bill.

"It's a start. Now we need to get the second part to work. Hopefully Roland likes what he sees."

From the pictures and video, I had there was little doubt he would.

Chapter 38

The call went out to meet with Roland Langer, using Dona's main cell phone, which I'd pieced back together. When he answered, I got an earful.

"Where the hell have you been?" I got several four-letter words in a row.

"So elegant," I said as he finished his tirade.

"Who the fuck is this?"

"As you can tell, Roland, this is not Dona," I stated. "I'm calling to see if we can get together and talk. I'm representing her, hoping we can come to an understanding."

"About what?" His voice was calmer, but I still could feel the tension.

"To see what can be done to release her from her contract with you."

"Who the hell are you?"

"In time. When and where can we meet?"

He would only see me at his place. I agreed, but only if we were outside on his front patio in plain sight. We had an understanding and now I was parked in his driveway about to get out. I was wearing my brown leather coat over a long-sleeve flannel shirt, with blue jeans, hiking boots, and my black and purple Rockies ball cap on, all to keep my six-foot frame warm. Under the jacket in my shoulder holster was my Beretta for insurance, and a bulletproof vest Bill had given to me for protection. The weather was cold but reasonable for December, with sun and temps close to fifty degrees. There was a pretty good wind making it feel colder, but there was no way I was going inside his home. I had no desire to experience his torture chamber.

Walking up, I was met by the steely glare of Dirk; I kept my distance. The brute had a good fifty pounds on me and most of it appeared to be muscle under his black leather bomber jacket. I pointed for him to lead the way and found the table and chairs on the brick patio about twenty-five yards from the front. I took a seat, so I was facing the house, one eye always watching Dirk, whose anger was obvious when he first saw me. Not only had I gotten him arrested but I'd killed his partner.

In a few minutes out lumbered Roland. He was tall and skinny, with a shaved head and goatee. He walked stiffly in his tight beige slacks, black winter boots and heavy brown parka one would wear in a blizzard of below-zero weather. His hands were in his pockets, which made me nervous, but Dirk was the trigger man and his hands were in plain sight for now. Roland plopped into a chair and Dirk came over and whispered in his ear.

"You are the detective," said Roland. "Jarvis Mann, from what I'm told."

"Guilty as charged."

"You are the one responsible for killing one of my men," Roland stated.

"In my defense, I was fired upon first. I was merely defending myself. A felony was being committed and after firing at me and injuring me, I returned fire." I reached for the area on my arm where I was stuck, the wound healing nicely.

"He was struck in the neck—a rather nasty way for him to die."

"Lucky shot."

"Not for him."

All I could do was nod.

"Let's be clear, my man Dirk here is anxious to put you down. Sometime and somewhere, he wants a piece of you."

"I understand."

"Also know if you are wearing a wire, it won't work. We have sophisticated electronic jamming equipment on our entire properly. I can admit to many things and no one would hear it, even with a boom microphone pointed at us. Nothing but static will be recorded."

"I'm not here to register a confession. I'm here for Dona."

"Brave of you to come here."

"Not brave, but prudent. If you look out there you see a plain-clothes police car. In it sits a Detective Mallard, whom you may have heard of. He is there as my insurance; I walk out of here after we talk. Any threat to me will bring more trouble for you."

I was lying. It was actually Bill sitting in the car, but a desk duty officer didn't carry the weight of a Detective. And I knew Mallard wouldn't go along with the plan.

"I've met Mallard and I have no fear of him."

Apparently, name dropping wouldn't scare Roland.

"Maybe, but he still is the police and they love bad guys like you. He will make your life a living hell. All when you could have listened to what I have to say. It may prove to be fruitful to your libido."

"OK, so you want to discuss Dona. What about her? You apparently know where she is."

"I do. She is hiding from you because she fears you. She is under the impression you are about to replace her with someone younger, which means one last deadly trip to your basement."

Roland smiled. "Why does she believe this?"

"I didn't get complete details, but she seemed pretty convinced. You have a past record of dumping your toys when they get to a certain age or no longer can satisfy your needs."

"Perhaps. But why is it any of your business?"

"I feel sorry for her. She has had a tough life and I figured she deserves better."

Roland chuckled.

"Did she fuck you into feeling pity for her?"

"She offered and I declined."

"A shame; she is highly skilled sexually. One of the reasons why I've kept for so long. She is adept at providing the variety of pleasure I require."

"So why replace her?"

"Because I can. I grow weary of the same pussy and ass each day and night. Even if I sprinkle in some other female flesh here and there, it becomes boring. Also, she betrayed me."

"Really. How?"

"Oh come now, Jarvis Mann, PI. I know and you know how. You were working for Jack's ex-wife trying to catch him cheating. You knew he and Dona had a side thing going on."

"So why didn't you end it?"

"We didn't learn of it until the fateful night."

"When you shot Jack dead and burned the salon down."

"Perhaps. Or the situation got out of hand and he was killed accidentally. All I know is he owed me money and we were trying to collect. My men were pushing him around and defiant Jack blurted out he was fucking Dona to show he was better than me. Merrick got upset, pulled his gun and he and Jack fought. It went off and Jack was dead. They torched the place to cover their tracks."

Stupid. I wanted to say it out loud, but resisted.

"Dona left out of fear," I stated. "You don't want her anymore and probably want to take out your anger on her. Why not let her go and get on with your life? I may be able to hook you up with some sweet tail making you forget her."

"Maybe I've already got a replacement."

Time to stroke his ego.

"Possibly. You are a man of quality. I doubt you'd pick someone quickly. Why not search the field and make sure what you have will be as tasty as Dona was when you first found her. She was sweet, wasn't she?"

"Undoubtedly," Roland replied sheepishly. "You have someone in mind."

"Actually, some place, with a broad, so to speak spectrum, to choose from. Do you have a computer?"

Roland had Dirk bring him a notebook. I placed the USB drive on the table and he plugged it in. Under the folder "Hustle" I told him to begin opening files. With each he opened his eyes lit up and his breathing increased, blood rushing to his lower regions.

"Like what you see?" I asked.

"Who is this?" he said.

"She calls herself Leather. I've experienced her pleasures and she is highly skilled, too. Though, she is probably a little old for your taste. Nevertheless, she is extraordinary."

"Oh, I'd still enjoy her. She'd love my dungeon."

"There are a couple of videos, too."

He viewed those, the volume high to hear the moans and groans, in between the sex talk. Each video was played to its conclusion. As riled up as he was, I was expecting him to be smoking a cigarette after the climax.

"So where is this place?" Roland asked.

"In Greeley—it's called The Hustle."

"Why would I want to go all the way up there?"

"Take a trip up and see what you find. They will even arrange a private demo for you. If you don't care for what you find, you've only lost a few hours. From your reaction to the pictures and video, I would say you'll get an afternoon to remember. Leather and her friends are quite good at their craft. I speak from experience."

"Why do this? What is in it for you?"

"I'm a good Samaritan helping a poor woman out."

"Bullshit. We know some about you—barely making a living working from case-to-case. Scraping to pay the bills. How much do you get for this?"

"Enough to make it worth my while. Is this a problem?"

Roland sat back smiling, as if we'd found a common ground. He went through the pictures again, studying them like a surgeon examining the x-rays on his next patient. He licked his lips when he was finished. He appeared to be hooked.

"Organize a time for me to go up for a private demo and when I mean demo I want some skin-on-skin time with several ladies. If you can arrange it, I will go. No guarantees, but if I'm satisfied, I may see it in my heart to release Dona from her obligations, so long as she keeps her mouth shut. Hell, I'd even give her some traveling money to leave the state where we'll never cross paths again."

"Sounds fair. What day and time?"

He told me, and I pulled out my cell phone and called Leather. She said she'd call me back after speaking with her boss.

"Jarvis, you've shared with me," said Roland. "Now I'm going to share with you."

He clicked the buttons on the large fifteen-inch notebook, turned the screen around so I could see the image. It was a video with a young woman in it, tied to a table completely nude, her mouth gagged. Her legs were spread wide apart and one after another naked men would climb on top and rape her. Then she was rolled over and attacked from behind. Finally, the last man came to her, stood her up, her body limp from the torture, removed the gag and grabbed her arm, and begin hitting her until she fell to the ground. Picking her up again, he smashed her face first on the table, slid himself inside of her and with a knife began stabbing her slowly with each thrust, her screaming getting louder, until finally with one last stab of the blade and his manhood, killed her in a bloody climatic conclusion, nearly making me physically sick.

"You see Jarvis, when someone betrays me, they suffer. Keep this in mind if you are scheming to double-cross me."

The threat was clear, though I had to ask one other thing.

"It's probably stupid, but I have to ask," I said. "What did you pay Dona's boyfriend for her?"

Roland laughed out loud, a laugh that would ice over Florida.

"Five hundred dollars. Of course, after we took her, my men returned, took the money from him and killed him. Couldn't have him blabbing to everyone about selling his girlfriend."

"What happened to the body?"

"Who knows? Probably used it to make canned Spam," Roland answered with a grim smirk.

No surprise. The man was a cold-blooded killer; there was no other way to say it. I would have to watch my back for the rest of my life with him around.

My cell phone rang, and it was a call from Leather confirming the time for the private demo. All agreed, so I left in my car. I couldn't shake the images of what I'd seen in the horrific video, violence beyond imagination. Once outside the security gate, I pulled over and threw up, the disgust overwhelming me.

Chapter 39

I was spent, needing some rest—and dammit, escape! Wanting to see Melissa was deep in my soul, resting high above, the agony was lurking. She was my outlet and release point. I wanted to run over to her place and wait for her to get home, hold on tight and sleep up close. Either via text or call I had not heard from her in days. I didn't want to push it, for I knew she had her own serious work to deal with. Sitting patiently wasn't easy.

Not feeling much like food, I returned to my temporary home and headed straight to the basement and plopped on the bed, doing my best to close my eyes. I fell asleep dreaming of being near Melissa, but not being able to touch her. Reaching, but not finding her. It scared me as I saw her getting further and further from me. In the distance, I saw someone grab her, a scary macabre face looking a whole lot like Roland's. He was about to do ungodly and unspeakable acts to her and I couldn't stop him. I was running towards her with long strides, though getting no closer to her, as if slipping on ice. I had to save her from the horrible evil. I was the only one who could. I tried to call out but couldn't speak, the terror paralyzing my vocal chords. I sat bolt upright in bed yelling, *No!*

Looking around, I realized where I was, understanding it was a dream, reality coming back into focus. I was thirsty and now hungry; the LED clock showed it was after midnight. I heard someone walking around upstairs, the ceiling above me creaking. I silently walked up the stairs and followed the noises. I wasn't sure who would be up at this hour, but I wanted to make sure someone hadn't broken in. I'd been cautious to verify no one was following after leaving Roland's. There was no reason for him to track me back to Kate's house, but then again, I didn't always have the foresight to anticipate everything. Sounds and light came from the kitchen and I found Kate raiding the refrigerator for food and wine. She was wearing white pajama tops and bottoms with fuzzy brown slippers, and in the glow of the fridge I could see right through them, so I could tell she didn't have anything on underneath. Doing my best not to startle her, I failed. She turned and saw me, jumping an inch or so off the ground.

"Damn!" she shouted. "Jarvis, you scared the crap out of me!"

I tried not to stare at her, which was challenging, as she was lavishly put together for someone of around fifty. The light behind her left little to the imagination. If she noticed my gawking, she didn't let on.

"Sorry, I didn't mean to. I heard noise and wanted to make sure it wasn't trouble."

"I was having a challenging time sleeping," she said. "A little cheese and wine usually works to make me drowsy. Well, mostly the wine. Would you care to join me?"

The offer sounded serene, so we sat at her dining room table, the light above dimmed, creating a cozy atmosphere. She had two glasses, some white Riesling, Wisconsin cheddar and a knife for cutting. I poured while she hacked off several slabs for each of us. Her long hair was free of her signature twisted ponytail, a static frizz to it from having been slept on. It was as raw as I'd ever seen her, and still she was attractive.

"How are you holding up?" I asked of her after a bite.

"OK," she replied. "I'm pretty bored. With no business to run, I have way more time on my hands. I'm down there every day checking on progress, making sure the work is done right. Mostly, I'm in the way because they know what they are doing. I clean the house like it hasn't been done in years to pass the time. Reading every book I have, some I haven't read in years. Watch a little TV and find most of it boring or disturbing. Can't do any shopping, I don't have the money to spend. I'm running out of things to do."

"Any timeframe on when the salon will be ready?"

"Probably after Christmas, though I forgot to mention that you can move back in Sunday morning. They'll be all done with the lower level Saturday afternoon. Could even bed down that night, if you're anxious to get out of here."

"Not anxious, but happy to be getting back to where I'm used to sleeping. I appreciate your putting me up."

She reached over and touched my arm. "No problem, Jarvis. I'm sorry my personal life spilled over into yours. Even though I hired you to catch Jack and now to find his killer, I didn't want it to mess with your love life. I expected you to be gone a night or two and stay with Melissa. I hope there isn't any trouble there?"

I really didn't want to burden her with my problems, but talking about it seemed the right thing to do.

"There is some tension there. We haven't talked for a few days."

"Is it because of this case?"

"Yes, but there's more. She has concerns about me staying here."

"Why?"

"You, mostly."

"Me? She is jealous?"

"Probably; with good reason, though. I had an issue with a female client a few months back. I became involved physically with her. Melissa and I had started dating and the other woman said some things about her that I believed. I stopped seeing her and ended up getting seduced into what turned out to be a mess."

"The lady you shot at Dave and Busters?"

"Yep."

"Oh, man. I didn't realize.

"It was a stupid mistake. Something I'm amazed she forgave me for. Once you screw up like this it's hard not to wonder if it could happen again."

Kate took a long sip of wine and followed it with some cheese. She rested her hand on mine and I tensed up. She sensed it, but didn't remove it.

"Jarvis, you are an attractive man. And damn, when I was younger I would have jumped you in a heartbeat. But I'm still trying to get over my husband, and I'm not a let's-fuck kind of lady anymore. I need to find myself and when it's time, find a good man my age to hopefully rock my world again. It's way too soon for sex, and too early to jump in bed for the hell of it. Melissa has nothing to worry about from me."

"I know it and I told her," I said. "I've even told her I loved her to ease her mind."

"Didn't calm her concerns any?"

"No. She couldn't respond back in kind—at least not yet."

"I know what it's like," she replied. "I was able to get beyond the wedge, or in my case a wall, with Jack the first time. The second time I couldn't, it was too much to overcome. I will say if she is worth it, hang in there. You'll find each other if it's meant to be."

She patted my hand and pulled it away. We enjoyed a little more cheese, and she downed another glass, the last gulp bringing on a deep yawn.

"Well, the wine is kicking in," Kate stated. "I'm going to head to bed. Can you put this away when you're done?"

"Be glad to. And again, thanks for putting me up and letting me bend your ear."

She got up from the table and headed towards the stairs. I watched her walking slowly, my imagination in overdrive on what she would be like in bed for the first time since I'd known her. Odd, but I do this with many women I see. She turned around, noticing me leering at her, and smiled.

"Thanks for the staring at my body," she said happily, "now and earlier. I hope you enjoyed the view. It's fabulous to know the old broad can still turn the head of a young stud."

She walked up the stairs slowly, and I'd never look at her as only my landlord ever again.

Chapter 40

Saturday came, and I started gathering together my stuff I'd brought to Kate's with plans to move back this evening. It was wonderful to have a place to stay, but I was ready to get back to my own residence and bed. All my clothes had been cleaned, all the furniture too. Carpeting had been freshly shampooed and the walls painted. A little food to restock the kitchen and I was set.

I still hadn't heard from Melissa, so, having a fair amount of energy, I decided to spend the afternoon working out. I ran, lifted, punched and swam all the vigor out of me I could. My body had healed up nicely and was strong and quick as ever. I knew tomorrow was the big day where all the parties would meet in Greeley. I had to be there to broker the deal, get them all together. Physically I was ready to go, but mentally I was still trying to find myself. It didn't matter; I had to be there and sell the whole thing. If I could walk out of there in one piece, everyone with smiles on their faces, I would have accomplished a lot. This was only the beginning. One step at a time. Patience, again, was the key. More internal pep talks required.

After finishing, exhaustion enveloping me, I showered and hit the grocery store and then met the contractor at my place. We walked through, and once I was satisfied, he handed over a key and left me. I pulled out a beer and sat down, turning the TV on. Tired and alone, I nodded off for some time until I heard the door opening, Melissa in all her beauty standing before me, carrying some takeout with her. She threw her arms around me, kissing me for a long time. She was wearing black jeans, a silk blouse, heavy jacket and black boots with heels where we could almost see eye to eye.

"Are you hungry?" she said. "Tony paid for dinner for us. Another case finalized successfully. He told me to get some food, expense it and go see Jarvis."

"How'd you know I was here?" I asked.

"I stopped by Kate's first and talked for a minute. Said you were moving back and were feeling down about us. She gave me a little advice."

"Which was?"

"Show up at your door and jump your bones?"

"Were those her exact words?"

"No, but this was…" She preceded to whisper in my ear their conversation, strolling towards the bedroom, removing her clothes along the way.

I walked after her. "What about dinner? Won't it get cold?"

"That is what ovens and microwaves are for. Besides you'd don't want me to get cold, do you?"

I followed in hot pursuit, stripping as fast as I could. When I made it to the bedroom, she was completely naked, her beauty with or without clothing was immense, the surge in my body intensifying. I needed a release from all the good and the bad from this last week. My whole being had been tense and, finally, I had what I coveted. No foreplay for this moment, but good old-fashioned hot lovemaking, her legs wrapped around me. It wouldn't be long, though neither of us cared, as we had been waiting for this moment. We both cried out within minutes. It may have been a quickie, but it was an eye-popping one.

In each other's arms we rested, catching our breath. After cleaning up and putting on some clothing, we warmed up our food and sat at the table eating. She had brought some roasted chicken, mashed potatoes and gravy, coleslaw and rolls. I provided a couple of bottles of beer to complete the meal. We ate silently, each of us staring at the other. I wanted to blurt out again how I felt about her, the languor of desire still fresh on my mind, but I held off. There was so much to talk about, but I wanted her to start it and I didn't want to push.

When finished, we retired to the sofa and she curled up against me. I tossed a blanket over to keep us warm. Her body radiation was nearly sufficient without the cover.

"Jarvis, we need to talk," she said after several minutes of silence.

"I'm all ears."

Her head was on my chest, her eyes staring off into the kitchen, not wanting to meet mine while she spoke.

"I've held off telling you how I felt after what you told me over the phone. Relationships can be hard for me. So, I'm cautious."

I sat and listened. I could feel her pulse pounding in her chest. She was nervous talking about this.

"When the 'L' word was used in the past it rarely lasted. My fault, their fault, it didn't matter. After our initial false start and your dalliance with Emily, putting myself out there is challenging."

"Perfectly understandable," I said. "I'm grateful you gave us another shot."

"Can you guarantee it won't happen again?"

I paused to choose my words carefully.

"Absolutes are difficult when it comes to my life." I replied. "I can tell you for the past weeks I've had strippers giving me lap dances that could be classified as borderline intercourse and a woman who is a sex slave throwing herself at me because it's the only life she knows. Each time, I resisted because you were on my mind—the person I most wanted to be with. I can't guarantee anything because this has been a weakness for me in the past. It is a work in progress and I have some growing to do. What I can say is, I'm trying to be a better man to be with you."

"What about me going back to school?"

"If it's what you want to do, I'm all for it."

"It will be difficult. It provided stress to my previous relationship."

"Yes, it will be. So will being involved with a private detective whose cases tend to gravitate to the seedy side of life. All we both can do is try and see where it leads."

"I do want to finish my schooling and be a lawyer. I've already registered at Colorado University to start up again after the first of the year."

"I'm happy for you and will help however I can. I'm thankful to have met you all those months ago."

"As am I, although without Janet it may never have happened."

"The receptionist at Bristol & Bristol?"

"Yes. She commented you were cute. I answered her 'yes' and she encouraged me to give you my card. Said it was time for me to get back on the horse. It had been some time since I'd dated. If I didn't, she said she would."

"Wow, as I recall she didn't even give me a second look."

"She is coy with men. Being pretty, she doesn't need to be overt. They usually fall all over her to get her number."

"Well, I'm glad she pushed you. I guess I owe her some flowers."

"She is also the one who said to give you another chance. Though if you fucked up again, I should cut them clean off."

Though the image was not pleasant, I had to laugh.

"Can we make it despite our failings?" Melissa said.

200

"No reason not to try. I'd rather try and fail than not try at all. I care about you. I love you."

She stopped talking, and I saw tears in her eyes. She threw her arms around me and squeezed me tightly.

"I love you, too," she said into my ear.

Little more needed to be said as we lost ourselves in the moment.

Chapter 41

I sat in the Mustang, the heater running, the teen temps chilling the car. My mind went through all the events of the last month; so much happening, if someone had described them to me I likely wouldn't have believed a word. Too surreal to be factual: the cases on two fronts, now coming together. It was a hairy mess, but I was in a hairy business sometimes. It was a big gamble, what I aimed to accomplish. If I pulled this off it would be a miracle. Normally I didn't trust in them, but today I was trying to stay positive.

There were a few cars in the parking lot already, so The Hustle group likely was inside, getting prepared, dressed or undressed in this case. About ten past eleven, Roland's car rolled in, an expensive black BMW, all shiny and freshly washed. Out stepped Dirk from the passenger side, and another new man from the driver's side I'd not seen before. He was tall and muscular, with goatee, dressed in all black, with a lengthy coat and leather driving gloves. His head was covered with an Oakland Raiders ball cap, his long blonde hair sticking out the back in a ponytail. He opened the door for Roland and his skinny frame stepped out, freakish as always. I joined them at the front entrance.

"Jarvis Mann," said Roland. "Are we ready to do this?"

I nodded.

"This is my new man, Rocky," he said. "His job is to watch after you. Do anything stupid and he is to kill you. Is this clear?"

"Nothing is going to happen unless you start it," I stated, keeping an emotionless expression. "I'm here for the payday and to set Dona free. Let's go inside so the show can commence."

Through the entry way I noticed the guard I'd fought with previously was there. He wanted to pat each of us down, but Dirk and Rocky would have none of it. He called for Mack and Grady, who came as backup.

"My men are carrying," stated Roland. "They either keep their weapons or we walk. You have my word nothing will happen so long as the event remains civil. I'm an important man who requires protection."

The three men scrutinized the scene, and Grady made a quick call. After talking with someone, they agreed to let us in with our guns. I was relieved. I was also armed with a new .38 I'd picked up to replace the one the police were still holding. It was reassuring to have it on my back hip, hidden by my brown leather jacket. It was my only backup on this day, which I hoped I would not need. All eyes were upon me: Dirk, Mack, Grady and now Rocky, with a steely gaze, the first three with an axe to grind, the fourth ready to shoot me if necessary. I was in the lion's den and felt like a chunk of raw meat the cats were savoring to tear to pieces, from the glances I was receiving. Calm on the outside but nervous on the inside, I did my best to keep everyone in my field of view, eyes on a swivel alert for the slightest threat. I pulled out a big piece of gum and began chewing, finding it calming.

Roland reached the front table and scanned the empty stage.

"Who is running this show?" he asked out loud. "I'm a busy man."

Out from the back room walked Marquis, all calm and cool-looking, in his expensive tailored white suit and polished shoes. He strolled over to Roland and put out his hand, but he refused to shake on anything for now.

"I am the proprietor of this establishment," Marquis said, pulling it back. "What shall I call you?"

"Sir for now," answered Roland. "No names are necessary. I'm here to see the merchandise."

The way it was said made you think he was there to see furniture or a car. To him it was a sex garage sale. I felt like a pimp bringing all of them together. Another new tagline: The Pimp Detective.

"OK," replied Marquis. "Ladies to the stage."

Out they all marched, in assorted sizes and races. All were wearing high-heeled shoes, a G-string and no top. There were eleven girls altogether and each smiled brightly. Their ages barely legal, eighteen to early twenties. I wasn't sure the age limit for a place that served liquor, but I imagined a couple of them were too young. Of course, no patron would ever complain, and certainly Roland wouldn't.

"Please ladies show me your stuff," commanded Roland. "Twirl around, bend over so I can see your ass. Rub your hands on your body. I want to see you play with yourself. The more you enjoy, the more likely you'll get a big, hard tip from me."

Roland laughed at his own joke, and his two guards chuckled

203

nervously, well after he started. I sat and smiled, but it was all an act. I never imagined the sight of several beautiful, naked women to be a turn-off, but this whole scene felt sickening.

All the ladies did as they were told, some more enthusiastically than others. Roland marched back and forth watching, his tongue sticking out ever so slightly. A couple of them leaned their backsides towards him and he grabbed and rubbed some flesh. Each squealed excitedly to add to the show. Roland stopped for a minute to check over everyone and turned to Marquis.

"There is someone I don't see here," he said. "She was in one of the pictures. Wildly pretty, all dressed in leather and older, maybe in her later thirties. I generally don't like them older, but she interested me. Is she here too?"

"I will check," said Marquis. "For now, why don't you pick one of your favorites and she can dance for you." He walked to the back room.

"You," said Roland, pointing to one of the girls, while taking a seat.

She was one I wasn't familiar with. She appeared Hispanic, barely eighteen, with long black hair, plump firm rear end, long legs and deep brown complexion. She stepped down off the stage and started dancing, moving round and round, shaking her butt, twisting and rubbing up against him. He grabbed at her and yanked her onto his lap, as she was facing away from him. I tensed when he pulled out a knife, but he used it to cut her G-string so now she was completely naked. She grounded herself into him and he seemed to release himself, so he could penetrate her. She moaned as she slipped up and down on him. I was watching the worst of a porn movie.

"I thought you were interested in me," came the voice of Leather walking into the room. "You should save the hard-on for the playroom."

"Plenty more where it came from," said Roland. "I have an instant on switch."

Leather had her black leather outfit on, covering her midsection and little else. Her hair was tied in a ponytail and she had a riding crop in her hand that she rubbed between her legs. She took her finger and began to suck on it, as if he needed any additional teasing to arouse him.

"Maybe you should try all the girls and see if you can keep up. If you can make it through them all, you can have me. Save the best for last. Come, Juanita, you can continue in the playroom and see what his stamina is like. The rest of you line up and wait your turn."

Juanita stood up and started walking towards the back room, her ass wiggling in excitement. Roland zipped himself up and followed her, like an animal in heat. The stage cleared and the rest of us sat. A waitress came to each of us asking if we wanted any food or drink. I had no appetite and declined. Standing, I moved to leave. Dirk motioned for Rocky to stop me and we faced eye-to-eye. His stare was unnerving, but I stood firm and wasn't about to back down.

"I believe I've held up my end of the bargain," I said. "No reason for me to hang around. Your boss will be busy for some time. If he needs me, he knows where I'll be." I pulled out a business card and handed it to him.

Rocky looked at Dirk, and he waved to let me pass. I walked out, glad to be out of the lion's den. I'd need to shower to remove the stench of what I saw. Like the video, it would be a long time before I could forget it. I'd accomplished what I wanted, knowing it would be a matter of time before the two criminal elements collided and would come looking for me, unless they killed each other first. If only I was so lucky.

Chapter 42

When I returned home Melissa was waiting, sitting on the sofa reading a book. The title appeared to be law-related, which I was happy to see. She closed it up, bookmark in place and smiled.

"Finished with your PI duties for the day?" Melissa asked.

"Yes. I'm yours to do with as you please," I replied.

"Come here," she stated with a sultry smile.

Excitedly, I did.

It felt refreshing to have someone there for me, to forget the future troubles brewing. Since she had Monday off, our next day-and-a-half was wonderful. Try as I might, I couldn't stay in bed with her the whole time. Snow had fallen in the afternoon, so we remained inside, talked about life and made love as much as my body would allow. In her arms, linked physically as only two in love can be, it all didn't matter anymore. No dead bodies, no threats, no twisted sex games for money. Night turned to day, leading to shopping and a pleasant drive in the snowy foothills, dinner out and movie. It was a wonderful relaxing time together. If I'd ever felt more alive in my life, I couldn't remember when.

We discussed our immediate futures, planning a trip over the holiday. She always had the two weeks off over Christmas and New Year's. I didn't care for flying much, but with her with me, the fear didn't seem so bad. We talked about a vacation to Acapulco, Cancun, Jamaica or Hawaii; anyplace warm, in the sun and away from the cold and snow. She was going to research some costs, but I didn't care, and would pay what it took to get lost with her for a while.

Her work week ahead was going to be light, so we planned to see each other every night. I stayed at her place one night, the next at mine. The rest of my time was spent putting together bills for my two cases, with hopes for another case to show up at my door. I followed up with all parties to see how everyone was doing. First call was to Dona.

"I'm getting stir crazy," she said.

"It will be over soon. Give it another week."

"There is only so much TV I can take. I need to shop, go out to eat, meet someone. There is only so much a girl can do to satisfy herself without a man."

I let it go.

"Be patient. Once it's all over you can come and go as you please. May even get a bonus from Roland to move away and start over. You need to decide what you're going to do to make a living. Screwing for pay isn't a way of life."

"I'm thinking about it. Finding what else I'm good at isn't easy."

I told her to work on it, stay hidden and said goodbye. Next call was to Kate.

"How is your place?" she asked. "Did they do a decent job?"

"It's great," I responded, "though it's a bit loud during the day when they are working upstairs. I'm certain it won't be much longer."

"Two weeks is what they are predicting, earlier if we're lucky. I'm trying to keep busy but it's hard. School is ending and we are going to take a trip to see my mother."

"It will do you good. Stay through the holidays." I explained to her why.

"Oh my! It sounds dangerous!"

"Could be. That's why it's best for you to be out of town. Once you return, it should be all over."

"How is Melissa?"

"Never been better, thanks for asking."

"I'm pleased for you both. You deserve to be happy."

I couldn't agree more.

"Enjoy your time at your mother's. Don't worry about a thing here. I'll make sure they finish up the salon and have it ready for the New Year. I want to be at the ribbon cutting and be your first customer."

Kate laughed and we said our goodbyes. Next it was Bill, but we agreed to meet at Boone's for an afternoon beer when his shift ended. When I arrived, he was sitting at the bar, a mug in front and another waiting for me.

"So where are we at?" he asked.

"No news yet," I said. "I got them all together on Sunday and it was a veritable festival of horniness. Roland was busting at the seams to get at those girls. I felt like a sex broker hooking him up with them."

"They are likely lost already, doing whatever they can to make a buck. If it wasn't you, it would be someone else. Your job is to save us and not them." Bill stopped to take a long drink of his favorite local beer. "The question is, when will it all come to a head?"

"Soon—when it boils over and whoever comes out of it alive."

"With any luck none of them, though I doubt it. Someone will remain standing and they will come after you; come after all of us."

I knew the possibility existed when the plan was put into place, and I was ready for when it happened. The waiting was the hard part, along with watching for the ensuing storm.

"Everything in place on your end?" I asked.

"Yes, we are prepared," Bill replied. "I'm not completely happy Ray is sticking around, though I'm glad he is willing to face up to the mess he is responsible for. He'll learn from it. Hopefully he lives to take advantage of the education."

"Let's hope we all live through it."

Bill picked up the tab for the beer and I headed to Melissa's to spend the night. Her place was much larger and nicer than mine, and I'd grown accustomed to it, feeling more at home with each evening spent there. The following day I met her at Bristol & Bristol for lunch with some of her work comrades, including Janet the receptionist, to whom I had flowers delivered as promised. It was a fun meal on the Sixteenth Street Mall, where I became acquainted with them for the first time. While walking back to the office this Friday afternoon, my cell phone rang. I recognized the number and asked if I could call them back. When we arrived, I requested privacy and Melissa took me to one of the smaller conference rooms, which was still the size of Rhode Island.

"Is it good news or bad?" I said after hitting redial.

"Mostly bad," said Trey, the Greeley cop. "There was a disturbance at The Hustle this morning. Seems a private party got out of hand. A few people got hurt and several arrested. Apparently, your man Roland was not happy about something. I have a feeling he discovered he was being recorded doing the deed."

"No luck them all killing each other off?"

"No. One guy got stabbed, a few scuffles, some blood and bruises. We arrived in full force before any shooting. All the major parties were arrested."

"Are they still in jail?"

"For now. They should all be out late today, early tomorrow at the latest. You better watch your back. You know they will be gunning for you."

All I could say was "yes" and "thanks." I proceeded to type out several text messages of warnings to those involved, hitting send and waiting for a response. Once I got them I walked out of the room and found Melissa in her office, a bouquet of roses sitting on one corner I had sent to her. I came in and closed the door, went around the desk and kissed her.

"Wow, what was that about?" she said.

"Wanted to show you how I felt," I answered. "I enjoyed lunch with your friends. They are a lovely group of people."

"They like you, too."

"I need to do something for the next couple of days, so I won't be able to see you. I wanted to make sure you understood. It's related to these last two cases and I need to keep you at a distance for your own safety."

"So, you are in danger?"

"I'm not certain. It's best to keep you out of the crossfire."

It wasn't totally true, for I was in danger, but I didn't want to alarm her. She looked concerned, as I wasn't the best at lying when it came to women. Transparency with the ladies was one of my biggest failings.

"Can we at least be together tonight?"

I thought long and hard about it. I doubted they knew Melissa or where she lived, so one additional night at her place probably wasn't dangerous.

"If we go straight to your place and stay in, it should be OK."

"Can we pick up some takeout? You know me, I don't have much food in the house other than something to nuke."

I smiled. "Sure. I'll hang around here if it's alright. Get done early and we can get home all the sooner."

"Somebody appears anxious. Did you have something in mind?"

"I did, but if I told you now I think we'd have to do it right here on your desk."

A sexy smile launched across Melissa's face when hearing my statement. She stood up, walked over to her door and pressed the button to lock it, turned and started unbuttoning her top.

"Tell me what you had in mind…"

Chapter 43

The next day, she convinced me to drive her to the mall against my better wishes, but it was hard not to spend time with Melissa, as her will was strong. One of my other failings with women was being easily talked into things against my better judgment. I had to go to my place first to get my gun. I didn't have it with me and I wasn't about to be unarmed. Once retrieved, we drove out heading for Park Meadows. We got a mile or so down the road when I noticed a tail. It was the black BMW driven by Dirk. I cursed myself for taking Melissa with me; I hadn't expected them to come after me so quickly. I now needed to get her to someplace safe.

"Be prepared to do what I tell you," I said with as much seriousness as I could.

"What?"

"Listen. We are being followed. You need to do what I ask and not hesitate. I tell you to run, please run and don't look back. I tell you to duck, then duck. Don't question me or think you should do something different. OK?"

Melissa hesitated in responding, but finally said, "yes."

It was early enough in the morning, so traffic wasn't horrible yet on Evans. My plan was to get on the highway and go as fast as possible, trying to create some distance. I cut down University and hopped on the I-25 and quickly got up to speed. The BMW was on my tail and now a second smaller sports car with lots of horsepower had joined them. It pulled up and was in front of me. I tried to switch lanes and pass, but they continued to blanket me, the rear car squeezing me from the back. There was enough traffic on the highway, so I was trapped. We neared the Hampden exit so I steered off at the last second, exiting at full speed, my fresh tires moaning while holding the road. The car in front had to brake and back up to catch the off ramp, while the rear car was still on my tail. I approached the intersection, the light red, but I ran it going right and barely missing a car. I began blowing my horn to warn them, the BMW still following, weaving to miss the traffic. I roared the Mustang to high speed and pulled away. Soon on the left was a small shopping center and I plowed through, crossing over and up the ramp quickly, making a left into the parking lot. Pulling up in front of a Starbucks, I slammed the brakes to stop near the entrance.

"Now Melissa, out of the car and run inside," I yelled. "And don't look back."

She reached out to touch me, but I hollered again for her to go. She got out of the car right when the BMW pulled up in front at an angle to block the Mustang. I tried to back up, but the other car spun right behind to cut me off from the rear. I got out of the car with my gun drawn and fired once into the BMW, missing my target, rushing the shot. Screams came from all around me, patrons in the parking lot bolting in fear from what was happening before them. From behind, someone grabbed me and knocked the Beretta out of my hand. I was grabbed around the neck and shoulders, try as I might I couldn't get loose. I heard a scream, which sounded like Melissa hollering to leave me alone. My head grew heavy from the sleeper hold. I tried to yell at Melissa to run inside, but only saw blackness with no sense of what else was happening.

Later, I sensed movement but couldn't tell where I was. It was dark and there wasn't much air. My head still was murky and I was out again. Sometime later I felt the car come to a stop; I noticed there was sunlight, and I was pulled from where I was and dragged across the ground, tossed unceremoniously into the dirt and gravel by Rocky. My eyes started to focus and I felt someone on top of me. I recognized the perfume and when I could see again realized it was Melissa. I had hoped she had escaped, but she hadn't. She was a wild card I hadn't counted on in my scenario.

"You didn't get away," I said, my voice cracking.

"I'm sorry, Jarvis," Melissa answered. "I thought they were going to kill you and I couldn't run away. The other one grabbed me and tossed me in the back of his car—said he'd shoot you if I resisted."

I didn't want to tell her they were going to kill us anyway.

"It's OK," I said. "Help me up."

"You may want to stay down for now, asshole," said Dirk, "at least until everyone else shows up."

Doing as I was told, since I was trying to get my wits and strength back, I glanced around to see where I was. It appeared to be an old work zone of some kind, obviously no longer in use. The ground was cold but dry, the recent snow having melted in the warm daytime December temps, which hovered in the fifties. We were in an open area devoid of trees, a couple of beat-up mobile buildings nearby. I had no idea where we were or how far we had traveled. Using stealth, I removed some fingerless gloves from my pockets and covered my hands.

"Do you know where we are?" I asked of Melissa.

"Somewhere south and east," she said. "I was so scared at first I wasn't paying attention. Once I settled down, I made some mental notes. I think we are somewhere east of Parker."

Absorbing my surroundings, it did appear we were in prairie land, with no other structures nearby. It may have been an old rock quarry site where they pulled minerals from the earth and processed them via equipment I had spotted. No one else was around—no vehicles and no other people. Why they picked this spot was hard to say, but it would be easy to hide our bodies in one of the holes where the product had been removed and replaced with fresh dirt. Not the type of burial I had hoped for, and way sooner.

In a few minutes, Mack and Grady's Cadillac arrived. They forcefully pulled out Ray and Raven, walking them over to us. Grady dragged Bill from the trunk, looking a little worse for the wear, with a swelling lip and bloody nose. I knew he wouldn't go easily and had paid the price. There was a welt under Grady's eye too, so he'd at least landed one punch. The three of them came over and I got to my feet, giving them the impression I was hobbled, using the illusion to my advantage.

"Appears you put up a struggle, Bill," I stated.

"Difficult to fight fair when there are two of them and each armed. I did my best."

"Old man, you need to shut up or I'll knock you down again," said Grady.

Bill gave him a hard stare, but remained silent. Ray seemed scared, but Raven appeared defiant, her face showing anger. I had warned them this might be coming and made sure they understood what to do if taken. Don't let them feed on your fear. Hopefully I heeded my own advice.

"You doing OK, Ray?" I asked.

"Fine," he answered. "I can't believe this—I thought you two bozos were my friends."

Mack stepped over and slugged Ray in the stomach. In his defense he didn't drop to his knees, but did bend over, gasping for air. Raven with her tall boots kicked Mack in the shins. He hopped up and down several times in pain. I tried not to laugh, but did smile broadly. Mack, once the agony subsided, went over to retaliate, but Ray stepped in between.

"What are you going to do, boy?" Mack said.

"Don't you dare touch her," Ray said, the fear now gone from his face. "Do what you want to me, but leave her alone or I swear…"

"Oh, we'll do what we want to her and do it over and over again until she begs us to kill her."

Raven lunged, but Ray halted her. He turned to face her, hugging her tightly.

"Isn't this sweet," said Grady.

"Is she as good screwing as the other girls you nailed at The Hustle?" said Mack.

"I guess we'll find out," replied Grady, while sexually gesturing with his hips.

"Show a little class, gentlemen," I said. "I know it goes against your nature, but give it a shot. You might even like it."

Both turned to come after me but stopped when two cars approached. The first contained Roland, with a different man driving. He slithered out and pulled out Dona with him, flinging her to the ground. Somehow, he had found her and now I had another wild card to deal with.

From the next car Marquis stepped out of the driver's seat, while out the passenger side came Leather, dressed all in black leather, with a fur cap and coat on which probably were tortured a hundred minks to manufacture. She walked over and stood at the center of the group, Marquis walking two steps behind her. She came in front of me and slapped me hard across the face. It was a good slap, though not the hardest I'd ever gotten from a woman.

"Before me stands the silent partner," I said while rubbing my face.

"You crossed the wrong woman," she stated firmly. "Now all around you will pay dearly."

Over to Melissa she stepped, looking her up and down. She took the back of her hand and ran it down her face and across her chest. Melissa tensed up, not appreciating the touching, but held her ground.

"Very nice," said Leather. "How is she in bed, Jarvis? I bet she is a wonder at fucking. The boys will find out and maybe even I'll have a taste."

She leaned over to lick Melissa's face, but Melissa stepped back this time.

"Oh come on, honey. Haven't you ever been kissed by a woman before? You might like it."

"Well, I see where Mack and Grady get their manners from," I said. "I'll say to you what I told them, show some class, lady."

She turned to face me with a pleasing expression.

"The only thing I'm going to show you is your balls after I have them cut off. While you are bleeding to death we are going to take your sweet honey and poke her in every hole she has."

"Is this what you did to Ariela before you killed her?" I asked.

She smiled brightly, licking her lips.

"The boys had some fun before snuffing her and dumping the body."

"At their leader's beck and call."

"Of course. She had to pay for letting you get the drop on us and stealing our hard drive with the recordings."

"You were there, too."

"She vouched for you. Said you were easy pickings. Had no problem giving you a hard-on when she gave you a lap dance, and she believed we could manipulate you. Silly bitch was always weak. She had a soft spot for Ray before understanding all he wanted was pussy, hers and others he could taste." She turned to Ray and Raven. "Is this your latest honey, Ray? She seems so exotic. Of course, he screwed all denominations at the club."

"You killed Ariela?" asked Ray.

"No one told you this?" said Leather.

"No."

"Had our pleasures and dumped her in a cornfield," said Mack.

"Dad, did you know this?"

Bill came over and placed his arm around him.

"I'm sorry. It was my decision not to tell you."

"Why?"

"I was afraid it would set you back on the progress you had made."

"You can't shield me from bad news. I'm not a kid anymore. That's why I'm here to face up to the mess I caused."

"I know, and I'm proud of the man you're becoming standing

214

with you here today. I want all the best for you, son—to be free, happy and with someone you love." He glanced over at Raven and smiled. "Fault me all you want, but I always have your best interests at heart…because I love you."

Ray's eyes met his father's, saying all that needed to be said. Bill put his arms around and gave him a solid hug.

"Can we get on with this?" stated Roland. "Too touching for me. All talk and no action is boring."

"No different with you, Roland, murdering Jack and torching the salon," I said.

There was no smile for him, only a growl.

"As I told you before, they didn't mean to kill him, but we would have. I had other ideas of how to make him pay. I would have peeled his skin off a layer at time, if given the chance, before killing him. He had it coming for stealing my money and screwing my girl. Would have been more fun, but one doesn't always get what they want."

"How did you find Dona?" I asked.

He grabbed her by the hair, lifting and kissing her, biting her on the lip until it bled, licking it as if it was sweet.

"Dumb bitch has been using her credit card; only a matter of time before we tracked her down."

I thought I'd gotten them all from her, but she must have held one back.

"What will become of her?"

Roland laughed, a horrid sound that made my skin crawl.

"Remember that video I showed you," he said, "of the whore who betrayed me? Well, I have an encore planned for Dona that will pale in comparison. It will be a glorious multi-hour finale before she breathes her last breath."

Dona attempted to break free, but Roland held on with one hand while grabbing her in the crotch with the other. She screamed out in pain, his fingers digging in.

"What happened at The Hustle?" I said, trying to bring his attention back to me. "I heard there was a scuffle."

"Pretty slick you putting us together," he replied after releasing his grip. "You knew they'd record me and try to blackmail me. While fucking three of them I saw the camera and called to my boys to come and destroy their equipment. Dirk stabbed the guy at the front entrance. A fight ensued and guns were drawn. The cops showed up before any shots were fired and dragged us all in. Sweet Leather and I had an opportunity to converse. We put two and two together, surmising what you had done. We now had a common enemy to strike back at. We coordinated our resources and here we are."

"I had hoped you'd all shoot each other and that would be the end of it—silly of me."

"Poor planning on your part," said Roland. "Now you're here and will die. Like Leather said, we will enjoy your two sweet ladies first and there won't be a damn thing you can do about it."

"Once we finish with all of you," added Leather, "we will track down Ray's mother and sister and do a number on them. They weren't around when we grabbed Ray."

Rachael and Monika had gone to Kansas to visit relatives, per Bill's insistence. Ray wouldn't go and wanted to see this to the end. Raven, of course, was sticking with Ray.

"Next, we'll find your other client, the ex-wife of Jack," added Roland. "I want a piece of her too since she is the one who hired you. Bring her to my chamber and have my way until she begs me to kill her. Schedule a doubleheader with her and Dona."

"Wow, can you all really be this evil?" I asked. "You seem like a cliché. Something you'd see in bad B-movie. I almost want to laugh; it's such a bad script you've written. A movie I'd walk out on."

I did laugh, out loud so all could hear. I wasn't showing fear, though it was there underneath my skin. Still thinking I was wobbly Dirk stepped over and took a swing at me, which I slipped and gave him a roundhouse punch to the ear, staggering him and sending a shiver up my arm. I was flexing my hand to bring back the feeling. I was glad I put on my fingerless leather gloves to provide some protection.

"I know you want a piece of me, Dirk, for killing your partner. Come on, let's see what you've got."

Removing my coat, I stepped back and away from the group, creating space, luring him, bouncing on my toes, thinking I was Ali against Foreman. Dirk was larger and heavier, probably in fair shape, with lots of muscle but lacking in speed. I doubted he was as fast as I was, so quickness was my friend. He lunged towards me, trying to grab me. I stepped to the side and banged him again with both hands cupped together on the back of the head. He went to his knees but was back up again showing he was tough. As he turned I kicked him in the groin, but it didn't land flush, as he twisted enough it didn't have the full impact, though he did gasp and buckle over some. I punched again with a right, but he rolled to the ground and I missed. Flexing my hands to keep the blood flowing and the stinging at bay, I continued to dance. He bounced up and charged me, so I hit him right-left, but he muscled through, getting me in a grasp, lifting me and squeezing with all his might. My arms were free, so I popped him on both ears, and gouged at his eyes with my thumbs. He dropped me in pain, and since he couldn't see I hit him with another combo, elbowed him in the left temple, and kicked his legs out from under him. Backward he fell, hitting the ground with his head. With no quit in him, he still got to his feet, though he was swaying and likely seeing halos. I was about to finish him off when Roland yelled.

"Enough! Rocky, kill him!"

"No, I want him to die slowly," stated Leather. "I want him to see the horrible things we do to his girl."

Melissa screamed while Bill moved in front to hold and shield her. I turned around to face Rocky, still flexing my hands. He had a Glock in one gloved hand and pulled out my Beretta from his pocket and pointed it at me. I heard Roland yell "do it" and Rocky tossed me the gun, and drilled Dirk in the head, dropping him dead to the gravel. I grasped the Beretta and turned and shot Mack twice in the chest before he could raise his weapon, while Rocky nailed Grady with one bullet to the skull. We both turned our sights on the remaining three. Marquis slumped to the ground whimpering in fear. Leather stood tall and defiant, but didn't appear to be armed. Roland had grabbed Dona and held her in front of him, a gun pointed at her head.

"I don't know what the fuck happened," yelled Roland. "The two of you stay back, or I'll kill her."

Leather looked at Marquis on the ground and kicked him.

"You pussy," she said. "I should have known you'd wimp out."

"Leather, you'd better join him," I said.

"Oh, you won't shoot a woman," she said, "you haven't the balls."

She was right, I wouldn't; killing a woman wasn't in my DNA, as

217

I had proved at Dave and Busters several months earlier. Rocky though, had no problem with it, turning and shooting her in the head like the other two without a second thought. Startled, Roland flinched enough so Dona tried to wrestle the gun from him, gouging at his eyes, a burning anger giving her new strength. In the struggle, the weapon went off and down she fell. Roland turned towards me, blood streaming down his face from the scratches. His gun hand raised and before aiming I put two bullets into his chest with lethal accuracy, knocking him straight back a few feet, now dead and descending to the depths of hell where he belonged.

I went over to check on Dona. She was bleeding badly, and I attempted to apply pressure to the chest wound. She winced in pain and you could see the life was draining from her.

"Hang in there," I said to her.

"It's OK," she said. "I'm free now. I really wanted to find something else I was good at like you said, Jarvis, but I couldn't. All I ever was good at was being a whore. So maybe in the next life…" Her eyes stared up at me, though lifeless now, and she was gone. She never stood a chance and it made me sad.

Roland's driver had taken off during the melee. So other than Marquis, everyone else was dead. The scene was a mess, with bodies everywhere. It wasn't a pretty site. Rocky walked over to Marquis and before I could say anything, shot him in the back of the head, adding to the body count. He handed me his gun, a tape recorder and microphone, my cell phone and began walking away. With blood on my hands, I went over and cradled Melissa, sensing she was in shock, which made two of us. Bill took my phone and dialed 911.

Chapter 44

The better part of a week had passed as I drove west on 6th Avenue. So much had happened since the shootout, I couldn't recall it all. The entire endeavor was a blur. Police, paramedics and the coroner came. Reporters swarmed in droves and had to be held back. Everyone was in shock at the carnage. We were grilled for hours and days on end. It wasn't over, either. The men and woman who died were bad people, so no one cared much; but still they couldn't let something like this go without questioning. All our stories were the same. We had been kidnapped, threatened and attacked, and had killed to save our own lives. With Bill being a police officer, it helped. The recording of the confessions that Rocky captured of Roland and Leather didn't hurt either. It all seemed unreal, but true. It had gone down, but not the way I had thought it would. Killing was going to be a last resort, but the precision of Rocky's shot told me otherwise. I was on my way to question this at the office of the man who had arranged his presence, Brandon Sparks.

Melissa had been in shock as I suspected, and needed medication to help her. She stayed in the hospital for a day, and when I brought her home, she told me she had some thinking to do and would call me. Our two-week vacation was now in jeopardy, as was our relationship. I hated she had been there to see it all, and cursed myself for letting her be dragged into this mess. For now, the reservations for Hawaii had not been cancelled. I held out hope a trip would heal us. All we had to do was get on the plane, get in the air and land in paradise.

My phone rang and it was Trey again. Good news would have been pleasant to hear.

"The Hustle burned to the ground last night," he said. "Nothing left of the place."

"Anyone hurt?"

"No. The place has been closed since the massacre. Lots of accelerant all over. It was a pretty old building and by the time the fire department arrived, it was a total loss. Ownership is in question, so the city will likely condemn it and it will be leveled, the land sold off to someone who will use it for something a little more upscale, or so we hope."

"A playground for kids would be a positive change of pace," I stated. "Maybe I can get someone to buy it and build one."

"Good luck," Trey said and hung up.

When I arrived at the office, Sue was there to greet me. I followed her to an elevator and we went down to the lower level. I was quiet, not doing my usual banter with her.

"No sexist remarks from you today?" Sue said.

"Not feeling playful," I replied.

"Sorry to hear. I actually enjoy the exchanges between us. For a man, you have some spunk."

The door opened and we stepped out.

"And you have a fine ass!"

"That's more like it. If you didn't have a dick, you might be worth exploring." She turned and went back into the elevator. "Mr. Sparks is down the hall, third room on the right." I think I saw her smile ever so slightly before the door closed.

I located the sign saying "Shooting Range." Once inside, I saw another female from behind walking away and out the other exit. There was something familiar about her, but I couldn't explore further as Brandon walked out of one of the stalls, protective glasses covering his eyes, ear protection around his neck. He came and crushed my hand in glee.

"So good to see you, Jarvis," he said happily. "Welcome to my gun range, where I can stay sharp and work out my frustrations on a paper target shaped like my enemies."

From what I could see there were eight stalls, the other end a few hundred feet away. It was odd seeing something like this in the bowels of a building, but for a man like Brandon Sparks, nothing was out of the question.

"Quite a setup," I said.

"Care to fire off a few rounds?"

"I didn't come armed."

"Won't be a problem; I have several handguns for you to choose from. I believe you carry a Smith and Wesson .38 and a Beretta PX4 9MM."

No surprise he knew the weapons I used.

"I came to talk. Should we head upstairs? It appears we aren't alone."

There was one other person a couple stalls down, shooting.

"Nothing you can't say down here."

"I'm a little concerned about what happened at the quarry. It didn't go off like we had talked about."

"You mean the killing?"

"Yes."

"Well, as I've told you before, my men are free-thinkers and don't always do what I tell them."

Frowning, I did my best not to lose my temper.

"Come on, Brandon, I find it hard to believe. You run a tight ship and your men are loyal. I think they do precisely as you tell them. I'm not certain you are telling me exactly what you have planned."

"Jarvis, the best plan is a flexible one. You are too rigid sometimes. What happened was for the greater good. These were bad people whom no one will miss. The world is a better place since they are gone."

"What of the one innocent woman who died, Dona?"

"Collateral damage; a shame, but she was a woman who, in the next life, may find peace. She hardly had much of one from what I have heard in this one."

"Your man shot and killed two unarmed people, who didn't need to die."

Brandon shrugged as if swatting a fly. He felt nothing, which I couldn't do, even if they were bad people who would kill me in a heartbeat.

"What of Roland's operation?"

"It will be handled, with new management. His house will be gutted and the torture chamber replaced with a game room for civilized people."

"You will oversee the new management?"

"No comment." He said it with a grin.

"And the driver who got away?"

"Of no concern; it's been handled."

"I heard The Hustle burned down."

"Another cleanup job. It will be rezoned and become capitalism at its finest. Something to bring needed revenue to Greeley."

"Buy the land and build a playground there for kids to use. Make is something useful. We don't need another multi-storied building or a shopping center."

"Interesting suggestion. I'll consider it once the dust has settled.

Might be a nice tax write-off."

All I could do was sigh and shake my head, feeling like a fool. I had been desperate and used a dangerous man for dangerous work. I should be happy I was out of this mess, but I wasn't.

"Look, Jarvis, you came to me and the job is done. It's not how you'd hoped it would turn out, but it's for the best. Your friends are safe and free now to live their lives. I have repaid my debt to you. Now you will be this famous PI who took out six dangerous people on your own. You will be a legend now. The press will be begging you for an exclusive interview. Potential clients will be knocking on your door, begging you to help them, willing to pay top dollar. Increase your rates. This will be a boom for your career."

"But at what cost?"

"You worry too much. If you are so worried about what happened, you should talk to the man who was responsible and tell him of your concerns."

Brandon led me over to the stall where the man was shooting. He had fired off sixteen rounds and was retrieving the target. From behind I saw he hit center mass or between the eyes with each shot. He turned around, a serious look on Rocky's face, his long hair flowing freely today. He reloaded his Glock, the same model he'd turned over to me at the scene and holstered it. Pulling off the paper, he folded and slapped it on my chest, causing me to take a step back.

"You're welcome," he said, while gracefully gliding out of the room, leaving behind a powerful presence.

I may have met the most dangerous man I'd ever encountered, and deep down I was thrilled he had been on my side.

Chapter 45

On the drive home I called Melissa but got no answer. Christmas was a couple days away and I wanted to be with her. I had to leave the dangerous world behind. Our flight was tomorrow and I needed to know if I should pull out my luggage. While contemplating, my phone rang and it was her.

"Sorry I missed your call," Melissa said. "How are you?"

"Better, now that I hear your voice," I replied. "And you?"

"Still a bit shaky. Trying to decide what to do."

"Pack and go away with me. I need you. We both need a break after what we've been through."

"I don't know if I will ever forget it."

"We can try. I want to see you in your bikini, walk hand-in-hand on the beach with you. Together we can return to some semblance of a real life. No guns and no violence. Two weeks of only you and me."

There was silence and I think I heard a sob or two.

"Please, Melissa. It is the only way we will know what we are to each other."

"OK."

"And the bikini?"

"Yes."

"The revealing lingerie you got from Victoria Secret?"

"Not much material so it fit easily in the suitcase."

"Little lady, you're already packed? I should have known since you did this to me once before."

"Yes, I was packing today. I wanted to make sure you still wanted to go. If not, I was going to order Domino's pizza and hope for the best."

I laughed out loud and loved the humor. The healing was starting and soon we'd be together.

"The deliveryman would only disappoint you like before," I said. "I'm the man for the job. You are my gal. I can't wait to see you every hour for two straight weeks."

"I can't wait to see you. I love you!"

If I hadn't been such a hard-ass macho guy, I'd have cried.

"I love you, too. I will be there bright and early tomorrow to pick you up."

"Why don't we start the vacation now and you come and stay the night? I've been missing you badly and want you."

"You took the words right out of my mouth. Be there in an hour or two. Have to run home and get my stuff."

A surge of excitement filled me on the rest of the drive home. With her in my corner, I could get past all this pain and violence, even if only for a little while. Arriving at my place, there was a familiar car parked in front. I saw her standing by my stairwell, a beauty only eclipsed by Melissa, but whose deviant behavior nearly cost me my profession and current relationship. She stood there looking as she always did, the girl next door with a sex appeal to drive men wild.

"Hello, Jarvis," said Emily White, dressed in expensive black jeans, black boots, pink blouse and a long brown leather jacket.

"It's good to see you," I said. "You are looking wonderful."

I wasn't lying, she was stunning! Her hair was a little shorter, but still the same brownish-blonde I remembered with a wave to it.

"Can we talk?" she said.

"Sure. Come in where it's warmer."

Once inside I asked if I could take her coat, but she declined. I offered for her to sit down, but again she said no. She had something on her mind by the expression on her face.

"You are looking good yourself," Emily said. "Brandon mentioned you wanted to talk with me, but said I should wait until I was through therapy and I was ready."

"How has the therapy gone?"

"Not too badly," she replied. "I know I've learned some things about myself; come to terms about my behavior. I need to make amends for some of the things I've done."

"Have you contacted Mark and Jim?"

Mark was her ex-husband, while Jim was a married man she'd had an affair with. In both cases, she had manipulated them with her feminine wiles.

"I have, and did my best to explain."

"How did it go?"

"Fair-to-poor with both of them. Mark listened, but I know he won't forgive me completely. Jim left calling me a bitch and a slut. It's to be expected. My therapist warned me the reactions might not be pleasant. It's as much for me as it is for them."

"Now you're here to make amends with me?"

"Sort of; in your case it's a little harder. You are the one I had deep emotions for. It wasn't love per se, but the passion was real and exciting. I had deeper feelings for you. I was exploiting them."

"You were exploiting me, too, wanting me to eliminate the other men in your life. I'm not certain how you can have deeper feelings for me, when you schemed to get me to kill them for you."

"It was part of the excitement—got me off. Foreplay of the mind, imagining you doing those nasty things for me. I know now it was wrong. I did want you. I still want you."

Looking at her, I could see the flush of arousal on her face I'd seen before. I had been weak giving into her previously. If it weren't for Melissa I would probably push her against the wall and take her in a second, even knowing it was a horrible idea, my male hormones taking over. Today. I would resist the temptation. I had to resist...

"Emily, you are one of the sexiest woman I've ever met," I said. "No matter how tempting, and believe me you are, I must decline. I'm in a strong relationship now with someone I do care for. I hope you understand."

A frown overcame her face, almost a pouting child face. She upped the ante by opening her coat to show off her braless ample bosom, her nipples pointing through the blouse, like two darts aimed at my eyes.

"Are you sure you won't reconsider?" Emily said. "Wouldn't you like to explore my body as you did before? Enjoy my curves and folds. Use your hands, fingers and tongue to drive me wild."

I counted to ten before responding. *Be strong, Jarvis!*

"I'm certain. I won't betray my lady's trust."

More pouting filled her expression.

"So, is it Melissa?"

I probably shouldn't have answered, but I said, "yes."

"I was able to persuade you before."

She rubbed her body with her hands, her eyes closed, her head thrown back to add to the sexy drama. It seemed a last ditch desperate attempt to seduce me, but I held my ground. It seemed her therapy had not been totally successful.

"Emily, please don't do this. You can find someone to care about you without throwing yourself at them."

Again, the pouting face appeared. She toyed with the buttons on her blouse, releasing one, then two to show more of her cleavage, her breasts nearly exposed. Her hands reached the next button and stopped.

"I know, but damn how I wanted you; one more glorious time of you inside of me. But it appears no matter what I try it won't happen."

"No, it won't. I'm sorry."

"So am I. Because I did want to fuck you before I shot you."

From out of her coat pocket she pulled a 9MM gun and pointed it at me. She held it expertly with both hands. It was at this moment I came to realize the backside of the woman I saw at Brandon's shooting range was hers.

"Been practicing at Brandon's office, I see."

"Yeah, been working with his help and one of his men's. Big, good-looking man with long hair and a scar above his right eye. I never got his name but sure liked the cut of his figure. I might have to thank him in my special way since you weren't willing."

"Your plan is to kill me?" I asked.

"No. I had to promise Brandon not to. He likes you for some reason, though he never could explain why. He said I could put a bullet in you like you did me. But you had to live through it and be able to work again. He appreciates having a PI in his back pocket."

I let the slam go, though I wondered myself sometimes.

"Come on, Emily. What will you accomplish by shooting me?" I took a step forward, but she tensed up, so I stopped.

"I'll feel better about the pain you put me through; all the physical agony from the hole in my leg which still hurts today. I need you to feel what I felt."

I made a quick move and she fired, aiming downward. I twisted as the bullet caught me in the back of the upper thigh. I crumbled down in instant pain, the burning feeling running up my spine. Once on the floor I felt for the spot and noticed the warm blood. I closed my eyes to try and manage the agony, but failed. She had gotten what she wanted. I now knew how she felt when I shot her.

"Damn, this hurts," is what I shouted out.

"Yes, it does," she answered, while grabbing a kitchen towel and tossing it to me.

"Satisfied?" I said while using it to apply pressure.

"On one level, yes," Emily said, "on another, no. Like I said, I would have preferred to fuck you first."

She put the gun back in her coat pocket. She kneeled next to me, her exposed breasts falling out her mostly open blouse. She grabbed my face and kissed me with a fiery passion, replacing the pain for a split second with desire. If she had led with this kiss in the first place I might not have been able to resist. When finished she stood up, closed her top and headed for the door.

"You won't see me again—I'm moving away," she stated. "I wished we'd have enjoyed the pleasure before the pain, but beggars can't be choosers. Since I'm all worked up, I'll find my gun trainer and do him a few times."

She opened the door and glanced back at me with a wicked expression.

"Oh, and Brandon wanted me to tell you he owes you again. Although if you tell the police I shot you, there will be dire consequences."

She was out the door and, hopefully, out of my life. But damn, that kiss would be difficult to forget, like the pain in my backside. I reached for my cell phone to call 911 before I passed out. My only other thought was how I was going to explain this to Melissa; our vacation appeared to be in jeopardy. It would be hard to look good in my swim trunks with a hole in my ass!

Thanks for reading *Twice As Fatal*. I hope you enjoyed it and would greatly appreciate if you would leave a review on Amazon to help an Indie Author. It is the greatest gift you can give us!!

And check out the other books in the *Jarvis Mann Detective Series* of which there are 8 to read. Read the books in this order for the best experience: *The Case of the Missing Bubble Gum Card, Tracking a Shadow, Twice as Fatal, Blood Brothers, Dead Man Code, The Case of the Invisible Souls, The Front Range Butcher* and *Mann in the Crossfire*. All are available on Amazon in eBook format including two boxsets, along with paperback versions, and on Kindle Unlimited.

And you can check out my *Divine Devils* Suspense/Thriller series. Read the three books in this order for the best experience: *The Divine Devils, Fallen Star: The Divine Devils Book 2* and *Sold Souls: The Divine Devils Book 3.* All are available in eBook, paperback and on Kindle Unlimited.

Find all my books via this link:
https://www.amazon.com/R-Weir/e/B00JH2Y5US

If you want to reach out, please email me at:

author@rweir.net

Receive a free eBook copy of my *Jarvis Mann PI* book, *Tracking A Shadow*. All you need to do is sign up for my newsletter on my website.
https://rweir.net

Follow R Weir, Jarvis Mann, and Hunter Divine on these social sites as I appreciate hearing from those who've read my books:

https://www.facebook.com/randy.weir.524
https://www.facebook.com/JarvisMannPI
https://twitter.com/RWeir720
https://www.instagram.com/rweir720/

Thanks for reading. Stay Safe, Happy and Healthy!!

Made in the USA
Middletown, DE
04 December 2022

15983478R00139